A. Roman and Company publishers, James M. Hutchings

Scenes of Wonder and Curiosity in California

Illustrated with over one hundred engravings - A tourists guide to the Yo-Semite

Valley

A. Roman and Company publishers, James M. Hutchings

Scenes of Wonder and Curiosity in California
Illustrated with over one hundred engravings - A tourists guide to the Yo-Semite Valley

ISBN/EAN: 9783337188191

Printed in Europe, USA, Canada, Australia, Japan

Cover: Foto ©Andreas Hilbeck / pixelio.de

More available books at **www.hansebooks.com**

SCENES

OF

WONDER AND CURIOSITY

IN

CALIFORNIA.

ILLUSTRATED WITH OVER ONE HUNDRED ENGRAVINGS.

A TOURIST'S GUIDE

TO THE

YO-SEMITE VALLEY;

THE BIG TREE GROVES—THE NATURAL CAVES AND BRIDGES—THE QUICKSILVER MINES OF
NEW ALMADEN AND HENRIQUITA—MOUNT SHASTA—THE FARALLONE ISLANDS, WITH THEIR SEA LIONS
AND BIRDS—THE GEYSER SPRINGS—LAKE TAHOE, AND OTHER PLACES OF INTEREST.

ALSO

GIVING OUTLINE MAP OF ROUTES TO YO-SEMITE AND BIG TREE GROVES—TABLES OF DISTANCES—
RATES OF FARE—HOTEL CHARGES, AND OTHER DESIRABLE INFORMATION FOR THE TRAVELLER.

BY J. M. HUTCHINGS,
(OF YO-SEMITE.)

NEW YORK AND SAN FRANCISCO:
A. ROMAN AND COMPANY, PUBLISHERS.
1870.

PREFATORY NOTE FROM PUBLISHER.

SINCE the completion and appointments of the great Overland Railway have made travelling to the Pacific Slope easy, pleasant, speedy, and safe, a general desire has arisen for information concerning its remarkable scenery, the cost of travelling, distances, hotel charges, etc.

The cordial reception this volume has received in California, where hitherto it has only been known, and the often expressed wish for its more general circulation, has led to the belief that a revised edition, giving the desired information, would supply a present need, and prove acceptable to the public.

The author's twenty years' experience in California has made him familiar with its history and progress; a long time devoted to studying and sketching its most interesting features, and an actual residence of six years in the wonderful Yo-Semite, together with his loving appreciation of the beautiful, have very naturally fitted him to write instructively and feelingly upon the subject.

Through his efforts, moreover, the attention of the public was first called to its sublime scenes, and for years he has, in many ways, been earnestly engaged in extending a knowledge of its glories.

New York, May 2, 1870.

CONTENTS.

CHAPTER I.

CHAPTER II.

CHAPTER III.

CHAPTER IV.

CHAPTER V.

CHAPTER VI.

CHAPTER VII.

CHAPTER VIII.

CHAPTER IX.

CHAPTER X.

CHAPTER XI.

CHAPTER XII.

CHAPTER XIII.

LIST OF ILLUSTRATIONS.

SCENES OF WONDER AND CURIOSITY

IN

CALIFORNIA.

THE MAMMOTH TREES OF CALAVERAS.

SECTION OF MAMMOTH TREE.
From Photograph by T. Houseworth & Co.

CHAPTER I.

"God of the forest's solemn shade!
 The grandeur of the lonely tree,
That wrestles singly with the gale,
 Lifts up admiring eyes to Thee,
But more majestic far they stand,
 When, side by side their ranks they form
To wave on high their plumes of green,
 And fight their battles with the storm."

PEABODY.

IT is much to be questioned if the discovery of any wonder, in any part of the world, has ever elicited as much general interest, or created so strong a tax upon the credulity of mankind, as the discovery of the mammoth trees of California. Indeed, those who first mentioned the fact of their existence, whether by word of mouth or by letter, were looked upon as near, very near, relatives of Baron Munchausen, Captain Gulliver, or the celebrated Don Quixote. The statement had many times to be repeated, and well corroborated, before it could be received as true; and there are many persons who, to this very day, look upon it as as a somewhat doubtful "California story;" such, we never expect to convince of the realities we are about to illustrate and describe, although we do so from our own personal knowledge and observation.

HOW THE CALAVERAS GROVE WAS FIRST DISCOVERED.

In the spring of 1852, Mr. A. T. Dowd, a hunter, was employed by the Union Water Company, of Murphy's Camp, Calaveras county, to supply the workmen engaged in the construction of their canal, with fresh meat, from the large quantities of game running wild on the upper portion of their works. Having wounded a bear, and while industriously following in pursuit, he suddenly came upon one of those immense trees, that have since become so justly celebrated throughout the civilized world. All thoughts of hunting were absorbed and lost in the wonder and· surprise inspired by the scene. "Surely," he mused," this must be some curiously delusive dream!" but the great realities standing there before him, were convincing proof, beyond a doubt, that they were no mere fanciful creations of his imagination.

When he returned to camp, and there related the wonders he had seen, his companions laughed at him and doubted his veracity, which previously they had considered to be very reliable. He affirmed his statement to be true, but they still thought it "too much of a story" to believe—thinking that he was trying to perpetrate upon them some first of April joke.

For a day or two he allowed the matter to rest—submitting,. with chuckling satisfaction, to the occasional jocular allusions to "his big tree yarn," and continued his hunting as formerly. On the Sunday morning following, he went out early as usual, and returned in haste, evidently excited by some event. "Boys," he exclaimed, "I have killed the largest grizzly bear that I ever saw in my life. While I am getting a little something to eat, you make preparations to bring him in. All had better go that can possibly be spared, as their assistance will certainly be needed."

As the big tree story was now almost forgotten, or by common consent laid aside as a subject of conversation ; and, moreover, as Sunday was a leisure day—and one that generally hangs the heaviest of the seven on those who are shut out from social intercourse with friends, as many, many Californians unfortunately are—the tidings were gladly welcomed ; especially as the proposition was suggestive of a day's excitement.

Nothing loath, they were soon ready for the start. The camp was almost deserted. On, on they hurried, with Dowd as their guide, through thickets and pine groves ; crossing ridges and cañons, flats and ravines ; each relating in turn the adventures experienced, or heard of from companions, with grizzly bears and other formidable tenants of the forests and wilds of the moun-

tains; until their leader came to a dead halt at the foot of the
tree he had seen, and to them had related the size. Pointing to
the immense trunk and lofty top, he cried out, "Boys, do you now
believe my big tree story? That is the large grizzly I wanted
you to see. Do you still think it a yarn?"

Thus convinced, their doubts were changed to amazement, and
their conversation from bears to trees; afterward confessing that,
although they had been caught by a ruse of their leader, they
were abundantly rewarded by the gratifying sight they had
witnessed; and as other trees were found equally as large, they
became willing witnesses, not only to the entire truthfulness of
Mr. Dowd's account, but also to the fact, that, like the confession
of a certain Persian queen concerning the wisdom of Solomon,
"the half had not been told."

Mr. Lewis, one of the party above alluded to, after seeing these
gigantic forest patriarchs, conceived the idea of removing the
bark from one of the trees, and of taking it to the Atlantic states
for exhibition, and invited Dowd to join him in the enterprise.
This was declined; but, while Mr. Lewis was engaged in obtaining a suitable partner, some one from Murphy's Camp to whom
he had confided his intentions and made known his plans, took up
a posse of men early the next morning to the spot described by
Mr. Lewis, and, after locating a quarter section of land, immediately commenced the removal of the bark, after attempting to
dissuade Lewis from the undertaking.* This underhanded proceeding induced Lewis to visit the large tree at Santa Cruz, discovered by Fremont, for the purpose of competing, if possible,
with his *quondam friend;* but finding that tree, although large,
only nineteen feet in diameter and 286 feet in height, while that
in Calaveras county was thirty feet in diameter and 302 feet in
height, he then turned his steps to some trees reputed to be the
greatest in magnitude in the state, growing near Trinidad, Klamath

---

* In the winter of 1854, we met Mr. Lewis in Yreka, and from his own lips received
this account; and we think it no more than simple justice to him here to make a
record of the fact, that such an unfair and ungentlemanly violation of confidence may
be both known and censured, as it well deserves to be.

county; but the largest of these he found only to measure about twenty-four feet in diameter, and two hundred and seventy-nine feet in height; consequently, much discouraged, and after spending about five hundred dollars and several weeks' time, he eventually abandoned his undertaking.

But a short season was allowed to elapse after the discovery of this remarkable grove, before the trumpet-tongued press proclaimed the wonder to all sections of the state, and to all parts of the world; and the lovers of the marvellous began first to doubt, then to believe, and afterward to flock from the various districts of California, that they might see, with their own eyes, the objects of which they had heard so much.

No pilgrims to Mohammed's tomb at Mecca, or to the reputed vestment of our Saviour at Treves, or to the Juggernaut of Hindostan, ever manifested more interest in the superstitious objects of their veneration, than the intelligent and devout worshippers of the wonderful in nature and science, of our own country, in their visit to the Mammoth-Tree Grove of Calaveras county, high up in the Sierras.

Murphy's Camp, then known as an obscure though excellent mining district, was lifted into notoriety by its proximity to, and as the starting-point for, the Big-Tree Grove, and consequently was the centre of considerable attraction to visitors.

PRINCIPAL ROUTES TO THE CALAVERAS GROVE.

As very many persons will doubtless wish to visit these remarkable places, and as we cannot in this brief work describe all the various routes to these great natural marvels, from every village, town, and city in the state—for they are almost as numerous and diversified as the different roads that Christians seem to take to their expected heaven, and the multitudinous creeds about the way and manner of getting there—we shall content ourselves by giving the principal ones; and, after having recited the following quaint and unanswerable argument of a celebrated divine to the querulous and uncharitably disposed members of his flock, we shall, with the reader's kind permission, proceed on our journey.

"There was a Christian brother—a Presbyterian—who walked up to the gate of the New Jerusalem, and knocked for admittance, when an angel who was in charge, looked down from above and inquired what he wanted. 'To come in,' was the answer. 'Who and what are you?' 'A Presbyterian.' 'Sit on that seat there.' This was on the outside of the gate; and the good man feared that he had been refused admittance. Presently arrived an Episcopalian, then a Baptist, then a Methodist, and so on, until a representative of every Christian sect had made his appearance; and were. alike ordered to take a seat outside. Before they had long been there," continued the good man, "a loud anthem broke forth, rolling and swelling upon the air, from the choir within; when those outside immediately joined in the chorus. 'Oh!' said the angel, as he opened wide the gate, 'I did not know you by your names, but you have all learned one song—come in! come in! The name you bear, or the way by which you came, is of little consequence compared with your being here at all.' As you, my brethren," the good man went on—"as you expect to live peaceably and lovingly together in heaven, you had better begin to practice it on earth. I have done."

As this allegorical advice needs no words of application either to the traveller or the Christian, in the hope that the latter will take the admonition of Captain Cuttle, "and make a note on't," and an apology to the reader for this digression, we will enter at once upon our pleasing task.

Those who start from San Francisco, for the Yo-Semite Valley or the Mammoth-Tree Groves, should first proceed to Stockton. This can be done by two routes: one *via* the Western Pacific railroad, and the other by steamboat. If the former, the distance is ninety miles, time four hours, ten minutes, and the starting point is the Alameda Ferry, at eight o'clock, A.M., and four o'clock, P.M. If the latter, you repair to the Broadway wharf a little before four o'clock, P.M., and the boat will arrive in Stockton in time next morning for the six o'clock stage. This having been the route most generally traveled, we shall confine our attention mainly to it.

There probably is not a more exciting and bustling scene of

STEAMBOATS LEAVING THE WHARF—THE ANTELOPE FOR SACRAMENTO, AND THE BRAGDON FOR STOCKTON.

business activity in any part of the world, than can be witnessed on almost any day, Sunday excepted, at Broadway street wharf, San Francisco, at a few minutes before four o'clock P.M. Men and women are hurrying to and fro; drays, carriages, express-wagons, and horsemen, dash past you with as much rapidity and earnestness as though they were the bearers of a reprieve to some condemned criminal, whose last moment of life had nearly expired, and, by its speedy delivery, thought they could save him from the scaffold. Indeed, one would suppose, by the apparent recklessness of manner in riding and driving through the crowd, that numerous limbs would be broken, and carriages made into pieces as small as mince-meat; but yet, to your surprise, nothing of the kind occurs, for, on arriving at the smallest real obstacle to their progress, animals are suddenly reined in, with a promptness that astonishes you.

On these occasions, too, there is almost sure to be one or more intentional passengers that arrive just too late to get aboard, and who, in their excitement, often throw an overcoat or valise on the boat, or overboard, but neglect to embrace the only opportune moment to get on board themselves, and are consequently left behind, as these boats are always punctual to their time of starting.

With the reader's consent, as he may· be a stranger to the various scenes of our beautiful California, we will bear him company, and explain some of the objects we may see. As it is always cool in San Francisco on a summer afternoon, we would invite him to please put on his overcoat or cloak, and let us take a cosy seat together on deck; and, while the black volumes of smoke are rolling from the tops of the funnels, and our boat is shooting past this wharf, and that vessel now lying at anchor in the bay, or, while numerous nervous people are troubled about their baggage, asking the porter all sorts of questions, let us have a quiet chat upon the sights we may witness on our trip.

The first object of interest that we find after leaving the wharves of the city behind, is

ALCATRACES, OR PELICAN ISLAND.

ALCATRACES ISLAND.

This, we see, is just opposite the Golden Gate, and about half way between San Francisco and Angel Island. It commands the

THE MAMMOTH TREES OF CALAVERAS.

entrance to the great bay of San Francisco, and is but three and a half miles from Fort Point.

This island is one hundred and forty feet in height above low tide, four hundred and fifty feet in width, and sixteen hundred and fifty feet in length ; somewhat irregular in shape, and forti- fied on all sides. The large building on its summit, about the centre or crest of the island, is a defensive barracks or citadel, three stories high, and in time of peace will accommodate about two hundred men, and, in time of war, at least three times that number. It is not only a shelter for the soldiers, and will with- stand a respectable cannonade, but from its top a murderous fire could be poured upon its assailants at all parts of the island, and from whence every point of it is visible. There is a belt of forti- fications encircling the island, consisting of a series of Barbette batteries, mounting, altogether, about ninety-four guns—twenty- four, forty-two, sixty-eight, and one hundred and thirty-two pounders.

The first building that you notice, after landing at the wharf, is a massive brick and stone guard-house, shot and shell proof, well protected by a heavy gate and drawbridge, and having three em- brasures for twenty-four pound howitzers, that command the approach from the wharf. The top of this, like the barracks, is flat, for the use and protection of riflemen. Other guard-houses, of similar construction, are built at different points, between which there are long lines of parapets sufficiently high to preclude the possibility of an escalade ; and back of which are circular plat- forms for mounting guns of the heaviest calibre, some of which weigh from nine to ten thousand pounds. In addition to these, there are three bomb-proof magazines, each of which will hold ten thousand pounds of powder. On the south-eastern side of the island is a large furnace for the purpose of heating cannon balls, and other similar contrivances are in course of construction.

Unfortunately, there is no natural supply of water on the island, so that all of that element which is used there is taken from Saucelito. In the basement of the barracks is a cistern, capa- ble of holding fifty thousand gallons of water, a portion of

2

which can be supplied from the roof of that building in the rainy season.

Appropriations have been made for the fortification of this island, to the amount of eight hundred and ninety-six thousand dollars; and about one hundred thousand dollars more will complete them. From forty to two hundred men have been employed upon these works since their commencement in 1853.

At the south-eastern end of the island is a fog-bell, of about the same weight as that at Fort Point, which is regulated to strike by machinery once in about every fifteen seconds.

The whole of the works on this island are under the skilful superintendence of Lieutenant McPherson, who very kindly explained to us the strength and purposes of the different fortifications made.

The lighthouse, at the south of the barracks, contains a Fresnel lantern of the third order, and which can be seen, on a clear night, some twelve miles outside the heads, and is of great service in suggesting the course of a vessel when entering the bay.

Yet, as we are sailing on at considerable speed across the entrance to the bay, toward Angel Island, we must not linger here, even in imagination; especially as we can now look out through the far-famed Golden Gate; the golden-hinged hope of many, who, with lingering eyes, have longed to look upon it, and to enter through its charmed portals to this land of gold. How many, too, have longed and hoped, for years, to pass it once again, on their way out to the endeared and loving hearts that wait to welcome them, at that dear spot they still call "*Home!*" God bless them!

Now the vessel is in full sail, and steamships that are entering the heads, as well as those within that are tacking, now on this stretch, and now on that, to make way out against the strong north-west breeze that blows in at the Golden Gate for five-eighths of the year, are fast being lost to sight, and we are just abreast of

ANGEL ISLAND.

This island, but five miles from the city of San Francisco, was granted by Governor Alvarado to Antonio M. Asio, by order of the government of Mexico, in 1837; and by him sold to its present owners in 1853. As it contains some eight hundred acres of excellent land, it is by far the largest and most valuable of any in the bay of San Francisco, and the green wild oats that grow to its very summit, in early spring, give excellent pasturage to stock of all kinds; while the natural springs, at different points, afford abundance of water at all seasons. At the present time there are about five hundred sheep roaming over its fertile hills. A large portion of the land is susceptible of cultivation, for grain and vegetables.

From the inexhaustible quarries of hard, blue, and brown sandstone that here abound, have been taken nearly all of the stone used in the foundations of the numerous buildings in San Francisco. The extensive fortifications at Alcatraces Island, Fort Point, and other places, have been faced with it; and the extensive government works at Mare Island have been principally built with stone from these quarries; yet many thousands of tons will be required from the same source, before the fortifications and other government works are completed. Clay is also found in abundance, and of an excellent quality for making bricks.

In 1856 Angel Island was surveyed by United States Engineers, for the purpose of locating sites for two twenty-four gun batteries, which are in the line of fortifications required, before our magnificent harbor may be considered as fortified. The most important of these batteries will be on the north-west point of the island, and will command Racqoon Straits; and, until this is built, our navy yard at Mare Island, and even the city of San Francisco itself, cannot be considered safe, inasmuch as, through these straits, ships of war could easily enter; if, by means of the heavy fog that so frequently hangs over the entrance to the bay, or other cause, they once passed Fort Point in safety. But here we are just opposite

RED ROCK.

This singular looking island was formerly called Treasure, or Golden Rock, in old charts, from a traditionary report being cir-

VIEW OF RED (OR TREASURE) ROCK.

culated of some large treasure having been once carried there, by early Spanish navigators. In charts of recent date, however, it is sometimes called Molate Island, but is now more generally known as Red Rock, from its general color.

There are several strata of rock, of different colors—if rock it can be called—one of which is very fine, and resembles an article sometimes found upon a lady's toilet-table—of course in earlier days—known as rouge-powder. Besides this there are several strata of a species of clay or colored pigment, of from four to twelve inches in thickness, and of various colors. Upon the beach numerous small red pebbles, very much resembling cornelian, are found. There can be but little wonder it should be called "Red Rock," by plain, matter-of-fact people like ourselves. It is covered with wild oats to its summit, on which is planted a flag-staff and cannon. Several years ago its locater and owner, Mr. Selim E. Woodworth, took about half a dozen tame rabbits over to it, from San Francisco, and now there are several hundred.

As Mr. Woodworth, before becoming a benedict, made this his place of residence, he partially graded its apparently inaccessible sides; and at different points planted several ornamental trees. A small bachelor's cabin stands near the water's edge, and as this affords the means of cooking fish and sundry other dishes, its owner, and a small party of friends, pay it an occasional visit for fishing and general recreation. Several sheep roam about on the island; and, as they seldom drink water, they do not feel the loss of that which nature has here failed to supply.

But on, on, we sail, and pass Maria Island and the Two Sisters.

VIEW OF THE TWO SISTERS.

After leaving these behind, and shooting by Point San Pablo, we enter the large bay of that name; and are charmed with the fine table and grazing lands on our right, at the foot of the Contra Costa range of hills.

STRAITS OF CARQUINEZ.

VIEW OF THE STRAITS OF CARQUINEZ.

Just before entering the Straits of Carquinez, that connects the bays of San Pablo and Suisun, on our left, we obtain a glimpse of the government works at Mare Island and the town of Vallejo;

but as we shall probably have something to say about these points at some future time, we will now take a look at the straits. As the stranger approaches these for the first time, he makes up his mind that the vessel on which he stands is out of her course, and is certainly running toward a bluff, and will soon be in trouble if she does not change her course, but as he advances and the entrance to this narrow channel becomes visible, he concludes that a few moments ago he entertained a very foolish idea.

Now, however, the bell of the steamboat and a porter both announce that we are coming near Benicia, and that those who intend disembarking here, had better have their baggage and their ticket in readiness.

BENICIA.

One would suppose as the boat nears the wharf that she is going to run "right into it," but soon she moves gracefully round and is made fast; but while those ashore, and those aboard, are eagerly scanning each other, to see if there is any familiar face to which to give the nod of recognition, or the cordial waving of the hand in friendly greeting, we will take our seats, and say a word or two about this city.

Benecia was founded, in the fall of 1847, by the late Thomas O. Larkin and Roland Semple (who was also the originator and editor of the first California newspaper published at Monterey, August 15th, 1846, entitled *The Californian*), upon land donated them for the purpose by General M. G. Vallejo, and named in honor of the general's estimable lady.

In 1848, a number of families took up their residence here. During the fall of that year a public school was established, which has been continued uninterruptedly to the present. In the ensuing spring a Presbyterian church was organized, and has continued under its original pastor to the present time.

The peculiarly favorable position of Benicia recommended it, at an early day, as a suitable place for the general military head-quarters of the United States, upon the Pacific. Being alike convenient of access both to the sea-board and interior, and far enough from the coast to be secure against sudden assault in time of war, it was seen that no more favorable position could be selected, as adapted to all contingencies. These views met the approval of the general government; and accordingly extensive store-houses were built, military posts established, and arrangements made for erecting here the principal arsenal on the Pacific coast.

VIEW OF THE CITY OF BENICIA.

There already are erected barracks for the soldiers, and officers' quarters; two magazines, capable of holding from six thousand to seven thousand barrels of gunpowder of one hundred pounds each; two store-houses filled with gun-carriages, cannon, ball, and several hundred stand of small arms; besides workshops, etc.

About one hundred men have been employed, under the superintendence of Captain F. D. Calender, in the construction of an arsenal two hundred feet in length by sixty feet in width, and three stories in height, suitably provided with towers, loop-holes, windows, etc. Besides this, a large citadel is in course of erection. Two hundred and twenty-five thousand dollars have already been appropriated to these works, and they will most probably require as much more before the whole is completed.

Here, too, are ten highly and curiously ornamented bronze cannon, six eight-pounders and four four-pounders, that were brought originally from old Spain, and taken at Fort Point during our war with Mexico. The following names and dates, besides coats of arms, etc., are inscribed on some of them :

"San Martin, Ano. D. 1684."

"Poder, Ano. D. 1693."

"San Francisco, Ano. D. 1673."

"San Domengo, Ano. D. 1679."

"San Pedro, Ano. D. 1628."

As the barracks are merely a depot for the reception and transmission of troops, it is difficult to say how many soldiers are quartered here at any one time.

There are numerous other interesting places about Benicia, one of which is the extensive works of the Pacific Mail Steamship Company, where all the repairs to their vessels are made, coal deposited, etc., etc.

In 1853, Benicia was chosen the capital of the state by our peripatetic legislature, and continued to hold that position for about a year, when it was taken to Sacramento, where it still (for a wonder) remains.

And, though last, by no means the least important feature of Benicia, is the widely-known and deservedly flourishing boarding-school for young ladies, the Benicia Seminary, under the charge of Mr. and Mrs. Mills, founded in 1852, and in which several young ladies have taken graduating honors.

Next to this is St. Augustine's College for young men, under the superintendence of Rev. Dr. Breck, and which was established in 1853 ; adjoining which is the college of Notre Dame, for the education of Catholic children. These, united to the excellent sentiments of the people, make Benicia a favorite place of residence for families.

MARTINEZ.

Nearly opposite to Benicia, and distant only three miles, is the pretty agricultural village of Martinez, the county-seat of Contra Costa county. A week among the live-oaks, gardens, and farms in and around this lovely spot, will convince the most sceptical that there are few more beautiful places in any part of the state. A steam ferry-boat plies across the straits between this place and Benicia, every hour in the day. The Stockton boat always used to touch here both going and returning.

The run across the Straits of Carquinez, from Benicia to Martinez, three miles distant, takes about ten minutes. Then, after a few moments' delay, we again dash onward—the moonlight gilding the troubled waters in the wake of our vessel, as she plows her swift way through the Bay of Suisun, and to all appearance deepens the shadows on the darker sides of Monte Diablo, by defining, with silvery clearness, the uneven ridges and summit of that solitary mountain mass.

But now we must hurry on our way, as the steamboat is by this time passing the different islands in the Bay of Suisun, named as follows: Preston Island, King's, Simmons', Davis', Washington, Knox's, Jones', and Sherman's Island; while on our right, boldly distinct in outline and form, stands

MONTE DIABLO.

Almost every Californian has seen Monte Diablo. It is the great central landmark of the state. Whether we are walking in the streets of San Francisco, or sailing on any of our bays and navigable rivers, or riding on any of the roads in the Sacramento and San Joaquin Valleys, or standing on the elevated ridges of the mining districts before us—in lonely boldness, and at almost every turn, we see Monte del Diablo. Probably from its apparent omnipresence we are indebted to its singular name, *Mount of the Devil*.

Viewed from the north-west or south-east, it appears double, or with two elevations, the points of which are about three miles apart. The south-western peak is the most elevated, and is three thousand seven hundred and sixty feet above the sea.

For the purpose of properly surveying the state into a network of township lines, three meridians or initial points were established by the United States Survey, namely: Monte Diablo,

MONTE DIABLO, WITH A PORTION OF SUISUN BAY, FROM THE SULPHUR-SPRING HOUSE.

Mount San Bernardino, and Mount Pierce, Humboldt county. Across the highest peaks of each of these, a "meridian line" and a "base line" were run; the latter from east to west, and the former from north to south. The boundaries of the Monte Diablo meridian include all the lands in the great Sacramento and San Joaquin Valleys, between the Coast Range and the Sierras, and from the Siskiyou Mountains to the San Bernardino meridian, at the head of the Tulare Valley.

The geological formation of this mountain is what is usually termed "primitive;" surrounded by sedimentary rocks, abounding in marine shells. Near the summit there are a few quartz veins, but whether gold-bearing or not has not yet been determined. About one-third of the distance from the top, on the western slope, is a "hornblende" rock of peculiar structure, and said by some to contain gold. In the numerous spurs at the base, there is an excellent and inexhaustible supply of limestone.

At the eastern foot of the mountains, about five miles from the San Joaquin River, several veins of coal have been discovered, and are now being worked with good prospects of remuneration, as the veins grow thicker and the quality better, as they proceed with their labors.

It is said that copper ore and cinnabar have both been found here, but with what truth we are unable to determine. Some Spaniards have reported that they know of some rich mineral there; but do not tell of what kind, and, for reasons best known to themselves, will neither communicate their secret to others nor work it themselves.

If the reader has no objection, we will climb the mountain—at least in imagination, as the captain, although an obliging man enough, will not detain the boat for us to ascend it *de facto*—and see what further discoveries we can make.

Provided with good horses—always make sure of the latter on any trip you may make, reader—an excellent telescope, and a liberal allowance of luncheon, let us leave the beautiful village of Martinez at seven o'clock A.M. For the first four miles, we ride over a number of pretty and gently rolling hills, at a lively gait, and arrive at the Pacheco Valley, on the edge of which stands the flourishing little village of Pacheco. We now dash across the valley at good speed for eight miles, in a south-east direction, and reach the western foot of Monte Diablo, after a good hour's pleasant ride.

For the first mile and a half of our ascent we have a good wagon road, built in 1852, to give easy access to a quartz lead, from which considerable rock was taken in wagons to the Bay of Suisun, and, after being shipped to San Francisco, for the purpose of being tested, was found to contain gold, but not in sufficient quantities to pay for working it; for the next two miles, a good, plain trail to the main summit, passes several clear springs of cold water.

From the numerous tracks of the grizzly bears that were seen at the springs, we may naturally conclude that such animals have their sleeping apartments among the bunches of chaparal in the cañons yonder: and, if we should see the track-makers before we return, we hope our companions will keep up their courage and sufficient presence of mind to prevent themselves imitating Mr.

Grizzly at the spring—at least not in the direction of the settlements—and leave us alone in our glory.

As you will perceive, the summit of the mountain is reached without the necessity of dismounting; and as there are wild oats all around, and the stores of sundries provided have not been lost or left behind, suppose we rest and refresh ourselves, and allow our animals to do the same.

The sight of the glorious panorama unrolled at our feet, we need not tell you, amply repays us for our early ride. As we look around us, we may easily imagine that perhaps the priests who named this mountain may have climbed it, and as they saw the wonders spread out before them, recalled to memory the following passage of holy writ: "The devil taketh him [Jesus] up into an exceeding high mountain, and sheweth him all the kingdoms of the world, and the glory of them; and saith unto him, All these things will I give thee, if thou wilt fall down and worship me" (MATTHEW 4th, verses 8 and 9); and from this time called it *Monte del Diablo*. Of course, this is mere supposition, and is as likely to be wrong as it is to be right.

The Pacific Ocean; the city, and part of the bay of San Francisco; Fort Point; the Golden Gate; San Pablo and Suisun Bays; the government works at Mare Island; Vallejo; Benicia; the valleys of Santa Clara, Petaluma, Sonoma, Napa, Sacramento, and San Joaquin, with their rivers, creeks, and sloughs, in all their tortuous windings; the cities of Stockton and Sacramento; and the great line of the snow-covered Sierras; with numerous villages dotting the pine forests on the lower mountain range—are all spread out before you. In short, there is nothing to obstruct the sight in any direction; and, with a good glass, the steamers and vessels at anchor in the bay, and made fast at the wharves of San Francisco, are distinctly visible.

Stock may be seen grazing, in all directions, on the mountains. To the very summit, wild oats and chaparal alternately grow. In the cañons are oak and pine trees from fifty to one hundred feet in height; and, on the more exposed portions, there are low trees from twenty to thirty feet in height.

In the fall season, when the wild oats and dead bushes are perfectly dry, the Indians sometimes set large portions of the surface of the mountains on fire; and, when the breeze is fresh, and the night is dark, and the lurid flames leap, and curl, and sway, now to this side and now to that, the spectacle presented is magnificent beyond the power of language to express.

SAILING UP THE SAN JOAQUIN RIVER.

The Sacramento boat, we see, is going straight forward, and will soon enter the Sacramento River, up which her course lies; while ours is to the right, past "New York of the Pacific" (containing three dilapidated houses), touching at Antioch, the convenient depot of the Monte Diablo coal mines, just sufficiently long to discharge passengers and freight, we shoot up the San Joaquin.

The evening being calm and sultry, it soon becomes evident that, if it is not the height of the musquito season, a very numerous band are out on a freebooting excursion; and, although their harvest-home song of blood is doubtless very musical, it is matter of regret with us to confess that, in our opinion, but few persons on board appear to have any ear for it. In order, however, that their musical efforts may not be entirely lost sight of, they— the musquitos—take pleasure in writing and impressing their low refrain, in red and embossed notes, upon the foreheads of the passengers, so that he who looks may read, "Musquitos!" when, alas! such is the ingratitude felt for favors so voluntarily performed, that flat-handed blows are dealt out to them in impetuous haste; and blood, blood, blood, and flattened musquitos, are written, in red and dark brown spots, upon the smiter; and the notes of *those* singers are heard no more!

While the unequal warfare is going on, and one carcass of the slain induces at least a dozen of the living to come to his funeral and avenge his death, we are sailing on, on, up one of the most crooked and monotonous navigable rivers out of doors; and, as we may as well do something more than fight the little, bill-presenting, and tax-collecting musquitos, if only for variety, we will relate to the reader how, in the early spring of 1849, just before leaving our southern home on the banks of "The Father of Waters," the old Mississippi, a gentleman arrived from northern Europe, and was at once introduced. a member of our little family circle. Now, however strange it may appear, our new friend had never in his life looked upon a live musquito, or a musquito-bar, and, consequently, knew nothing about the arrangements of a good *femme de charge* for passing a comfortable night, where such insects were even more numerous than oranges. In the morning, he seated himself at the breakfast-table, his face nearly covered with wounds received from the enemy's proboscis, when an inquiry was made by the lady of the house if he had passed the night pleasantly. "Yes—yes," he replied with some hesitation; "yes—toler-a-bly pleasant; although—a—*small*—*fly*—annoyed me—somewhat!" At this confession we could restrain ourselves no longer, but broke out into a hearty laugh, led by our good-natured hostess, who then exclaimed: "Musquitos! why, I never dreamed that the marks on your face were musquito bites. I thought they might be from a rash, or something of that kind. Why, didn't you lower down your musquito-bars?" But, as this latter appendage to a bed, on the low, alluvial lands of a southern river, was a greater stranger to him than any dead language known, the "small fly" problem had to be satisfactorily solved, and his sleep made sweet.

Perhaps it may be well here to remark, that the San Joaquin River is divided into three branches, known, respectively, as the west, middle, and east channels—the latter named being not only the main stream, but the one used by the steamboats and sailing-vessels bound to and from Stockton—or, at least, to within four miles of that city, from which point the Stockton slough is used. The east, or main channel, is navigable for small, stern-wheel steamboats as high as Frezno City. Besides the three main channels of the San Joaquin, before mentioned, there are numerous tributaries, the principal of which are the Moquelumne, Calaveras, Stanislaus, Tuolumne, and Merced Rivers.

An apparently interminable sea of tules extends nearly one hundred and fifty miles, south, up the valley of the San Joaquin;

and when these are on fire, as they not unfrequently are, during the fall and early winter months, the broad sheet of licking and leaping flame, and the vast volumes of smoke that rise, and eddy, and surge, hither and thither, present a scene of fearful grandeur at night, that is suggestive of some earthly pandemonium.

NIGHT SCENE ON THE SAN JOAQUIN RIVER—MONTE DIABLO IN THE DISTANCE.

The lumbering sound of the boat's machinery has suddenly ceased, and our high-pressure motive power, descended from a regular to an occasional snorting, gives us a reminder that we have reached Stockton. Time, half-past two o'clock A.M.

At day-break we are again disturbed in our fitful slumbers, by the rumbling of wagons and hurrying bustle of laborers discharging cargo; and before we have scarcely turned over for another uncertain nap, the stentorian lungs of some employee of the stage companies announce, that "stages for Sonora, Columbia, Moquelumne Hill, Sacramento, Mariposa, Coulterville, and Murphy's, are just about starting."

The reader knows as well as we do, that it is of no use, whatever, to be in too great a hurry when we are sight-seeing; consequently, with his permission, we will allow the stages to depart without us this morning, and take a quiet walk about the city.

THE CITY OF STOCKTON.

This flourishing commercial city is situated in the valley of the San Joaquin, at the head of a deep navigable slough or arm of the San Joaquin River, about three miles from its junction with that stream. The luxuriant foliage of the trees and shrubs impress the stranger with the great fertility of the soil; and the unusually large number of windmills with the manner of irrigation. So marked a feature as the latter has secured to this locality the cognomen of "the City of Windmills."

The land upon which the city stands is part of a grant made by Governor Micheltorena, to Captain C. M. Weber and Mr. Gulnac, in 1844, who most probably were the first white settlers in the valley of the San Joaquin; although some Canadian Frenchmen, in the employ of the Hudson Bay Company, spent several hunting seasons here, commencing as early as 1834.

In 1813, an exploring expedition, under Lieutenant Gabriel Morago, visited this valley, and gave it its present name—the former one being "Valle de los Tulares," or Valley of Rushes. At that time, it was occupied by a large and formidable tribe of Indians, called the Yachicumnes, who, in after times, were for the most part captured and sent to the Missions Dolores and San Jose, or decimated by the small-pox, and now are nearly extinct. Under the maddening influence of their losses by death from that fatal disease, they rose upon the whites, burned their buildings and killed their stock, and forced them to take shelter at the Missions.

In 1846, Mr. Weber, reinforced by a number of emigrants, renewed his efforts to form a settlement; but the war breaking out, compelled him to seek refuge in the larger settlements, until the Bear flag was hoisted, when Captain Weber, from his knowledge of the country, and the devotedness of those who had placed

VIEW OF THE CITY OF STOCKTON, FROM THE WHARF, LOOKING EAST.

themselves under his command, was able to render invaluable aid to the American cause.

When the war was concluded, in 1848, another and successful attempt was made to establish a prosperous settlement here, but upon the discovery of gold it was again nearly deserted.

Several cargoes of goods having arrived from San Francisco, for land transportation to the southern mines, were suggestive of the importance of this spot for the foundation of a city, when cloth tents and houses sprung up as if by magic. On the 23d of December, 1849, a fire broke out for the first time, and the "linen city," as it was then called, was swept away, causing a loss of about two hundred thousand dollars. Almost before the ruins had ceased smouldering, a newer and cleaner "linen city," with a few wooden buildings, was erected in its place. In the following spring, a large proportion of the cloth houses gave place to wooden structures; and, being now in steam communication with San Francisco, the new city began to grow substantially in importance.

On the 30th of March, 1850, the first weekly Stockton newspaper was published by Radcliffe and White, conducted by Mr. John White.

On the same day, the first theatrical performance was given, in the Assembly Room of the Stockton House, by Messrs. Bingham and Fury.

On the 13th of May following, the first election was held—the population then numbering about two thousand four hundred.

June 26th, a fire department was organized, and J. E. Nuttman elected chief engineer.

On the 25th of the following month an order was received from the County Court, incorporating the city of Stockton, and authorizing the election of officers. On the 1st of August, 1850, an election for municipal officers was held, when seven hundred votes were polled, with the following result:—Mayor, Samuel Purdy; Recorder, C. M. Teak; City Attorney, Henry A. Crabb; Treasurer, George D. Brush; Assessor, C. Edmondson; Marshal, T. S. Lubbock.

On the 6th of May, 1851, a fire broke out that nearly destroyed

"THE PRAIRIE SCHOONER."

the whole city, at a loss of one million five hundred thousand dollars. After this conflagration, a large number of brick buildings were erected.

In 1852, steps were taken to build a City Hall; and about the same time, the south wing of what is now the State Asylum for the Insane, was erected as a General Hospital; but which was abolished in 1853, and the Insane Asylum formed into a distinct institution by an act of the Legislature. In 1854, the central building was added, and in 1855, the kitchen, bakery, dining-rooms, and bath-rooms were also added.

On the 1st of February, 1856, another fire destroyed property to the amount of about sixty thousand dollars; and on the 30th of July following, by the same cause, about forty thousand dollars' worth of property was swept away.

There are twelve places of worship in Stockton: two Presbyterian, two Baptist, an Episcopal, Congregational, Methodist Episcopal, Methodist Church South, German Methodist, Catholic, colored Methodist, and a Jewish synagogue.

Of newspapers published here, there are the *Stockton Independent*, daily and weekly, N. M. Orr & Co., proprietors; *San Joaquin Republican*, daily and weekly, H. C. Patrick & Co., proprietors; and the *Evening Herald*, daily, Wm. Biven, proprietor.

There are seven public schools here, with an aggregate attendance of 1,275 scholars, as follows: Washington, 350; Lafayette, 325; Franklin, 225; North, 100; South, 80; Vineyard, 125; Pacific, 70: Total, 1,275.

These are exclusive of several flourishing private schools, the success of which will prove how well they were conducted.

Stockton can boast of having the deepest artesian well in the state, which is one thousand and two feet in depth, and which throws out two hundred and fifty gallons of water per minute, fifteen thousand per hour, and three hundred and sixty thousand gallons every twenty-four hours, to the height of eleven feet above the plain, and nine feet above the city grade. In sinking this well, ninety-six different strata of loam, clay, mica, green sandstone, pebbles, etc., were passed through. Three hundred and forty feet from the surface, a redwood stump was found, imbedded in sand, from whence a stream of water issued to the top. The temperature of the water is 77° Fahrenheit—the atmosphere being only 60°. The cost of this well was ten thousand dollars.

One of the principal features connected with the commerce of this city, is the number of large freight wagons, laden for the mines; these have, not inappropriately, been denominated "prairie schooners," and "steamboats of the plains." One team, belonging to Mr. Warren, has taken one hundred thousand pounds to Mariposa in four trips, thus averaging twenty-five thousand per trip. Another team, belonging to Mr. Huffman, hauled thirty-two thousand from Staple's Ranche to Stockton. Twenty-nine thousand six hundred and eighty pounds of freight, in addition to seven hundred pounds of feed, were hauled to Jenny Lind—a mining town on the Moquelumne Hill road, twenty-seven miles from Stockton—by twelve mules. The cost of these wagons is from nine hundred to eleven hundred and fifty dollars. In length, they are generally from twenty to twenty-three feet on the top, and from eighteen to nineteen feet on the bottom. Mules cost upon the average three hundred and fifty dollars each; and some very large ones sell as high as one thousand four hundred dollars the span. One man drives and tends as many as fourteen animals, guiding and driving with a single line. These teams have nearly superseded the use of pack trains, inasmuch as formerly the number of animals in the packing trade exceeded one thousand five hundred, and now it is only about one hundred and sixty. It would be a source of considerable amusement to our eastern friends, could they see how easily these large mules are managed. They are drilled like soldiers, and are almost as tractable. When a teamster cracks his whip, it sounds like the sharp quick report of a revolver, and is nearly as loud.

Several stages leave Stockton daily, at six o'clock, A.M.: For Chinese Camp, fare, $7 (connecting at Chinese with stages for Big Oak Flat, Garrote, Hardin's Mill, Tamarack Flat, and at the latter place with saddle train to Hutchings', in Yo-Sem'ite, eleven miles distant. Also with Coulterville); Sonora and Columbia, fare, $8; for Copperopolis, fare, $6; Murphy's Camp, fare, $8; Calaveras Grove of Mammoth Trees, fare, $10. These fares, it should be remembered, are from Stockton through to the points named. On alternate days, at the same hour, for Mariposa, the Mariposa Mammoth Tree Grove, and Yo-Semite, fare to Mariposa, $10. A daily line is projected on this route.

The Western Pacific railroad, directly connected with the "Central Pacific" and "Union Pacific," passes straight through Stockton. Visitors who wish to see the Yo-Semite valley, or either grove of big trees, before going to San Francisco, should here leave the train, as every mile in either direction, on that great thoroughfare, would be that much out of the way.

Two new lines of railway are now being constructed: "The Stockton and Copperopolis," and "The Stockton and Tulare." The terminus of the former will be thirty-six miles, on the shortest, as well as on one of the most picturesque of routes, to both the Calaveras Grove and the Yo-Semite. The latter will pass a point some twelve miles west of "Snelling's," on the Merced River, and will convey passengers on the Mariposa route to within some ninety-five miles of Yo-Semite. Both these lines will afford pleasant and rapid transit over the dusty plains—now the least comfortable of any portion of the trip.

STOCKTON, VIA COPPEROPOLIS, TO THE CALAVERAS BIG TREES.

"All aboard for Copperopolis, Murphy's, and the Calaveras Big-Tree Grove," cries the coachman. "All set," shouts somebody in answer; when, "crack goes the whip, and away go we."

There is a feeling of jovial, good-humored pleasureableness that steals insensibly over the secluded residents of cities when all the cares of a daily routine of duties are left behind, and the novelty of fresh scenes forms new sources of enjoyment. Especially is it so when seated comfortably in an easy old stage, with the prospect before us of witnessing one of the most wonderful sights to be found in any far-off country, either of the old or new world. Besides, in addition to our being in the reputed position of a Frenchman with his dinner, who is said to enjoy it three times—first, by anticipation; second, in participation; and third, upon retrospection; we have new views perpetually breaking upon our admiring sight.

As soon as we have passed over the best gravelled streets of any town or city in the state, without exception, we thread our way past the beautiful suburban residences of the city of Stockton, and emerge from the shadows of the giant oaks that stand on either side the road. The deliciously cool breath of early morning, laden as it is in spring and early summer, with the fragrance of myriads of flowers and scented shrubs, we inhale with an acme of enjoyment that contrasts inexpressibly with the almost stifling and unsavory warmth of a liliputian state-room on board a high-pressure steamboat.

The bracing air will soon restore the loss of appetite resulting from, and almost consequent upon, the excitement created by the novel circumstances and prospects attending us, so that when we arrive at the first public-house for a change of horses, and breakfast is announced, it is not by any means an unwelcome sound. The inner man being allowed about fifteen minutes to receive satisfaction, and a fresh relay of horses provided, we are soon upon our way again. At the "twenty-seven mile house," we again "change" horses. By this time the day and the travellers all become warm together; and as the cooling land-breeze dies out, the dust begins to pour in by every chink and aperture, so that the luxurious enjoyments of the early morning depart in the same way that lawyers are said to get to heaven—by degrees.

Leaving Copperopolis, we pass through the mining towns of Angel's Camp, Vallecito, and Douglas Flat, arriving at Sperry & Perry's hotel in Murphy's Camp about dark. Early the next morning let us start for the Mammoth-Tree Grove.

ROAD TO THE MAMMOTH-TREE GROVE.

Leaving the mining town of Murphy's Camp behind, we cross the "Flat," and—about half a mile from town—proceed, upon a good carriage road, up a narrow cañon, now upon this side of the stream, and now on 'that,' as the hills proved favorable, or other-wise, for the construction of the road. If our visit is supposed to be in spring or early summer, every mountain side, even to the tops of the ridges, is covered with flowers and flowering-shrubs of great variety and beauty; while, on either hand, groves of oaks and pines stand as shade-giving guardians of personal comfort to the dust-covered traveller on a sunny day.

As we continue our ascent for a few miles, the road becomes more undulating and gradual, and lying, for the most part, on the top, or gently sloping sides, of a dividing ridge; often through dense forests of tall, magnificent pines, that are from one hundred and seventy to two hundred and twenty feet in height, slender, and straight as an arrow. We measured one, that had fallen, that was twenty inches in diameter at the base, and fourteen and a half inches in diameter at the distance of one hundred and twenty-five feet from the base. The ridges being nearly clear of an under-growth of shrubbery, and the trunks of the trees, for fifty feet upward, or more, entirely clear of branches, the eye of the traveller can wander, delightedly, for a long distance, among the captivating scenes of the forest.

At different distances upon the route, the canal of the Union Water Company winds its sinuous way on the top or around the sides of the ridge; or its sparkling contents rush impetuously down the water-furrowed centre of a ravine. Here and there an aqueduct, or cabin, or saw-mill, gives variety to an ever-changing landscape.

When within about four and a half miles of the Mammoth-Tree Grove, the surrounding mountain peaks and ridges are boldly visible. Looking south-east, the uncovered head of Bald Moun-tain silently announces its solitude and distinctiveness; west, the "Coast Mountain range" forms a continuous girdle to the horizon, extending to the north and east, where the snowy tops of the Sierras form a magnificent back-ground to the glorious picture.

While we have been thus riding and admiring, and talking and wondering, and musing concerning the beautiful scenes we have witnessed, the deepening shadows of the densely-timbered forest we are entering, by the awe they inspire—at first gently and imperceptibly, then rapidly and almost to be felt—prepare our minds to appreciate the imposing grandeur of the objects we are about to see, just as

> "Coming events cast their shadows before."

The gracefully-curling smoke from the chimneys of the Big-Tree Cottage, that is now visible; the inviting refreshment of the inner man; the luxurious feeling arising from bathing the hands and temples in cold, clear water—especially after a ride or walk—are alike disregarded. One thought, one feeling, one emotion—that of vastness, sublimity, profoundness, pervades the whole soul; for there

> "The giant trees, in silent majesty,
> Like pillars, stand 'neath Heaven's mighty dome.
> 'Twould seem that, perch'd upon their topmost branch,
> With outstretch'd finger, man might touch the stars;
> Yet, could he gain that height, the boundless sky
> Were still as far beyond his utmost reach,
> As from the burrowing toilers in a mine.
> Their age unknown, into what depths of time
> Might Fancy wander sportively, and deem
> Some Monarch-Father of this grove set forth
> His tiny shoot, when the primeval flood
> Receded from the old and changed earth;
> Perhaps, coeval with Assyrian kings,
> His branches in dominion spread; from age
> To age, his sapling heirs with empires grew.
> When Time those patriarchs' leafy tresses strew'd
> Upon the earth, while Art and Science slept,
> And ruthless hordes drove back Improvement's stream
> Their sturdy oaklings throve, and, in their turn,
> Rose, when Columbus gave to Spain a world.
> How many races, savage or refined,
> Have dwelt beneath their shelter! Who shall say

HOTEL AT THE CALAVERAS GROVE OF BIG TREES.

(If hands irreverent molest them not)
But they may shadow mighty cities, reared
E'en at their roots, in centuries to come,
Till, with the "Everlasting Hills" they bow,
When "Time shall be no longer!"*

Before wandering further amid the wild secluded depths of this forest, it will be well that the horse and his rider should partake of some good and substantial repast, such as he will here find provided, inasmuch as it is not always wisest, or best, to explore the wonderful, or look upon the beautiful, with an empty stomach, especially after a bracing and appetitive ride of fifteen miles. While thus engaged, let us explain some matters that we have reserved for this occasion.

* Extract from Mrs. Conner's forthcoming play of "The Three Brothers; or, the Mammoth Grove of Calaveras: a Legend of California."

A COTILLON PARTY OF THIRTY-TWO PERSONS DANCING ON THE STUMP OF THE MAMMOTH TREE.

The Mammoth-Tree Grove, then, is situated in a gently sloping, and, as you have seen, heavily-timbered valley, on the divide or ridge between the San Antonio branch of the Calaveras River and the north fork of the Stanislaus River; in lat. 38° north, long. 120° 10' west; at an elevation of 2,300 feet above Murphy's Camp, and 4,370 feet above the level of the sea; at a distance of ninety-seven miles from Sacramento City, and eighty-seven from Stockton.

When specimens of this tree, with its cones and foliage, were sent to England for examination, Professor Lindley, an eminent English botanist, considered it as forming a new genus, and accordingly named it (doubtless with the best intentions, but still unfairly) "Wellingtonia gigantea;" but through the examinations of Mr. Lobb, a gentleman of rare botanical attainments, who has spent several years in California, devoting himself to this interesting, and, to him, favorite branch of study, it is decided to belong to the Taxodium family, and must be referred to the old genus *Sequoia sempervirens;* and consequently, as it is not a new genus, and as it has been properly examined and classified, it is now known, only, among scientific men, as the *Sequoia gigantea* (sempervirens) and not "Wellingtonia," or, as some good and laudably patriotic souls would have it, to prevent the English from stealing American thunder, "Washingtonia gigantea."

Within an area of fifty acres, there are one hundred and three trees of a goodly size, twenty of which exceed twenty-five feet in diameter at the base, and, consequently, are about seventy-five feet in circumference!

WORKMEN ENGAGED IN FELLING THE MAMMOTH TREE.

But—the repast over—let us first walk upon the "Big-Tree Stump" adjoining the cottage. You see it is perfectly smooth, sound, and level. Upon this stump, however incredible it may seem, on the 4th of July, thirty-two persons were engaged in dancing four sets of cotillions at one time, without suffering any inconvenience whatever; and besides these, there were musicians and lookers-on. Across the solid wood of this stump, five and a half feet from the ground (now the bark is removed, which was from fifteen to eighteen inches in thickness), measures twenty-five feet, and with the bark, twenty-eight feet. Think for a moment; the stump of a tree exceeding *nine yards* in diameter, and sound to the very centre.

This tree employed five men for twenty-two days in felling it—not by chopping it down, but by *boring it off* with pump augers. After the stem was fairly severed from the stump, the uprightness of the tree, and breadth of its base, sustained it in its position. To accomplish the feat of throwing it over, about two and a half days of the twenty-two were spent in inserting wedges, and driving them in with the butts of trees, until, at last, the noble monarch of the forest was forced to tremble, and then to fall, after braving " the battle and the breeze" of nearly three thousand winters. In our estimation, it was a sacrilegious act; although it is possible, that the exhibition of the bark, among the unbelievers of the eastern part of our continent, and of Europe, may have convinced all the "Thomases" living, that we have great facts in California, that must be believed, sooner or later. This is the only palliating consideration with us for this act of desecration.

VIEW OF DOUBLE BOWLING-ALLEY ON TRUNK OF BIG TREE.

This noble tree was three hundred and two feet in height, and ninety-six feet in circumference at the ground. Upon the upper part of the prostate trunk is constructed a long double bowling-alley, where the athletic sport of playing bowls may afford a pastime and change to the visitor.

Now let us walk, among the giant shadows of the forest, to another of these wonders—the largest tree now standing; which, from its immense size, two breast-like protuberances on one side, and the number of small trees of the same class adjacent, has been named "The Mother of the Forest." In the summer of 1854, the bark was stripped from this tree by Mr. George Gale, for purposes of exhibition in the East, to the height of one hundred and sixteen feet; and it now measures in circumference, without the bark, at the base, eighty-four feet; twenty feet from base, sixty-nine feet; seventy feet from base, forty-three feet six inches; one hundred and sixteen feet from base, and up to the bark, thirty-nine feet six inches. The full circumference at base, including bark, was ninety feet. Its height is three hundred and twenty-one feet. The average thickness of bark was eleven inches, although in places it was about two feet. This tree is estimated to contain five hundred and thirty-seven thousand feet of sound inch lumber. To the first branch it is one hundred and thirty-seven feet. The small black marks upon the tree indicate points where two and a half inch auger holes were bored, into which rounds were inserted, by which to ascend and descend, while removing the bark. At different distances upward, especially at the top, numerous dates, and names of visitors, have been cut. It is contemplated to construct a circular stairway around this tree. When the bark was being removed, a young man fell from the scaffolding—or, rather, out of a descending noose—at a distance of seventy-nine feet from the ground, and escaped with a broken limb. We were within a few yards of him when he fell, and were agreeably surprised to discover that he had not broken his neck.

A short distance from the above lies the prostrate and majestic body of the "Father of the Forest," the largest tree of the entire group, half-buried in the soil. This tree measures in circumference, at the roots, one hundred and ten feet. It is two hundred feet to the first branch; the whole of which is hollow, and through

VIEW OF THE "FATHER OF THE FOREST."

which a person can walk erect. By the trees that were broken
off when this tree bowed its proud head, in its fall, it is estimated
that, when standing, it could not be less than four hundred and
thirty-five feet in height. Three hundred feet from the roots,
and where it was broken off by striking against another large
tree, it is eighteen feet in diameter. Around this tree stand the
graceful, yet giant trunks of numerous other trees, which form a
family circle, and make this the most imposing scene in the whole
grove. From its immense size, and the number of trees near,
doubtless originated the name. Near its base is a never-failing
spring of cold and delicious water.

Let us not linger here too long, but pass on to "The Husband
and Wife"—a graceful pair of trees that are leaning, with apparent affection, against each other. Both of these are of the
same size, and measure in circumference, at the base, about sixty
feet; and in height are about two hundred and fifty-two feet.

A short distance further is "The Burnt Tree;" which is prostrate, and hollow from numerous burnings—in which a person can
ride on horseback for sixty feet. The estimated height of this
tree, when standing, was three hundred and thirty feet, and its
circumference ninety-seven feet. It now measures across the
roots thirty-nine feet six inches.

"Hercules," another of these giants, is ninety-five feet in circumference, and three hundred and twenty feet high. On the
trunk of this tree is cut the name of "G. M. Wooster, June, 1850;"

so that it is possible this person may some day claim precedence to Mr. Dowd, in this great discovery.*   At all events, it was through the latter that the world became acquainted with the grove. There are many other trees of this group that claim a passing notice; but, inasmuch as they very much resemble each other, we shall only mention them briefly.

THE CONE, AND FOLIAGE OF THE MAMMOTH TREES—FULL SIZE.

The " Hermit," a lonely old fellow, is 318 feet in height, and 60 in circumference; exceedingly straight and well formed.

* Since writing the above, we have made the acquaintance of Mr. Wooster, who disclaims all title to the discovery, although of the same party; and gives it to W. Whitehead, Esq., who, while tying his shoe, looked casually around him, and saw the trees, June, 1850.

The "Old Maid"—a stooping, broken-topped, and forlorn-looking spinster of the big-tree family—is two hundred and sixty-one feet in height, and fifty-nine feet in circumference.

As a fit companion to the above, though at a respectful distance from it, stands the dejected-looking "Old Bachelor." This tree, as lonely and as solitary as the former, is one of the roughest, bark-rent specimens of the big trees to be found. In size it rather has the advantage of the "Old Maid," being about two hundred and ninety-eight feet in height, and sixty feet in circumference.

Near to the "Old Bachelor" is the "Pioneer's Cabin," the top of which is broken off about one hundred and fifty feet from the ground. This tree measures thirty-three feet in diameter; but, as it is hollow, and uneven in its circumference, its average size will not be quite equal to that.

The "Siamese Twins," as their name indicates, with one large stem at the ground, form a double tree about forty-one feet upward. These are each three hundred feet in height.

Near to them stands the "Guardian," a fine-looking old tree, three hundred and twenty feet in height, by eighty-one feet in circumference.

The "Mother and Son" form another beautiful sight, as side by side they stand. The former is three hundred and fifteen feet in height, and the latter three hundred and two feet. Unitedly, their circumference is ninety-three feet.

The "Horseback Ride" is an old, broken, and long prostrate trunk, one hundred and fifty feet in length, hollow from one end to the other, and in which, to the distance of seventy-two feet, a person can ride on horseback. At the narrowest place inside, this tree is twelve feet high.

"Uncle Tom's Cabin" is another fanciful name, given to a tree that is hollow, and in which twenty-five persons can be seated comfortably (not, as a friend at our elbow suggests, in each other's laps, perhaps!) This tree is three hundred and five feet in height, and ninety-one feet in circumference.

The "Pride of the Forest" is one of the most beautiful trees of this wonderful grove. It is well-shaped, straight, and sound;

and, although not quite as large as some of the others, it is, nevertheless, a noble-looking member of the grove, two hundred and seventy-five feet in height, and sixty feet in circumference.

THE "THREE GRACES."

4

The "Two Guardsmen" stand by the roadside, at the entrance of the "clearing," and near the cottage. They seem to be the sentinels of the valley. In height, these are three hundred feet; and in circumference, one is sixty-five feet, and the other sixty-nine feet.

Next—though last in being mentioned, not least in gracefulness and beauty—stand the "Three Sisters"—by some called the "Three Graces"—one of the most beautiful groups (if not *the* most beautiful) of the whole grove. Together, at their base, they measure in circumference ninety-two feet; and in height they are nearly equal, and each measures nearly two hundred and ninety-five feet.

Many of the largest of these trees have been deformed and otherwise injured, by the numerous and large fires that have swept with desolating fury over this forest, at different periods. But a small portion of decayed timber, of the Taxodium genus, can be seen. Like other varieties of the same species, it is less subject to decay, even when fallen and dead, than other woods.

Respecting the age of this grove, there has been but one opinion among the best informed botanists, which is this—that each concentric circle is the growth of one year; and as nearly three thousand concentric circles can be counted in the stump of the fallen tree, it is correct to conclude that these trees are nearly three thousand years old. "This," says the *Gardener's Calendar,* "may very well be true, if it does not grow above two inches in diameter in twenty years, which we believe to be the fact."

Could those magnificent and venerable forest giants of Calaveras county be gifted with a descriptive historical tongue, how their recital would startle us, as they told of the many wonderful changes that have taken place in California within the last three thousand years !*

* Almost eight miles from here is the wonderful " South Grove," by far the largest and finest grove of *Sequoias* yet discovered in California. It contains 1,380 trees, many of them of the most magnificent proportions. We measured ten trees that were twenty-one feet larger in circumference than any others in either of the groves. Through the prostrate trunk of one tree, resembling an immense tube, we could have driven one of the heaviest Concord stages, crowded with passengers, a distance of 200 feet. The trip can be made there and back in one day from the Calaveras Grove.

CHAPTER II.

THE CAVES OF CALAVERAS COUNTY.

"Nature—faint emblem of Omnipotence!
Shaped by His hand—the shadow of His light;
The veil in which He wraps His majesty,
And through whose mantling folds He deigns to show,
Of His mysterious, awful attributes
And dazzling splendors, all man's feeble thought
Can grasp uncrushed, or vision bear unquenched."
                                    STREET'S POEMS.

THE MOUTH OF THE CAVE.

AFTER the visitor has lingered long among the scenes we have just described, he will feel that he

"Could pass days
Stretched in the shade of those old cedar trees,
Watching the sunshine like a blessing fall—
The breeze like music wandering o'er the boughs,
Each tree a natural harp—each different leaf
A different note, blent in one vast thanksgiving."

Yet he may entertain a desire to look upon other wonders that

"Are but parts of a stupendous whole,"

and pay a visit to the natural caves. These caves are situated on McKinney's Humbug, a tributary of the Calaveras River, about fourteen miles west of the mammoth trees, sixteen miles south, by the trail, from Moquelumne Hill, seven miles north, from Murphy's Camp, nine miles east of San Andreas, and near the mouth of O'Neil's Creek.

They were discovered accidentally, in October, 1850, by Captain Taylor, who, with others, was engaged in mining on this creek, and who, having finished their mid-day repast, were spending the interval, before resuming their afternoon's work, in shooting at a mark near the back of their cabin. Mr. Taylor, having just fired his rifle, proceeded to examine the mark, and having hit the centre, proposed that it should be placed at a greater distance than any at which they had ever before tried their skill; and was looking out for a tree upon which to place it, when he saw a hole among the rocks. He immediately went to it, and, seeing that the aperture extended into the mountain for some distance, he called to his companions, and they conjointly commenced to explore it.

But let us not keep the reader waiting; and as the following excellent description from the *Pacific* is so truthfully descriptive of this curiosity, we transcribe it for this work.

"The entrance is round a jutting angle of a ledge of rocks, which hides the small mining town adjacent from sight.

THE ENTRANCE.

"Only the house of the proprietor is to be seen. The country around is wild and romantic. Provided with adamantine candles, we entered through a small doorway, which had been blasted out to a sufficient size. Thence we crept along twenty-five or thirty feet, threading our way through an irregular and difficult passage, at first descending rapidly, but afterward level. Sometimes we were forced to stoop, and at others to bend the body in accordance with the seam of the rocks which constitute the passage. Suddenly we emerged into a large vault or room, about sixty feet in length by twenty in breadth, with an irregular roof, running up in some places thirty feet. This room is called

THE COUNCIL CHAMBER.

"The walls are dark, rough, and solid, rather than beautiful. Descending a little to the south-west, we again made our way through a long, low passage, which led to another room of half the size of the Council Chamber. Rising from the floor of this room, by another narrow passage, we soon came into a third large room, of irregular construction. The roof ascends, until lost to sight in perfect darkness; here, as far up as the eye, assisted by the dim taper, can reach, the lime depositions present a perfect resemblance to a vast cataract of waters rushing from an inconceivable height, in a perfect sheet of foam, leaping from one great shelf of jutting rock down to others, onward, widening as they near, in exact perspective. This room is called

THE CATARACT.

"And well does it deserve the name. Next we descended a short distance, by another passage, and entered a small, round room, in the centre of the roof of which runs up a lofty opening, sixty feet high, of singular appearance. This apartment is called

THE CATHEDRAL.

"Turning back by the Cataract, we passed an easy way by a deep well of water upon the left, and very singular small pools or reservoirs on the right. Leaving these, we soon entered a spacious room, full one hundred feet square, and of fair proportionate height. Through another low opening, we entered yet another great room, near the centre of which stands a large, dark structure, the perfect likeness of a full-robed Roman Bishop, minus the head; whence the name for the room, the

BISHOP'S PALACE.

"Descending through another small opening, we entered a room beautifully ornamented with pendents from the roof, white as the whitest feldspar, and of every possible form. Some like garments hung in a wardrobe, every fold and seam complete; others like curtains, with portions of columns, half-way to the floor, fluted and scolloped for unknown purposes; while innumerable spear-shaped stalactites, of different sizes and lengths, hung from all parts; giving a beauty and splendor to the whole appearance surpassing description. Once, as the light was borne up along a glorious fairy stairway, and back behind solid pillars of clear deposits, and the reflected rays glanced through the myriads of varying forms, the whole—pillars, curtains, pendents, and carved work, white as snow, and translucent as crystal—glistened and shone, and sparkled with a glory that surpassed in splendor all that we had seen in art, or read in fable. This is called

THE BRIDAL CHAMBER.

VIEW OF THE BRIDAL CHAMBER.

"Immediately at the back of this, and connected with it by different openings, is another room, now called

MUSICAL HALL.

"It is so called from the fact, that, on one side, suspended from a singular rock, that has the character of a musical sounding-board, hang a large number of stalactites, arranged in a line very large at one end, and gradually increasing in size toward the other, so that, if with a rod you strike the pendents properly, all the musical tones, from a common bass to a very high key, can be produced in perfection, ringing loud and clear through the halls, as a well-toned instrument.

"Here the present exploration of the cave terminates, at the distance of about one-sixth of a mile from the entrance."

THE HOTEL.

In 1853 it was taken up, under a pre-emption right, by Messrs. Magee and Angel, who erected a large and substantial hotel adjoining the cave, for the convenience of the public, at a cost of about four thousand five hundred dollars. This hotel is commodious and comfortable, and we shall long remember the enjoyment of our visit, and the personal attention we received from the agreeable and enterprising proprietors.

VIEW OF THE HOTEL AT THE CAVE.

VIEW OF THE UPPER SIDE OF UPPER NATURAL BRIDGE.

CHAPTER III.

THE NATURAL BRIDGES OF CALAVERAS COUNTY.

" Here the great Architect
Did, with curious skill, a pile erect
Of carved marble."
CAREW.

THESE bridges are situated on Cayote Creek, about half way between Valicita and McLane's Ferry, on the Stanislaus River, and
hold a high rank among the varied natural objects of interest and

beauty abounding in California. The entire water of Cayote Creek runs beneath these bridges. The bold, rocky, and precipitous banks of the stream, both above and below the bridges, present a counterpart of wild scenery, in perfect keeping with the strange beauty and picturesque grandeur of their interior formation.

THE UPPER BRIDGE.

Approaching the upper bridge from the east, along the stream, the entrance beneath presents the appearance of a noble Gothic arch of massive stone-work, thirty-two feet in height above the water, and twenty-five feet in width at the abutments; while the rock and earth above, supported by the arch, are thirty or more feet in thickness, and overgrown to some extent with trees and shrubbery.

Passing under the arch, along the border of the creek, the walls, extend upward to an almost perfectly formed and pointed arch, and maintaining their width and elevation; but with here and there an irregularity, serving, however, to heighten the interest of the beautiful scene presented. Along the roof, or arch, hang innumerable stalactites, like opaque icicles, but solid as the limestone, or marble, of which they are formed.

As we advance, the width of the arch increases to nearly forty feet, and in its height to fifty feet; and here it really seems as though nature, in her playful moments, determined for once, in her own rude way, to mock the more elaborately-worked objects of art. Yet, as more in accordance with reality, we think that from such fine natural formation, the noble Gothic order of architecture was first suggested.

Here the spacious roof (with a little aid from the imagination) is made to resemble an immense cathedral, with its vaulted arches supported by innumerable columns along the sides, with here and there a jutting portion, as though an attempt had been made to rough-hew an altar, and corridor with massive steps thereto; while stalactites, springing from the bottom and sides, would appear like waxen candles, ready to be lighted, but for the muddy sediment which has formed upon them.

Nor is this all, for near the foot of the altar is a natural basin of pure water, clear as crystal, as though purposely for a baptismal font.

Numerous other formations, some of them peculiarly grotesque, and others beautiful, adorn the sides and roof of this truly magnificent subterranean temple; one of these, the "rock cascade," is a beautiful feature, as it bears a striking resemblance to that which would result from the instantaneous freezing, to perfect solidity, of a stream of water rolling down the rocky sides of the cavernous formation. Others resemble urns and basins; all formed from the action of, and ever filled to their brims with, clear cold water, as it trickles from the rocks above.

LOWER SIDE OF UPPER NATURAL BRIDGE.

Approaching the lower section of this immense arch, its form becomes materially changed, increasing in width, while the roof, becoming more flattened, is brought down to within five feet of the water of the creek. The entire distance through or under this vast natural bridge is about ninety-five yards.

THE LOWER BRIDGE.

Nearly half. a mile down the creek from the bridge described, is another, with its arched entrance differing but little from the one already described, in size, but the form of the arch is quite different, being more flattened and broader at the top. Advancing beneath its wide-spreading arch, and passing another beautiful fount of water, issuing from a low, broad basin, wrought by nature's own hand, we arrive at a point where a roof and supporting walls present the appearance of a magnificent rotunda, or arched dome, sixty feet in width, but with a height of only fifteen feet.

THE UPPER SIDE OF LOWER NATURAL BRIDGE.

Here, too, are numberless stalactites, hanging like opaque icicles from above, while the rocky floor, where the creek does not receive the trickling water from above, is studded thick with stalagmites of curious and beautiful forms. The length of this arch is about seventy yards.

These natural bridges give to the locality an interest exceeded by few in the State; they form the most remarkable natural tunnels known in the world, serving as they do for the passage of a considerable stream through them.

The entire rock formation of the vicinity is limestone, and various are the conjectures relative to the first formation of these natural bridges or tunnels. Some believing them to have been formed by the rocky deposit contained in, and precipitated by, the water of countless springs, issuing from the banks of the creek, that, gradually accumulating and projecting, at length united the two sides, forming these great arched passages. Others believe that, as these bridges are covered many feet in depth with rock and earth, these natural tunnels were but so many subterranean passages or caverns, formed, we will not attempt to say *how*, but as other caverns are, or have been, in nearly all limestone formations; for were these subterranean passages to exist in the adjoining hills or mountains, with either one or two arches of entrance, they would be called caverns. But, by whatever freak of nature formed, they are objects of peculiar interest, and will well repay the summer rambler, among the mines and mountains, the trouble of visiting them. Our wonder is that so few, comparatively, have visited these singular specimens of nature's architecture.

THE YO-SEMITE VALLEY.

THE YO-SEMITE WATERFALL, TWO THOUSAND SIX HUNDRED AND THIRTY-FOUR FEET IN HEIGHT.

From a Photograph by C. L. Weed.

CHAPTER IV.

"Where rose the mountains, there to him were friends;
Where rolled the ocean, thereon was his home;
Where a blue sky and glowing clime extends,
He had the passion and the power to roam;
The desert, forest, cavern, breakers' foam,
    Were unto him companionship."
                                        Childe Harold.

"If thou art worn and hard beset
With sorrows, that thou wouldst forget;
If thou wouldst read a lesson that will keep
Thy heart from fainting, and thy soul from sleep—
Go to the woods and hills."
                                        LONGFELLOW.

THE reader knows as well as we do, that, although it may be
of but little consequence in point of fact, whether a spirit of ro-
mance, the love of the grand and beautiful in scenery, the suggestions or promptings of a fascinating woman—be she friend, sweet-
heart, or wife—the desire for change, the want of recreation, or
the necessity of a restoration and recuperation of an overtasked
physical or mental organization, or both—whatever may be the
agent that first gives birth to the wish for, or the love of travel;
when the mind is thoroughly made up, and the committee of ways
and means reports itself financially prepared to undertake the
pleasurable task—in order to enjoy it with luxurious zest, we
must resolve upon four things: *first*, to leave the "peck of troub-
les," and a few thrown in, entirely behind; *second*, to have none
but good, suitable, and genial-hearted companions; *third*, a sufficient supply of personal patience, good humor, forbearance, and
creature comforts for all emergencies; and, *fourth*, not to be in a
hurry.   To these, both one and all, who have ever visited the Yo-
Semite Valley, we know will say—Amen.

As there are but few countries that possess more of the beautiful and wildly picturesque than California, it seems to us a sin to
neglect to cultivate the knowledge and inspiration of it.   Especi-

ally as her towering and pine-covered mountains; her wide-spread valleys, carpeted with flowers; her leaping waterfalls; her foaming cataracts; her rushing rivers; her placid lakes; her ever green and densely timbered forests; her gently rolling hills, covered with blooming shrubs and trees, and wild flowers, give a voiceless invitation to the traveller to look upon her and admire.

Whether one sits with religious veneration at the foot of Mount Shasta, or cools himself in the refreshing shade of the natural caves and bridges, or walks beneath the giant shadows of the mammoth trees, or stands in awe looking upon the frowning and pine-covered heights of the Yo-Semite Valley, he feels that

"A thing of beauty is a joy forever,"

and that the Californian's home will compare, in picturesque magnificence, with that of any other land.

In later years, other employments and enjoyments have been entertained as worthy the attention of the residents and visitors of this coast, than money-making. Now, there are many who throng the highway of elevating and refining pleasure, in spring and summer, to feast the eye and mind upon the beautiful. In the hope, though humbly, of fostering this feeling, we continue our sketches of the most remarkable and interesting, among which doubtless stands the great Yo-Semite Valley.

THE CIRCUMSTANCES THAT LED TO ITS DISCOVERY.

The early California resident will remember, that during the spring and summer of 1850, much dissatisfaction existed among the white settlers and miners on the Merced, San Joaquin, Chowchilla, and Frezno Rivers and their tributaries, on account of the frequent robberies committed upon them by the Chook-chan-cie, Po-to-en-cie, Noot-cho, Po-ho-ne-chee, Ho-na-chee, Chow-chilla, and other Indian tribes on the head waters of those streams. The frequent repetition of their predatory forays having been attended with complete success, without any attempted punishment on the part of the whites, the Indians began seriously to contemplate the practicability of driving out every white intruder upon their hunting and fishing grounds.

At this time, James D. Savage had two stores, or trading-posts, nearly in the centre of the affected tribes; the one on Little Mariposa Creek, about twenty miles south of the town of Mariposa, and near the old stone fort; and the other on Frezno River, about two miles above where John Hunt's store now is. Around these stores those Indians who were most friendly, used to congregate; from them and his two Indian wives, Eekino and Homut, Savage ascertained the state of thought and feeling among them.

In order to avert such a calamity, and without even hinting at his motive, he invited an Indian chief, who possessed much influence with the Chow-chillas and Chook-chan-cies, named José Jerez, to accompany him and his two squaws to San Francisco; hoping thereby to impress him with the wonders, numbers, and power of the whites, and through him the various tribes who were malcontent. To this Jerez gladly assented, and they arrived in San Francisco in time to witness the first celebration of the admission of California into the Union, on the 29th of October, 1850,* and they put up at the Revere House, then standing on Montgomery street.

During their stay in San Francisco, and while Savage was purchasing goods for his stores in the mountains, José Jerez, the Indian chief, became intoxicated, and returned to the hotel about the same time as Savage, in a state of boisterous and quarrelsome excitement. In order to prevent his making a disturbance, Savage shut him up in his room, and there endeavored to soothe him, and restrain his violence by kindly words; but this he resented, and became not only troublesome, but very insulting; when, after patiently bearing it as long as he possibly could, at a time of great provocation, unhappily he was tempted to strike Jerez, and followed it up with a severe scolding. This very much exasperated the

* The news of the admission, by Congress, of California into the Union, on the 9th of September, 1850, was brought by the mail steamer "Oregon," which arrived in the Bay of San Francisco on the 18th of October, 1850, when preparations were immediately commenced for a general jubilee throughout the State on the 29th of that month.

Indian, and he indulged in numerous muttered threats of what he would do when he went back among his own people. But, when sober, he concealed his angry resentment, and, Indian-like, sullenly awaited his opportunity for revenge. Simple, and apparently small as was this circumstance, like many others equally insignificant, it led to very unfortunate results; for no sooner had he returned to his own people, than he summoned a council of the chief men of all the surrounding tribes; and from his influence and representations mainly, steps were then and there taken to drive out or kill all the whites, and appropriate all the horses, mules, oxen, and provisions they could find.*

Accordingly, early one morning in the ensuing month of November, the Indians entered Savage's store on the Frezno, in their usual manner, as though on a trading expedition, when an immediate and apparently preconcerted plan of attack was made with hatchets, crow-bars, and arrows; first upon Mr. Greeley, who had charge of the store, and then upon three other white men named Canada, Stiffner, and Brown, who were present. This was made so unexpectedly as to exclude time or opportunity for defence, and all were killed except Brown, whose life was saved by an Indian named " Polonio" (thus christened by the whites), jumping between him and the attacking party, at the risk of his own personal safety, thus affording Brown a chance of escape, which he made the best of, by running all the way to Quartzburg, at the height of his speed.

Simultaneously with this attack on the Frezno, Savage's other store and residence on the Mariposa was attacked, during his absence, by another band, and his Indian wives carried off. Similar onslaughts having been made at different points on the Merced, San Joaquin, Frezno, and Chow-chilla rivers, Savage concluded that a general Indian war was about opening, and immediately commenced raising a volunteer battalion. At the same time a requisition for men, arms, ammunition, and general stores,

* These facts were communicated to us by Mr. J. M. Cunningham (now in the Yo-Semite valley), who was then engaged as clerk for Savage, and was present during the altercation between him and the Indian.

5

was made upon the Governor of the State (General John McDougal), which was promptly responded to by him, and hostilities were at once begun.

Doctor L. H. Bunnell, an eye-witness, belonging to the Mariposa battalion, has kindly favored us with the following interesting account of this campaign:

"Preparations were being made for defence, when the news came of the sack of Savage's place on the Frezno, and of two men killed, and one wounded; and close on this report came another, of the murder of four men at Doctor Thomas Payne's place, at the Four Creeks; one of the bodies being found skinned. The bearer of the news was one who had escaped the murderous assault of the Indians by the fleetness of his horse, but with the loss of an arm, which was amputated, soon after this event, by Doctor Leach, of the Frezno.

"These occurrences so exasperated the people, that a company was at once raised and despatched to chastise the Indians. They found and attacked a large rancheria, high up on the Frezno. During the fight, Lieutenant Stein was killed, and William Little severely wounded. It is not known how many Indians were killed, but the whites assert that in that battle they did nothing to immortalize themselves as Indian fighters. Most of the party were very much dissatisfied with the result of the fight; and while some left for the settlements, others continued in search of the Indians.

"In a few days it was ascertained that some four or five hundred Indians had assembled on a round mountain, lying between the north branches of the San Joaquin, and that they invited attack. They were discovered late in the afternoon; but Captain Boling and Lieutenant Chandler were disposed to have a 'brush' with them that evening, if for no other reason than to study their position. Their object was gained, and the captain, with his company, was followed by the Indians on his return from reconnoitring, and annoyed during the night.

"In the morning volunteers were called for, to attack the rancheria. Thirty-six offered, and at daylight the storming commenced with such fury as is seldom witnessed in Indian warfare. The rancheria was fired in several places at the same time, in accordance with a previous understanding, and as the Indians sallied from their burning wigwams, they were shot down, killed, or wounded. A panic seized many of them, and notwithstanding the fear in which their chief, 'José,' was held, at such a time his authority was powerless to compel his men to stand before the flames, and the exasperated fury of the whites. José was mortally wounded, and twenty-three of his men were killed upon the ground. Only one of Captain Boling's party (a negro who fought valiantly) was touched, and he but slightly. It is not my purpose to eulogize any one, but it is right to say, that that battle checked the Indians in their career of murder and robbery, and did more to save the blood of the whites, as well as of Indians, than any or all other circumstances combined.

"In a subsequent expedition into that region after the organization of the battalion, which was in January, 1851, the remains of José were found still burning among the coals of the funeral pyre. The Indians fled at the approach of the volunteers, not even firing a gun or winging an arrow, in defence of their once loved, but dreaded chief.

"It will not, I think, be out of place in this connection, to repeat a speech *delivered* by Captain Boling on the eve of the expected battle. The captain's object was to exhort the men to do their duty. He commenced :—'Gentlemen—hem—fellow citizens— hem—soldiers—hem—fellow volunteers—hem'—(tremblingly)— and after a long pause, he broke out into a laugh, and said : 'Boys, I will only say in *conclusion*, that I hope I will fight better than I speak.'

"It was during the occurrence of the events that have been mentioned above, that the existence of an Indian stronghold was brought to light. When the Indians were told that they would all be killed, if they did not make peace, they would laugh in derision, and say that they had many places to flee to, where the whites could not follow them; and one place they had, which, if the whites were to enter, they would be corralled like mules or horses. After a series of perplexing delays, Major Savage, Captain Boling, and Captain Dill, with two companies of the battalion, started in search of the Indians and their Gibraltar. On the south fork of the Merced, a rancheria was taken without firing a gun; the orders from the Commissioners being in ' no case to shed blood unnecessarily ;' and to the credit of our race, it was strictly obeyed throughout the campaign, except in one individual instance.

" As soon as the prisoners had arrived at the rendezvous designated, near what is now called Bishop's Camp, Pou-watch-ie and Cow-chit-ty (brothers), chiefs of the tribes we had taken, despatched runners to the chief of the tribe living in the then unknown valley, with orders from Major Savage for him to bring in his tribe to head-quarters, or to the rendezvous.

"Next morning the chief spoken of, Ten-ie-ya, came in alone, and stated that his people would be in during the following day, and that they now desired peace. The time passed for their arrival. After waiting another day, and no certainty of their coming manifested, early on the following morning volunteers were called for to storm their stronghold.

" The place where the Indians were supposed to be living, was depicted in no very favorable terms; but so anxious had the men become, that more offered than were desired by Captain Boling for the expedition. To decide who should go, the captain paced off one hundred yards, and told the volunteers that he wanted men fleet of foot, and with powers of endurance, and their fitness could be demonstrated by a race. By this means he selected, without offence, the men he desired. Some, in their anxiety to go, ran bare-footed in the snow.

" All being ready, Ten-ie-ya took the lead as guide, very much against his inclination; and we commenced our march to the then unknown and unnamed valley. Savage said he had been there, but not by the route that we were taking. About half way to the valley, which proved about fifteen miles from the rendezvous, on the south fork, seventy-two Indians, women, and children, were met coming in as promised by Ten-ie-ya.

"They gave as an excuse for their delay the great depth of the snow, which in places was over eight feet deep. Ten-ie-ya tried to convince Major Savage that there were no more Indians in the valley, but the whole command cried out as with one voice, 'Let's go on.' The major was willing to indulge the men in their desire to learn the truth of the exaggerated reports the Indians had given of the country, and we moved on. Ten-ie-ya was allowed to return with his people to the rendezvous, sending in his stead a young Indian as guide.

"Upon the arrival of the party in the valley, the young Indian manifested a great deal of uneasiness; he said it would be impossible to cross the river that night, and was not certain that it could be crossed in the morning. It was evident that he had some object in view; but the volunteers were obliged to content themselves for the night, resolved to be up and looking out for themselves early in the morning, for a crossing, or way over the rocks and through the jungle into which they had been led. Daylight appeared, and with it was found a ford. And such a ford! It furnished in copious abundance, water for more than one plunge bath, and that, too, to some who were no admirers of hydropathy; or, judging from their appearance, had never realized any of its bounties.

" In passing up the valley on the north side, it was soon very evident that some of the wigwams had been occupied the night before; and hence the anxiety of the young Indian, lest the occupants should be surprised. The valley was scoured in all directions, but not an Indian could be found. At length, hid among the rocks, the writer discovered an old woman; so old, that when Ten-ie-ya was interrogated in regard to her age, he with a smile, said, that 'when she was a child, the mountains were hills.' The old creature was provided with fire and food, and allowed to remain.

"It having snowed during the night, and continuing to snow in the morning, the major ordered the return of the command, lest it should be hemmed in by snow. This was in March, 1851. Ten-ie-ya and others of his tribe asserted most positively that we were the first white men ever in the valley. The writer asked Major Savage, 'Have you not been in the valley before?' he answered, 'No, never; I have been mistaken; it was in a valley below this (since known as Cascade Valley), two and a half miles below the Yo-Semite.'

"On our return to the rendezvous where the prisoners had been assembled, we started for the Commissioners' camp on the Frezno. On our way in, about a hundred more Indians gave themselves up to Captain Dill's company. When within about fifteen miles of the Commissioners' camp, nine men only being left in charge, owing to an absolute want of provisions, the Indians fled—frightened, as it afterward appeared, by the stories told them by the Chow-chillas. Only one of their number was left; he had eaten venison with such a relish at the camp-fire of the whites as to unfit him for active duties; and on his awaking and finding himself alone among the whites, he thought his doom sealed. He was told that he had nothing to fear, and soon became reconciled.

"Upon the arrival, at the Commissioners' camp, of Captain Boling and his nine men, Von-ches-ter (!), a chief, was despatched to find and bring in the frightened Indians. In a few days he succeeded in bringing in about a hundred; but Ten-ie-ya with his people said he would not return.

"After a trip to the San Joaquin, which before has been alluded to, it was resolved to make another trip to the Yo-Semite Valley, there establish head-quarters, and remain until we had thoroughly learned the country, and taken, or driven out, every Indian in it. On our arrival in the valley, a short distance above the prominent bluff known as El Capitan, or as the Indians call it, Tu-toch-ah-nu-lah, which signifies in their language, The Captain, five Indians were seen and heard on the opposite side of the river, taunting us. They evidently thought we could not cross, as the river was so very high (this was in the early part of May), but they were mistaken, as six of us plunged our animals in the stream, swam across, and drove the Indians in among the rocks which obstruct the passage of animals on the north side of the valley; Captain Boling in the mean time crossing above the rocks, succeeded in

TU-TOCK-AH-NU-LAH, THREE THOUSAND THREE HUNDRED FEET ABOVE THE VALLEY.
From a Photograph by C. L. Weed.

taking them all prisoners. Three of these were kept as hostages, while two were sent to Ten-ie-ya with an order for his immediate presence. Of the three kept as hostages, two were sons of Ten-ie-ya, while the two sent with a message, were a son and son-in-law.

"The writer was despatched by Captain Boling to guard them against the fire of any scouting party they might encounter in the valley, and succeeded in saving them from an exasperated individual who was met returning with C. H. Spencer, Esq. (now of Chicago), who had been wounded while tracing out the hiding-places of the Indians. When the two sent for Ten-ie-ya left, they said he would be in by ten o'clock the next morning, and that he would not have ran away but for the stories told by the Chow-chillas. On the morning of the day Ten-ie-ya was expected, one of the three Indians escaped, having deceived the guard.

"Soon after, the two remaining were discovered untying themselves. Two men, instead of informing Captain Boling, that he might make more secure their fastenings, placed themselves near their arms to watch their movements, in order, if possible, to distinguish themselves. One was gratified; for as soon as the Indians bounded to their feet, freed from their fetters, they started to run; Ten-ie-ya's youngest son was shot dead—the other escaped.

"While this was occurring, a party was reconnoitring the scene of Spencer's disaster, and while there, discovered Ten-ie-ya perched upon a rock overlooking the valley. He was engaged in conversation, while a party cut off his retreat and secured him as a prisoner. Upon his entrance into the camp of the volunteers, the first object that met his gaze was the dead body of his son. Not a word did he speak, but the workings of his soul were frightfully manifested in the deep and silent gloom that overspread his countenance. For a time he was left to himself; but after a while Captain Boling explained to him the occurrence, and expressed his regrets that it should have so happened, and ordered a change of camp, to enable the friends of the dead boy to go unmolested and remove the body.

"After remaining inactive a day or two, hoping that the Indians might come in, a 'scout' was made in the direction of the Tuolumne. Only one Indian was seen, and he evidently had been detailed to watch our movements. Various scouts being made to little purpose, it was concluded to go as far up the river as possible, or as far as the Indians could be traced.

"The command felt more confidence in this expedition, from the fact that Cow-chit-ty had arrived with a few of the tribe mentioned before as having been taken on the south fork of the Merced. They knew the country well, and although their language differed a little from that of the Yo-Semite tribe, yet, by means of a mission Indian, who spoke Spanish and the various Indian tongues of this region, Ten-ie-ya was told if he called in his people they were confident that we would not hurt them. Apparently he was satisfied, and promised to bring them in, and at night, when they were supposed to hover around our camp, he would call upon them to come in; but no Indians came.

"While waiting here for provisions, the chief became tired of his food, said it was the season for grass and clover, and that it was tantalizing for him to be in sight of such abundance, and not be permitted to taste it. It was interpreted to Captain Boling, when he good humoredly said that he should have a ton if he desired it. Mr. Cameron (now of Los Angeles) attached a rope to the old man's body, and led him out to graze! A wonderful improvement took place in his condition, and in a few days he looked like a new man.

"With returning health and strength came the desire for liberty, and it was manifested one evening, when Mr. Cameron was off his guard, by his endeavor to escape. Mr. Cameron, however, caught him at the water's edge, as he was about to swim the river. Then, in the fury inspired by his failure to escape, he cried: 'Kill me if you like; but if you do, my voice shall be heard at night, calling upon my people to revenge me, in louder tones than you have ever made it ring.' (It was the custom of Captain Boling to ask him to call for his people.)

"Soon after this occurrence, it being manifest to all that the old man had no intention of calling in his people, and the provisions arriving, we commenced our march to the head waters of the Py-we-ah, or branch of the Merced, in the valley on which is situated Mirror Lake, and fifteen miles above the valley lake Ten-ie-ya. At a rancheria on the shore of this lake, we found thirty-five Indians, whom we took prisoners. With this expedition Captain Boling took Ten-ie-ya, hoping to make him useful as a guide; but if Cow-chit-ty, who discovered the rancheria, had not been with us, we probably would have gone back without seeing an Indian. In taking this rancheria no Indians were killed, but it was a death-blow to their hopes of holding out longer against the whites, for when asked if they were willing to go in and live peaceably, the chief at the rancheria (Ten-ic-ya was not allowed to speak) stretching his hand out and over the country, exclaimed: 'Not only willing, but anxious, for where can we go that the Americans do not follow us ?'

"It was evident that they had not much expected us to follow them to so retired a place; and surrounded as they were by snow, it was impossible for them to flee, and take with them their women and children.

"One of the children, a boy five or six years old, was discovered naked, climbing up a smooth granite slope that rises from the lake on the north side. At first he was thought to be a coon or a fisher, for it was not thought possible for any human being to climb up such a slope. The mystery was soon solved by an Indian who went out to him, coaxed him down from his perilous position, and brought him into camp. He was a bright boy, and Captain Boling adopted him, calling him Reub, after Lieutenant Reuben Chandler, who was, and is, a great favorite with the volunteers. He was sent to school at Stockton, and made rapid progress. To give him advantages that he could not obtain in Mariposa county at that time, he was placed in charge of Colonel Lane, Captain Boling's brother-in-law. To illustrate the folly, as a general thing, of attempting to civilize his race, he ran away, taking with him two very valuable horses belonging to his patron.

"We encamped on the shores of the lake one night. Sleep was prevented by the excessive cold, so in the gray of morning we started with our prisoners on our return to the valley. This was about the 5th of June; we had taken at the lake four of old Ten-ie-ya's wives and all of his family, except those who had fled to the Mono country, through the pass which we saw while on this expedition; and, being satisfied that all had been done that could be, and not a fresh Indian sign to be seen in the country, we were ordered to the Frezno. The battalion was soon after disbanded, and nothing more was heard of the turbulent Ten-ie-ya and his band of pillager Indians (who had been allowed once more to go

back to the valley upon the promise of good behavior), until the
report came of their attack upon a party of whites who visited
the valley in 1852, from Coarse-Gold Gulch, Frezno county.
Two men of the party, Rose and Shurbon, were killed, and a
man named Tudor wounded.

"In June, Lieutenant Moore, accompanied by one of Major Savage's men, A. A. Gray, and some other volunteers, visited the valley
with a company of United States troops, for the purpose of chas-
tising the murderers. Five of them were found and immediately
executed; the wearing apparel of the murdered men being found
upon them. This may shock the sensibilities of some, but it is
conceded that it was necessary in order to put a quietus upon the
murderous propensities of this lawless band, who were outcasts
from the various tribes. After the murder, Ten-ie-ya, to escape
the wrath he knew awaited him, fled to the Monos, on the eastern
side of the Sierra. In the summer of 1853, they returned to the
valley.

"As a reward for the hospitality shown them, they stole a
lot of horses from the Monos, and ran them into the Yo-Semite.
They were allowed to enjoy their plunder but a short time before
the Monos came down upon them like a whirlwind. Ten-ie-ya
was surprised in his wigwam, and, instead of dying the very poetic
death of a broken heart, as was once stated, he died of a broken
head, crushed by stones in the hands of an infuriated and wronged
Mono chief. In this fight, all of the Yo-Semite tribe, except
eight braves and a few old men and women, were killed or taken
prisoners (the women only taken as prisoners), and thus, as a tribe,
they became extinct.

"It is proper to say, what I have before stated, that the Yo-Semite Indians were a composite race, consisting of the disaffected of
the various tribes from the Tuolumne to King's River, and hence
the difficulty in our understanding of the name, Yo-Semite; but
that name, upon the writer's suggestion, was finally approved and
applied to the valley, by vote of the volunteers who visited it.
Whether it was a compromise among the Indians, as well as with
us, it will now be difficult to ascertain. The name is now well

established, and it is that by which the few remaining Indians
below the valley call it.

"Having been in every expedition to the valley made by volunteers, and since that time assisted George H. Peterson (Fremont's
engineer) in his surveys, the writer, at the risk of appearing ego-
tistical, claims that he had superior advantages for obtaining correct information, more especially as, in the first two expeditions,
Ten-ie-ya was placed under his especial charge, and he acted as
interpreter to Captain Boling.

"It is acknowledged that Ah-wah-ne is the old Indian name for
the valley, and that Ah-wah-ne-chee is the name of its original
occupants; but as this was discovered by the writer long after he
had named the valley, and as it was the wish of every volunteer
with whom he conversed that the name Yo-Semite be retained,
he said very little about it. He will only say, in conclusion, that
the principal facts are before the public, and that it is for them to
decide whether they will retain the name Yo-Semite, or have
some other.   L. H. BUNNELL.

"We, the undersigned, having been members of the same company, and through most of the scenes depicted by Doctor Bunnell, have no hesitation in saying, that the article above is correct.
                              "JAMES M. ROANE,
                              "GEO. H. CRENSHAW."

We cheerfully give place to the above communication, that the
public may learn how and by whom this remarkable valley was
first visited and named; and, although we have differed with the
writer and others concerning the name given, as explained in several articles that have appeared at different times in the several
newspapers of the day, in which Yo-ham-i-te was preferred, yet,
as Mr. Bunnell was among the first to visit the valley, we most
willingly accord to him the right of giving it whatever name he
pleases. At the same time, we will here enter the following reasons for calling it Yo-ham-i-te, the name by which we have been
accustomed to speak of it.

In the summer of 1855, we engaged Thomas Ayres, a well-known artist of San Francisco (who unfortunately lost his life by the wreck of the schooner Laura Bevan), to accompany us on a sketching tour to the Calaveras Big Trees and the valley above alluded to. Mr. W. Millard and A. Stair were also of the party.

When we arrived at Mariposa, we found that the existence even of such a valley was almost unknown among a large majority of the people residing there. We made many inquiries respecting it, and how to find our way there; but, although one referred us to another who had been there after Indians in 1851, and he again referred us to some one else, we could not find a single person who could direct us. In this dilemma we met Captain Boling, the gentleman spoken of above, who, although desirous of assisting us, confessed that it was so long since he was there, that he could not give us any satisfactory directions. "But," said he, "if I were you, I would go down to John Hunt's store, on the Frezno, and he will provide you with a couple of good Indian guides from the very tribe that occupied that valley."

We adopted this plan, although it took us twenty-five or thirty miles out of our way; deeming such a step the most prudent under the circumstances. Up to this time we had never heard or known any other name than "Yo-Semite."

Mr. Hunt very kindly acceded to our request, and gave us two of the most intelligent and trustworthy Indians that he had, and the following day we set out for the valley.

Toward night on the first day, we inquired of Kossum, one of our guides, how far he thought it might possibly be to the Yo-Semite Valley, when he looked at us earnestly, and said: " No *Yo-Semite! Yo-Hamite; sabe, Yo-Ham-i-te.?*" In this way were we corrected not less than thirty-five or forty times on our way thither, by these Indians. After our return to San Francisco, we made arrangements for publishing a large lithograph of the great falls; but, before attaching the name to the valley and falls for the public eye, we wrote to Mr. Hunt, requesting him to go to the most intelligent of those Indians, and from them ascertain the exact pronunciation of the name given to that valley. After attending to the request, he wrote us that " *the correct pronuncia-*

tion was Yo-Ham-i-te, or *Yo-Hem-i-te.*" And, while we most willingly acquiesce in the name of Yo-Semite, for the reasons above stated, as neither that nor Yo-Ham-i-te, but *Ah-wah-ne,* is said to be the *pure Indian* name, we confess that our preferences still are in favor of the pure Indian being given; but until that is determined upon (which we do not ever expect to see done now), *Yo-Semite,* we think, has the preference. Had we before known that Doctor Bunnell and his party were the first whites who ever entered the valley (although we have the honor of being *the first, in later years, to visit it and call public attention to it*), we should long ago have submitted to the name Doctor Bunnell had given it, as the discoverer of the valley.

At the time we visited it there was scarcely the outline of an Indian trail visible, either upon the way or in the valley, as all were overgrown with grass or weeds, or covered with old leaves; and nothing could be found there but the bleaching bones of animals that had been slaughtered, and an old acorn post or two, on which a supply of edibles had once been stored by the Indian residents.

Having thus explained the incidents and accidents connected with the early history of this remarkable place, we invite the courteous reader to give us the pleasure of his company thither, as we propose, with his kind permission, to act as "guide" for the occasion. But,

BEFORE STARTING ON THE TRIP,

Let us premise that almost every stranger who arrives on the Pacific Coast is frequently "at his wit's ends" to know how or where to obtain information upon the following subjects :—

1st. The direction and distances to the Yo-Semite Valley, and to the different groves of mammoth trees.

2d. The easiest, cheapest, most expeditious, and most picturesque routes to take, with the probable cost of transportation for himself and effects to each and all of these places.

3d. The best kind and probable amount of personal baggage necessary.

4th. The best general course for him to follow to secure safety, comfort, economy, and a comprehensive knowledge of the most remarkable points of interest.

Now, in order to make every tourist familiar with these facts, we must presume—a very impertinent piece of presumption, no doubt, in many instances—that they are not already in his possession. This point conceded, by way of commencement, we will place before him the following outline map of the different routes and points mentioned, so that he may see at a glance how they can be reached. With the map before you, a clear, general idea is obtainable.

STOCKTON, you will perceive, is the main starting-point. If, therefore, as we have before suggested, you are on the great Overland Railroad, and do not wish to go out of your way before visiting Yo-Semite, or the Big Tree Groves, you had better leave the train at Stockton.

From here there are three main routes: *First*, *via* Copperopolis and Murphy's Camp to the Calaveras grove of mammoth trees; thence back to Murphy's, through Sonora, Chinese Camp, and Big Oak Flat, to Yo-Semite. *Second*, *via* Knight's Ferry, Chinese Camp, and Big Oak Flat, to Yo-Semite. *Third*, by Hornitos, Mariposa, and the Mariposa grove of mammoth trees to Yo-Semite. One of the main travelled roads to Yo-Semite was formerly *via* Coulterville, Bower Cave, and Blacks to Yo-Semite. This recently has been, we regret to say, but little travelled. A new road now in progress may revive its old prosperity. It has our best wishes.

We now propose to give the following—

TABLES OF DISTANCES TO YO-SEMITE BY THE DIFFERENT ROUTES.

From Stockton, via the Calaveras Grove, to Yo-Semite.

		Miles.	Total.
	Copperopolis	36	
	Murphy's Camp	20	56
	Calaveras Grove	15	71
By Coach.	Back to Murphy's Camp	15	86
	Sonora	14	100
	Chinese Camp	10½	110½
	Big Oak Flat	12	122½
	Tuolumne South Grove Big Trees	29½	152
	Tamarack Flat	5½	157½
By Saddle Train.—Hutchings' Hotel. in Yo-Semite		11	168½

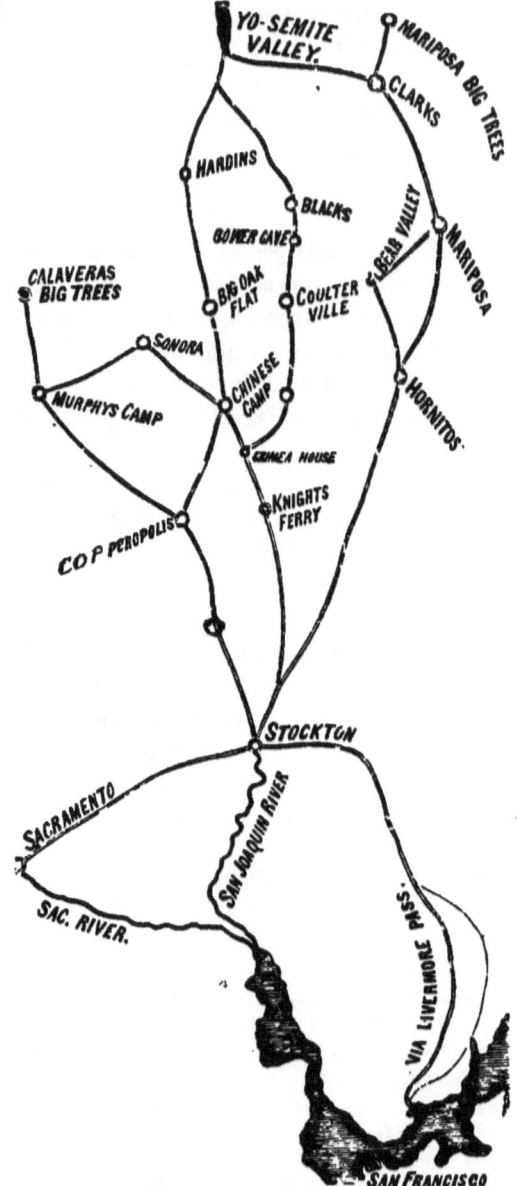

OUTLINE MAP OF ROUTES TO YO SEMITE AND THE MAMMOTH TREE GROVES.

From Stockton, via Knight's Ferry (or Copperopolis), and Chinese Camp, to Yo-Semite.

		Miles.	Total.
By Coach.	Knight's Ferry (or Copperopolis)	36	
	Chinese Camp	15	51
	Jacksonville	4	55
	Keith's Orchard and Vineyard	1½	56½
	Steven's Bar Ferry	1	57½
	Newhall & Culbertson's Vineyard	2½	60
	Kirkwood's	2	62
	Big Oak Flat	1	63
	First Garrote	2	65
	Second Garrote	2	67
	Sprague's Ranch	5½	72½
	Hamilton's Ranch	3½	76
	Hardin's Mill	7	83
	Bronson's Meadows	6	89
	Tuolumne South Grove Big Trees	3½	92½
	Crane Flat	¾	93¼
	Tamarack Flat	4¾	98
By Saddle Train.	Top of Yo-Semite Mountain	3	101
	Bottom of Yo-Semite Mountain	2¼	103¼
	Green Meadow Spring	1	104¼
	Opposite Bridal Veil Fall	¾	105
	Tu-tock-ah-nu-la (El Capitan)	1¼	106¼
	Sentinel Hotel	2¼	108½
	Hutchings' Yo-Semite Hotel	½	109

From Stockton, via Mariposa, and the Mariposa Mammoth Tree Grove, to Yo-Semite.

		Miles.	Total.
By Coach.	Salter's (Tuolumne River)	45	
	Snelling's (Merced River)	13	58
	Murray's Ferry (Merced River)	4	62
	Hornitos	8	70
	Bear Valley	9	79
	Mariposa	13	92
	Mormon Bar	1⅞	93⅞
	Spring House	1⅝	95½
	Bolton's	4⅝	100⅛
	Thompson's	2⅜	102½
	White & Hatch's	1¼	103¾
	Little Cut-Off	1½	105¼
	Forks of Road (take left hand)	1½	106¾

Horseback.	Lard's Ranch (Hogan's)	1	107¾
	South Fork Chowchilla	2	109¾
	Upper Crossing Chowchilla	1	110¾
	Summit Spring	¾	111½
	Big Creek Bridge	2⅜	113⅞
	Clark's Ranch (South Fork Merced)	1½	115⅜
	Mariposa Grove of Mammoth Trees, and back to Clark's	13	128⅜
	Camp Placido	3⅞	132¼
	Cold Water Creek	1½	133¾
	Alder Creek	¼	134
	Grass Creek	⅞	134⅞
	Empire Camp	1¼	136⅛
	Owl Camp	½	136⅝
	Green Spring Flat	2	138⅝
	Westfall's Meadow	¾	139⅜
	Mountain View House	1	140⅜
	Highest Point on Trail	1⅞	142¼
	Last Meadow	⅞	143⅛
	Inspiration Point	⅞	144
	Mount Beatitude (turning-off place)	¼	144¼
	Hermitage	1⅛	145⅜
	Fern Spring (foot of mountain)	2	147⅜
	Bridal Veil Fall	1	148⅜
	Cathedral Spires	1	149⅜
	Sentinel Hotel	2⅝	152
	Hutchings' Yo-Semite Hotel	½	152½

	Miles.
By the above tables it will be observed that the route from Stockton, *via* the Calaveras Big Tree Grove, to Yo-Semite is —157½ by coach, and 11 on horseback.	168½
Knight's Ferry (or Copperopolis) and Chinese Camp, to Yo-Semite —98 by coach and 11 on horseback.	109
Mariposa and Mariposa Big Tree Grove, to Yo-Semite —106¾ by coach, and 45¾ on horseback.*	152½

THE EASIEST, CHEAPEST, AND MOST EXPEDITIOUS ROUTE,

And one of the most picturesque in scenery, is, doubtless, that from Stockton, by Knight's Ferry (or if the Stockton and Copperopolis railroad has sufficiently progressed to allow it, *via* Copperopolis), to Chinese Camp, Big Oak Flat, Garrote, the Tuolumne South

* A turnpike road company has been formed, for the purpose of constructing a road to Clark's, and the Mariposa Big Tree Grove; so that during the summer of 1870 the distance, by this route, on horseback, may be very materially decreased.

Grove of Mammoth Trees, and Tamarack Flat, to Yo-Semite. The entire distance by this route being only 109 miles—ninety-eight of which are by coach,—and the total fare from Stockton to Hutchings', in Yo-Semite Valley, not exceeding $20. It should also be remembered by those whose time is very limited, that by this route the tourist passes directly through the Tuolumne South Grove of Mammoth Trees, several of which are remarkably fine specimens of the genus. Through, by stage and saddle, in two days.

Those persons who are unaccustomed to the fatigue of travel, and to whom comfort is as much of an object as sight-seeing, should not attempt the through trip in less than three days,— reaching Chinese Camp only the first day. Next in importance, the route,

VIA THE CALAVERAS GROVE OF MAMMOTH TREES, TO YO-SEMITE

claims our attention, not only on account of its being the first grove discovered, and the most celebrated, or from the wonderful size, height, and gracefulness of its trees,—and these are remarkable,—but for its close proximity to the finest grove of sequoias yet known in California. [For description of these groves see Chapter I.] By reference to the map and table of distances, page 80, it will be seen that our course lies through Copperopolis to Murphy's, distance fifty-six miles, and the fare $8; to Mammoth Tree Grove and back, thirty miles, fare $4; Murphy's to Sonora, fourteen miles, fare $2.50; Sonora to Chinese Camp, ten and a-half miles, fare $1.50; Chinese to Yo-Semite, fifty-eight miles, fare $13. Total distance 168½ miles,—157½ of which are by coach,—and the total fare for the round trip, $29. Time required to make the journey comfortably will be about as follows: first day, to Murphy's; second day, to and about the grove; third day, return to Murphy's, thence to Sonora and to Chinese Camp; fourth day, to Tamarack Flat; fifth, arrive at Hutchings', in Yo-Semite, about noon. One day should be added to this if a visit is paid to the large " South Grove," near to that of Calaveras.

ROUTE VIA MARIPOSA, AND THE MARIPOSA GROVE OF BIG TREES.

Owing to the magnificence and number of the big trees in the Mariposa groves, and the impressive views obtained of Yo-Semite from Inspiration Point and Mount Beatitude, many prefer this route to either of the others.   There can be no question that the scenes from the points named are unequalled; but whether they are to be enjoyed on entering the valley, or by a special visit from the valley, or after becoming familiar with the different objects of interest in and around the valley, and on leaving it, must be determined by the taste and wishes of the visitor.   Those who prefer to enter this way, by consulting the map and table of distances, page 80, will find that, after leaving Stockton, their course lies through the singular old mining town of Hornitos to Bear Valley, across the celebrated Mariposa or Fremont estate to Mariposa; distance ninety-two miles, fare $10.   Here saddle horses and guides have generally been obtained at the livery stables on the following terms: horses each per day, $2.50; guide per day, $3; board for guide, $3; horse for guide, $2.50,—making the cost per day for each guide, $8.50, exclusive of horse feed.   It is only just, however, to say that but little horse feed need be purchased until late in the summer and fall, as grass is tolerably abundant.   Other arrangements may be made during the season for making the round trip from and to Stockton for about $50 or $55, but what they will be we are now unable to say.

From Mariposa the road lies past the Mariposa Company's quartz mill, and over a pleasant, hilly country, dotted with oaks and pines, and numerous kinds of shrubs, to White & Hatch's, one of the neatest and most agreeable stopping-places to be found on either of the routes.   Past De Long's orchard to the foot of the Chowchilla Mountain; thence by a long and fatiguing climb (all mountain climbing generally partakes of this quality) to a delicious spring near the top of the divide, and which is nearly 6,000 feet above the sea, and some 2,800 feet above White & Hatch's. Thence the trail winds down a magnificently timbered and easy grade to Clark's ranch, on the South Fork of the Merced.   Clark's is about 4,180 feet above sea level. Here also very agreeable quarters will be found : and Mr. Clark, one of the old pioneers of this region, will take real pride and pleasure in looking out for your creature comforts, and by giving you every information in his power.

The road to the Mariposa Grove of Big Trees, here diverges from that for Yo-Semite, and is up a long and gradual ascent to an altitude above Clark's of some 1,500 feet. [For description of this grove, see Chapter V.]

From Clark's the trail continues up the side of the mountain in a dense growth of shrubbery nearly to the top of the divide, where it enters and continues through some of the finest stretches of forest, composed mainly of the yellow pine (*Pinus ponderosa*), the sugar pine (*Pinus lambertiana*), and the cedar (*Libocedrus decurrens*), to be found in any portion of the world. Then for a few miles it runs across green patches of meadow, or over low ridges and spurs, whence it threads among numerous clumps of silver firs (*Picea grandis* and *Picea amabalis*), and groves of "tamaracks" (*Pinus contorta*); and as you ride along, glimpses of the distant sierras are caught, upon whose lofty peaks, or in whose shadowy and sheltered gorges, snow lies eternally slumbering. You are now for the most part, about 7,000 feet above the sea. The highest portions of the trail being about 7,500 feet.

As you now descend, the dark purple haze at your right reveals a near approach to the goal of your anticipations,—the Mecca of this pilgrimage. Almost before the gratifying fact is realized, you have reached "Inspiration Point," and are standing out upon a bold promontory of rock, and with feelings all your own, are looking over the precipice of nearly three thousand feet, into the deep abyss. This is the first view obtained of Yo-Semite Valley. Mr. Sidney Andrews, in his correspondence to the *Boston Advertiser*, thus writes of this glorious scene :—

"Suddenly as I rode along, I heard a shout. I knew the valley had revealed itself to those who were at the front of the line. I turned my head away—I couldn't look until I had tied my horse. Then I walked down to the ledge and crawled out upon the overhanging rocks. I believe some men walk out there,—it's a dull clod of a soul who can do that. In all my life, let it lead me where it may, I think I shall see nothing else so grand, so awful, so sublime, so beautiful,—beautiful with a beauty not of this earth,—as that Vision of the Valley. It was only yesterday evening,—I cannot write of it yet. How long I sat there on the rocks I never shall know. I brought the picture away with me; I have only to shut my eyes and I see it as I saw it in that hour of hours. I think I shall see nothing else so sublime and beautiful, till, happily, I stand within the gates of the Heavenly City.''

As you are now some eight and a half miles from the hotel, however enchanting this spot may be, you must not linger here too long; but, bringing lunch, after you are rested, pay it another visit from the valley, and make a day of it. Besides, a really finer view than this is obtained a short distance below, on "Mount Beatitude," from whence a more comprehensive picture of the valley is realized. To see this, however, will require a short detour from the trail, and a little more time.

Presuming that you could not resist the temptation of witnessing the imposing view from Mount Beatitude—and knowing the impossibility of even approximating justice in any written description—you will think of it as you descend the mountain, and dream of it both by day and by night. Presently you come to the "Hermitage," a hollow sugar-pine tree that was the home of a solitary woodsman for nearly three months. One night, when the wind blew unpleasantly strong, he concluded that "discretion was the better part of valor," and vacated his nature-built cabin until the storm had subsided.

Fine views of the valley are obtained at almost every turning point and, while assisting to distract your attention from the long and somewhat difficult descent, reward you for the trouble of coming.

At the foot of the mountain you arrive at "Fern Spring." The cooling, bower-like shade of the trees and shrubs, and the clear and sparkling brightness of the water, bubbling up among rocks and green-matted foliage, united to its almost icy coldness, may, after your journey down, especially if both you and the weather are warm, tempt an indulgence in too hearty a draught. This, however, should be studiously resisted for the first day or two, as persons unaccustomed to the pure cold water of Yo-Semite are in danger of being uncomfortably troubled with diarrhœa.

Now as you ride across the Bridal Veil meadow, with the "Bridal Veil Fall" in full sight; rainbow hues are toying and playing with its beautiful rockets, and mists, and sprays ; but, knowing that a full afternoon can be well spent in such glorious companionship; and that the setting sun, with scenes of interest on either hand to be viewed as you ride up the valley, admonish not to linger here too long—you had better not tarry. Besides, by this time you will begin to feel that a refreshing glass of good California wine, a bath, dinner, and such other acceptable comforts as may be found at Hutchings' are not to be despised. Then, after you have rested and are comforted, sally out at your pleasure.

The time required to make this trip by Mariposa comfortably will be about as follows : First day, to Hornitos ; second day, to Mariposa (or to White and Hatch's, 11¼ miles farther), and in obtaining outfits of horses, etc. ; third day, to Clark's ; fourth day, to the Big Tree Grove and back ; fifth day, to Hutchings'. Those in a hurry can go to White & Hatch's the second day, to Clark's and the Big Tree Grove the third day, and to the Yo-Semite on the fourth.

THE KINDS AND AMOUNT OF PERSONAL BAGGAGE TO BE TAKEN.

This, you will allow, is a difficult matter for us to determine, and one that will require your generous forbearance and assistance. These questions settled, we will suppose that your good sense (no flattery is intended) will suggest at the start that all Saratoga trunks should be eschewed—even if their dimensions do not exceed those of an ordinary cottage or two. If you have one of moderate pretensions be sure and carefully examine its contents with the view of laying aside every thing that you know will not be wanted. Next, turn over your effects again, and reject every thing you feel that you could conscientiously do without. The reason for all this will be apparent when we inform you that after the coach (and its capaciousness) is left behind, every article you take will have to be carried on your saddle animal, or on a pack-mule, for the balance of the way.

Now, if health and comfort are studied, gentlemen will see that they have one extra of each of the following articles : One pair of good serviceable boots (not necessarily very heavy) that have been broken to the feet; one complete outfit of under-clothing ; one woollen over-shirt ; three or four pairs of hose (woollen should be preferred); one pair of strong pants (old ones, if not too easily torn, would be the best, as they will be good for nothing after returning) ; pocket-handkerchiefs, and a few other necessary articles. Ladies would do well by taking some of the hints thrown out to gentlemen—in providing themselves with woollen dresses of suitable strength, color, and texture, made in the Bloomer or other similar style, as such would be found to possess both comfort and adaptability; a durable linen riding-habit; boots that were made for wear more than for ornament; a warm shawl ; and by making choice of such other articles that will suit their wants, wishes, and tastes, without further enumeration from us.

At the best it will be difficult to give advice that will accord with every variety of condition and of circumstance. By way of illustration we may mention that an estimable and intelligent lady correspondent of a San Francisco paper visited Yo-Semite early in May, and finding the weather cool, advised every lady to go there warmly clad. Other ladies, later in the season, taking that advice, and finding the climate pleasantly warm, remarked, " How could Mrs. —— recommend us to come in such warm clothing ? when we return we will tell all *our* lady friends to choose none but light summer dresses ! "

Trunks can be taken wherever coaches can go. Beyond that, as they have to be packed upon mules, the expenses of transportation are necessarily increased. It is true that they can be safely left at the end of the stage route, but this would suggest the necessity of returning the same way. That necessity should always be avoided. It is much more satisfactory to be left fully at liberty to make your own choice ; and, where time and convenience will permit, to go in one way and out the other, so that the scenes upon one road, however beautiful, may afford a pleasing contrast to those of the other. Our advice, therefore, would be to leave your trunk in Stockton (unless you intend to spend some weeks or months in Yo-Semite), so that after you return from your ride in the mountains you may be refreshed by a bath and change of clothing, before taking the steamboat or cars for San Francisco or Sacramento.

Supposing, then, that you have concluded to leave your trunks behind, as a portion of the journey is on horseback, the most convenient receptacle for clothing will be a pair of saddle-bags. Next to these, a flexible valise is best. Gentlemen in a hurry will sometimes strap up all the clothing they expect to need in an overcoat, and tie it at the back of their saddle. Do not, however, suppose that it is impossible to pack in almost any thing, from a cooking range to a six-story house—in pieces,—but such things cost money. These remarks are only intended for those who wish to be economical in their expenditures. " *Nuf ced.*"

THE MOST ACCEPTABLE COURSE FOR A STRANGER TO PURSUE,

It is presumed, would be that which will obtain for him the greatest amount of enjoyment and information for the smallest amount of money. To secure these, experience has taught us that one cannot be too explicit in his directions. Therefore, the motive which prompts the following details, let us hope, will be considered a sufficient apology for their introduction.

HOTEL CHARGES IN SAN FRANCISCO.

San Francisco will doubtless be the central point of attraction. There, the new " Grand Hotel,"—leased by the former proprietor of the " Lick House,"—the " Cosmopolitan," and the " Occidental," are the principal hotels. Their charges are, we believe, $3 per day. Next come the " Russ House," " Brooklyn Hotel," and others, whose charges are from $2 to $2.50 per day. All prices in California, remember, are upon a gold basis. These hotels can all be reached by street-car, fare 6¼ cents, by making your destination known to the conductor. Cars are near to most of the wharves and railway termini. The obliging book-keepers and clerks at all first-class hotels will give you reliable information concerning the city and State.

Meals and beds, when travelling in California, will be from 50 cts. to $1 each—averaging about $3 per day. At Hutchings', in Yo-Semite, hotel charges are $3 50 per day, $20 per week, or $75 per month. At the Calaveras Grove of Mammoth Trees, and at Clark's,—the nearest house to the Mariposa Grove,—the prices are about the same. Perhaps it will not be far out of place here to say that meals, on the great overland railway, are from 75 cts. (in currency) to $1.25, and will average about $1 each. From Chicago to Omaha, a berth in a sleeping-car is $3 per night; from Omaha to Ogden, $4 per night, including its use in the day-time; from Ogden to San Francisco, $3 per day and night.

If you contemplate a visit to Yo-Semite, or the Big Trees,—and but few would go to California, and have the courage on their return to say that they had not been there,—send for the authorized Route Agent, *Edward Harrison, Esq.*, of the stage and saddle train companies,* and have a good talk and a clear understanding with him about every thing. Know exactly how much will be his full charge to convey you from San Francisco or Stockton to Yo-Semite, and back direct; how much if you wish to go by either grove of mammoth trees, and back. See, also, that the sum named includes guides, and saddle-horses in the valley, so that there shall be no annoying "extras." Once fully satisfied that every thing is "on the square" (as we say in California), pay him your fare, and receive from him a properly certified set of coupons for the trip.

* Where this gentlemen can be found or addressed, is generally published in some of the newspapers.

PRELIMINARY PREPARATIONS.

One word more before starting. Have you been accustomed to horseback riding? If you have not, you will add very much to the enjoyment of the trip by practising a little every day on some reliable animal; as experience in this gives a fearlessness of action that adds much to the pleasure of such a delightful ride.

Supposing that the reader has already formed one of our party as far as Stockton from San Francisco, in Chap. I.; and supposing, also, that he will give us the pleasure of his company on the shortest and easiest route to Yo-Semite, and especially as it is also one of the most picturesque,—besides being the freest from dust,—with the assurance, also, that the scenery on the others is substantially very similar, we will choose that, via Big Oak Flat.

It is nearly six o'clock A. M., and time to be off. The most to be desired of all places on a stage, is the one known as the " box-seat." This is with the coachman: for if he is intelligent, and in a good humor, he can tell you of all the sights by the way, with the personal history of nearly every man and woman you may meet, the qualities and "points" of every horse upon the road, with all the adventures, jokes, and other good things he has seen and heard, during his thousand and one trips, under all kinds of circumstances, and in all sorts of weather. In short, he is a living road encyclopædia, to be read and studied at intervals by the occupant of "the box-seat."

You saw that look and motion of the coachman's head? That was at once a sign of recognition and of invitation to the privileged seat at his side, as we are old acquaintances. But, as you are a stranger, and as every excursion of real pleasure—like the happiest experiences of social life—become dependent to a very great extent upon little courtesies and kindnesses that cost nothing, we wish to set a good example to the party, and to you, by foregoing selfishness, and by trying to secure that seat for you. No thanks are needed, as every pleasure is doubled by being shared. Now, supposing that you are the occupant of the "box-seat," we will make one suggestion—invite the driver to accept one of your best cigars, and as its smoke and fragrance are rising on the air, you will gradually become better acquainted, learning his secrets on the outside, while we are talking to those within. Now,

OFF FOR THE MOUNTAINS.

Leaving Stockton, then, we journey over a level and oak-studded plain to the "Twelve Mile House," where we change horses and take breakfast, which generally occupies fifteen to twenty minutes. Here we change horses. The country then gradually becomes gently rolling, and, although covered with wild flowers, is almost barren of trees or shrubs. We again change horses at the Twenty-five Mile House. At noon we reach Knight's Ferry, a small settlement on the Stanislaus River, where a group of sturdy miners probably is congregated in front of the hotel, and a bell announces that dinner is ready.

This was once one of the most flourishing of placer mining towns, but now, like many similar ones in the mining districts, its prosperity is on the wane. Being the seat of government for Stanislaus County, and surrounded by numerous ranches and vineyards, there is considerable life still manifest. Miners here frequently used to find garnets and opals in their mining sluices when cleaning them out at night. A fine stratum of yellow ochre, several feet in thickness, lies on the south bank of the river; also large masses of crude iron, in blocks containing scores of cubic feet each.

After taking refreshments, with loss of our appetites and forty-five minutes, we not only again change horses, but find ourselves and our baggage changed to another stage—as the newest and best-looking ones seem to be retained for the comparatively level and city end of the route, while the dust-covered and paint-worn are used for the mountains.

Shortly after leaving Knight's Ferry, we cross the "Stanislaus Bridge"—a very substantial structure—and wind to the left, over a spur of the celebrated "Table Mountain." This formation is very remarkable, from its being apparently level for some fifteen miles, and composed of volcanic scoria or trap. Beneath it, and in the bed of a now extinct river, very rich gravel diggings were discovered, which made several men wealthy. At different points upon our winding way, as we thread our course among the oak-studded hills, we obtain glimpses of this singular deposit.

About the middle of the afternoon we arrive at Chinese Camp, where, if we are wise and have time, we shall remain for the night, and place ourselves and our comforts in care of Count Solinsky, the obliging landlord of the "Garrett House," who will, if we wish it, cheerfully show us the interesting sights in and around the town. Whether we go or stay, our bags and baggage are here removed from the Sonora stage, and, if we want to continue our journey without delay, will be promptly placed upon the one bound for Garrote. In any event, let us see that our luggage is in our own safe-keeping before the stage leaves the door. A little trouble now will save us from much annoyance in the future.

FROM CHINESE CAMP TO TAMARACK FLAT.

An early start—preceded by a good cup of coffee—on a summer's morning, will prove to us the pleasantest portion of the day. The deliciously bracing "Champagne atmosphere" (as a lady friend of ours so naïvely expresses it) is quaffed with a delight and zest that makes itself felt through every portion of the human frame. Still on, on we roll, now over gently swelling hills, now along shallow ravines, then down a well-graded road to the Tuolumne River and Jacksonville. This village is supported mainly by river mining and the placer diggings of Wood's Creek. Within a stone's throw is one of the earliest fruit gardens in the State. A short drive above this will bring us to a shady flower-covered retreat, known as "Keith's Orchard and Vineyard." Here fruits of every rare variety known in the temperate zone can be found, and of the finest quality. Let us hope that we are just in their season. The grapes will be found especially large and fine in flavor. Let us not pass without testing their excellence, not forgetting the old adage, that fruit is gold in the morning, silver at noon, and lead at night.

About a mile above Keith's we cross the Tuolumne River on the Stevens' Bar Ferry, and drive up Moccasin Creek some two and a half miles to "Newhall and Culbertson's Vineyard." This is another of those delightful wayside tarrying-places where fruit of the finest quality is in abundance, and where we can obtain a glass of the most delicious white wine to be had in any portion of the State. It is but simple justice to these people to say that their charges are not only very reasonable, but always low.

For the next two miles our road is on the side of a mountain, covered with a dense mass of shrubbery, among which will be found the manzanita, buckeye, mountain mahogany, pipe wood, Indian arrow, granite wood, and numerous other kinds—all of which, if cut in the proper season, November to March, are hard and useful furniture woods, susceptible of a very high polish.

You will think this quite a mountain to climb—and it is. It will be well, however, to bear in mind, that, before we commence the descent toward Yo-Semite, we have to attain an altitude of nearly seven thousand feet; we must, therefore, commence ascending somewhere, and why not here? It will be a task upon our patience, perhaps, but as it seems to be a trial of both wind and muscle to the horses, we may surely console ourselves with the thought that we can stand it if they can. Up, up we toil, many of us on foot, perhaps, in order to ease the faithful and apparently overtasked animals, which puff and snort like miniature locomotives, while the sweat drops from them in abundance.

One quiet evening in the height of summer, after the sun had set, and the deep purple atmosphere—almost peculiar to California —had changed to sombre gray, we (the passengers) were wending our way up the mountain, on foot, and a little ahead of the stage, when a rustling sound, just below the road, startled us with its singular and suspicious distinctness, and dark, shadowy forms were gently threading their way among the bushes. Our hearts beat uncomfortably fast, and we instinctively felt for our revolvers, but they were in the stage. It should be told that at this time numerous robberies had been committed upon the highway by Joaquin, Tom Bell, and their respective gangs. "We are caught,"

whispered one. "They will rob, and perhaps murder us," suggested another. "We can die but once," bravely retorted a third.
"Let us all keep close together," pantomimed a fourth. "Who
goes there?" loudly challenged a fifth. "A friend," exclaimed
the ringleader of a party of miners who were climbing the steep
sides of the mountain just at our side, with their blankets at their
backs, all walking to town, and who had caused all our alarm;
and as he and his companions quietly seated themselves by the roadside, they commenced wiping off the perspiration, and gave us cordial salutation in good plain English. "Why, bless us, these men,
who have almost frightened us out of our seven senses, are fellow-
travellers!" "Couldn't you see that?" now valorously inquired
one whose knees had knocked uncontrollably together with fear
only a few moments before. At this we all laughed; and the
coachman, having stopped his stage, said, "Get in, gentlemen,"
and we had enough to talk and joke about until we reached Kirk-
wood's.

This brings us to the last-named place. Here we stop to water
the horses and change the mails and passengers to the Coul-
terville-bound stage—this being the turning-off point for the
latter-named town. We have by this time probably received
sundry admonitions from within that the comforting morning meal
has not, as yet, been duly furnished to a tenantless stomach,
accompanied, possibly, with the secret wish that Garrote and
breakfast are not far off. That it is only three miles, over a
tolerably good road, is at this time an encouraging thought.

As we jog along, we must not omit to notice the evidences of
mining on either hand, even if we forget the unpleasant fact that
a miner's labors almost invariably bring desolation to the landscape. Nor must we pass unseen the sturdy branch-lopped and
root-cut veteran trunk of a noble and enormous oak, some eleven
feet in diameter, still standing on our right; as it was from this
once famous tree that "Big Oak Flat," the village through which
we are passing, received its name. Then, however, its immense
branch-crowned top gave refreshing shadow to the traveller, and
beauty to the scene. We fear that many a year will have made

its faithful record before our virtues become sufficiently Christian to confess forgiveness to those who committed, or permitted, the vandal act of its destruction. We take real comfort in the thought that its storm-beaten, dead, and limbless form must daily administer stinging reproofs to every one whose act, or silence, gave sanction to the deed. "So mote it be!"

"Breakfast!" shouts the coachman (a musical sound indeed to us, even though his voice were cracked, and it isn't), as he "pulls up" at Savory's, the jovial and obliging landlord of the Washington Hotel, Garrote. We predict that if he knows that we are coming, and we are certain that he does, he will spread before us an excellent repast,—especially for a mining town. Perhaps it will not be out of place here to say, in all kindness, that no traveller should expect to find meals and accommodations in the mountains of California equal to those of the "Grand Hotel," the "Cosmopolitan," or the "Occidental," in San Francisco. And perhaps he doesn't. "If so, why so." Then we take it all back.

While the stage is settling our breakfasts, and we are advancing toward another euphoniously named mining camp, known as "Second Garrote" (we should like to "garrote" the name-givers of these villages until they repented), we must caution you against stopping (so soon after leaving Savory's, you know), at Chaffey & Chamberlain's; for their delicious pears and other fruits will be sure to tempt you to eat again, and it is a long way to the doctor's! Then, if you think of the amount of internal freight taken in but two miles below, ought you in conscience to add to it without paying extra? But this being the last orchard seen on this side of Yo-Semite; and this, moreover, being considered a "pleasure trip," we will accept of your pardon for mentioning such trifles as apples, hoping that you have sufficient caution not to allow the driver to see you cram them into your pockets, unless prepared to pay for "extra baggage." We will talk to him about a new road up the mountain while you have an eye to business.

A short ascent up a somewhat steep hill, brings us to the ups and downs of a ridge road, with timber and shrubbery on both sides. The large ditch we cross several times is that of the Golden

Rock Water Co.'s, constructed for the purpose of supplying the mining towns below with water for mining purposes. This work will be seen at different times until we pass the "Big Gap," where lie the broken fragments of a flume, once the pride of its engineers, as the finest wooden structure of the kind in the State, having a height of two hundred and sixty-four feet above the Gap, and a length of two thousand two hundred feet, costing the snug little amount of pocket change of eighty thousand dollars. A strong wind one night told the sad story, that "the best-laid plans of mice and men gang oft aglee," and made it the wreck you see. Now, a large iron tube placed upon the ground answers the purpose of the flume. This only cost, we are informed, some twelve thousand dollars. There is but little danger of this being blown over, that is one comfort. Our hope and wish is that it may not be inclined to go upon "a bender."

Calling at Sprague's Ranch to pay our respects to the owner, as we are largely indebted to the enterprise of Mr. Sprague for the construction of the new road to Hardin's; become refreshed if we need "refreshing;" change or water the horses; and, to avoid a side hill covered with loose volcanic scoria, pass through his farm on our winding way.

As we advance it is evident that the timber becomes larger, and the forest land more extensive. The gently rolling hills begin to give way to tall mountains; and the quiet and even tenor of the landscape changes to the wild and picturesque. An occasional deer may shoot across our track; or covies of quail, with their beautiful plumage and nodding "top-knots," whirr among the bushes. The robin and meadow lark and oriole may prove to us that they still have a love and a voice for music; and the "too coo-" ing of the dove tells that its voice "is still heard in our land." Instead of the eastern "woodpecker tapping at the hollow beach-tree," the red-headed Californian variety, known as the carpenter (*el carpintero*) woodpecker, may be seen busily engaged boring holes in the bark of a large pine-tree, and afterward carefully fitting and filling them up with acorns, or critically examining them apparently for his own amusement, or for purposes known only to himself. The reason for these are still, we believe, a mystery to naturalists. As the greatest activity in storing was in the fall, and the inspection went on at other seasons, it was for many years supposed that an instinctive provision for a coming want was the cause. But as this variety of woodpecker has seldom or never been seen feeding on the acorn, or on the supposed insect which it contained, some doubt has arisen as to the satisfactory nature of its occupation. Perhaps some student of the habits of this singular bird may give us some interesting facts connected with its history.

. While we are talking, the horses have again stopped before a neat house in a green meadow. This is "Hamilton's," near to the "Big Gap." We feel it a duty to mention every deserving wayside public-house, above the settlements, so that any traveller who, from either choice or necessity, wishes to eat, drink, or sleep, may know where to go. But as we must not tarry too long by the way, we will now say that seven miles above is "Hardin's Mill;" six miles farther is "Hodgden's," at the Bronson meadows; five miles farther is "Goburn's," at Crane Flat; and five miles farther brings us to "Tamarack Flat." These people having provided for the wants of the public, will be pleased to receive, we doubt not, such patronage as any may have to bestow.

Who, in feeble language, can fully disclose to us the grandeur of the scenery that opens before us a short distance east of the Big Gap? When the painter's art can build the rainbow upon canvas so as to deceive the sense of sight—when simple words can tell the depth and height, the length and breadth of a single thought— or the physician's skill delineate, beyond peradventure, the hidden mysteries of a living soul—then, ah! then, it may be possible.

Deep down in an abyss before us is a gulf—a cañon—of more than two thousand feet. The gleaming, silvery thread, seen running among boulders, is the Tuolumne River, a hundred feet in width. Its rock-ribbed sides, in places, show not a vestige of a tree or shrub. In others, its generous soil has clothed the almost perpendicular walls with verdure. As the eye wanders onward and upward it traces the pine-clad outlines of distant gorges whose tributary waters compose and swell the volume of the stream beneath us. To the right, surrounded by noble trees, can be discerned a bright speck—it is a waterfall a hundred feet in height and thirty feet in width. In the far distance, piercing the clouds, the snow-covered peaks of the sierras lift their glorious heads of sheen, while a beautiful purple haze casts its broad, softening mantle over all.

Our road, shaded by lofty pines and umbrageous oaks and cooled by a delicious breeze, lies safely near the edge of the precipice, the whole panorama rolled vividly out before us. It is such scenes as this that introduce refreshing change to such a journey. We know of no view equal to it, so far from the valley, on either of the other routes.

Crossing the bridge of the south fork of the Tuolumne, our course is upward for a considerable distance until we reach Hardin's, and possibly dinner. Beyond, we again cross the south fork, and still our course is upward, until we have reached a long stretch of elevated table-land that, for timber, is not excelled in any portion of the State. Large sugar-pine trees (*Pinus Lambertiana*) from five to ten feet in diameter, and over two hundred feet in height, devoid of branches for sixty or a hundred feet, and straight as an arrow, everywhere abound. Besides these, there are thousands of yellow pines (*Pinus ponderosa*), Douglas firs (*Abies Douglasii*), and cedar (*Libocedrus decurrens*), that are but little, if any, smaller or shorter than the sugar-pines. These forests are not covered up with a dense undergrowth, as at the east, but give long and ever-changing vistas for the eye to penetrate. Well might Mr. Horace Greeley write concerning them :—

" Here let me renew my tribute to the marvelous bounty and beauty of the forests of this whole mountain region. The Sierra Nevadas lack the glorious glaciers, the frequent rains, the rich verdure, the abundant cataracts of the Alps ; but they far surpass them—they surpass any other mountains I ever saw—in the wealth and grace of their trees. Look down from almost any of their peaks, and your range of vision is filled, bounded, satisfied, by what might be termed a tempest-tossed sea of evergreens, filling every upland valley, covering every hill-side, crowning every peak but the highest, with their unfading luxuriance.   That I saw, during this day's travel, many hundreds of pines eight feet in diameter, with cedars at least six feet, I am confident; and there were miles of such, and smaller trees of like genus, standing as thick as they could grow.   Steep mountain-sides, allowing these giants to grow, rank above rank, without obstructing each other's sunshine, seem peculiarly favorable to the production of these serviceable giants.   But the Summit Meadows are peculiar in their heavy fringe of balsam fir, of all sizes, from those barely one foot high to those hardly less than two hundred, their branches surrounding them in collars, their extremities gracefully bent down by the weight of winter snows, making them here, I am confident, the most beautiful trees on earth.   The dry promontories which separate these meadows, are also covered with a species of spruce, which is only less graceful than the firs aforesaid.   I never before enjoyed such a tree-feast as on this wearing, difficult ride." *

THE TUOLUMNE SOUTH GROVE OF BIG TREES.

Talking of trees, almost before we know it, we are entering the "Tuolumne South Grove" of mammoth trees, as our road lies directly through it.   These trees are of the same genus (*Sequoia gigantea*) as those of Calaveras, Mariposa, and other similar groves.   There are about thirty in this group.   Several of them are remarkably fine specimens of the Big Tree family.   Two of them, which grew from the same root, and unite a few feet above the base, are called " The Siamese Twins."   These are about one hundred and fourteen feet in circumference at the ground, and, consequently, about thirty-eight feet in diameter—of course, including both.   The bark has been cut on one side of one of these

* Mr. Greeley, we believe, rode from Bear Valley to the Yo-Semite—over sixty miles—in one day.   He had not, it is said, been in a saddle before for thirty years. The mule he rode was considered the hardest trotting brute in America; and Mr. G. (not the mule) being somewhat corpulent, there was but little unabrased cuticle left him.   Arriving at the hotel after midnight, he was lifted from his saddle, and at his own request, put supperless to bed.   A little after noon the same day, having speaking engagements to fulfill, he started back without even seeing the Lake, or the great sights on the main river—the " Vernal " and the " Nevada " falls.

and has been found to measure twenty inches in thickness. Near the "Twins" there are two others which measure seventy-four feet around their base. There is one black stump still standing that must have once represented a tree not less than one hundred feet in circumference. Within a few yards of this grows one of the finest representatives of this wondrous family to be found.

"Excelsior" being our motto, we shall soon reach "Crane Flat." These flats are grassy meadows, interspersed among the mountain districts, and are generally the heads of creeks or rivers, being almost always "springy." Of late years they are fed off by bands of sheep brought up from the plains when the feed there has become short or dry. Running upon or over trails, they are apt to obliterate all traces of the traveller's course, and where a short turn is made, great care is needed, by the inexperienced, to prevent being lost.

In the early spring the snow upon the main road being deep, a detour is here made from the regular course. At such a time we strike a little south of east, down the flat, past the front of the old cabin, carefully looking out for and following "the blazes." These "blazes" are axe marks in the trees. This is known as the "Old Coulterville Route;" and although, in addition to being several miles further round, a long mountain has to be descended and another one climbed, it is the safest and most speedy in the early spring. A guide, then, however, will be very necessary.

Let us hope that we can continue on the shortest and easiest route. This will be in a northeasterly course until we have surmounted the crest of the dividing ridge which separates the waters of the Tuolumne from those of the Merced. Here we are some seven thousand feet above the sea. From this ridge magnificent views of the distant landmarks and snow-covered peaks of the sierras open at brief intervals before us; while timber-covered ridges and gorges, like waves of the sea, stretch farther and farther away to the verge of the distant horizon; with an occasional mountain of verdureless rock, like an island, standing gloriously out as if to defy the further encroachments of those evergreen masses of pines. There does not seem to be a foot of ground over which we are passing that has not some novelty to charm us. But the lengthening shadows in silence admonish us not to tarry too long. Reluctantly we take a long lingering look, and commence our descent toward the wonderful valley.

The apparently omnipresent forest overarches our way; and beautiful firs (*Picea amabalis* and *Picea grandis*) and "tamaracks" (*Pinus contorta*) stand sentinel guard on every hand; while patches of stunted manzanita (*Arctostaphylos glauca*), with its evergreen leaves and fragrant, waxy-like blossoms, and different species of California lilac (*Ceanothus*), literally loading the air with its perfume, and brightening the landscape with its flowery plumes of purple or white, attract our attention, until, by a gentle declivity, we arrive at "Tamarack Flat."

Here, for the present at least, our stage ride will probably end, and that by horseback begin. Here, too, if we are not tired, we should walk about among the singular groups of granite rocks that surround the house. Their quaint forms and unique combinations of picturesque beauty, will well repay examination. These will make an agreeable interchange of rest and recreation for a few hours. The house itself, and its accommodations, will be found to be, like the scenery around it, somewhat meagre perhaps, but we trust with enough of enjoyment in it to make the visit a remembrance of pleasure.

Now, the novelty of the circumstances and situation to many may be fruitful of confusion, or disappointment, or dissatisfaction, and even of discord, if the following motto is not inscribed upon every one's intent and purpose:

"SELFISHNESS IS BANISHED FROM OUR PARTY."

This being cheerfully and unanimously conceded, we predict for all a delightful trip. To secure its immediate as well as ultimate success, permit us to make one or two suggestions before starting: *First,*—Let there be one chosen leader for the party, whose excellent judgment and considerate attention shall be beyond question. Then, after mutual conference with each other upon any desirable movement, let him execute the wishes of the majority. Two heads, we grant, are better than one in consultation, but not in execution. *Second*,—In the selection of horses see to it that the easiest and best is secured for the most aged, or most weakly, or the most timid. And if experience teaches that an error has been committed, and that after all either possesses the favorite animal, let us promptly offer it to the one our better nature tells us should be the rider. *Third*,—Start and keep as nearly as possible together. Do not " straggle." If it is perceived that one of our friends has not the knowledge of riding, or the daring to keep up with us, let us not leave them, but rein in, and keep them company. We shall thus make them our devoted friends, and surely this would be a better reward than the boast that we had reached the hotel first, and secured the best rooms. The most thorough enjoyments of life are those which arise in generous and sympathetic consideration for, or concession to, the wants and wishes of others.

Before mounting let the guide examine and see that every saddle is perfectly safe. There should be no neglect, or doubt, about this; for, although there is no real danger, due precaution will avoid any. " All ready ? " Then,

"HO! FOR YO-SEMITE."

The gentle undulations and gradual declivities of the trail give opportunity for renewed confidence, both in ourselves and in our horses. This will leave us at liberty to notice the continuation of the glorious forest: the singular and attractive groupings of the rocks, additional to the conformation of numerous isolated specimens, one of which (on our right) resembles, and is named, "The Decanter," and another, "The Sphynx."

About two and a half miles from Tamarack Flat, we arrive at Cascade Creek, across which is a rude bridge; almost immediately after crossing which it will be well for the whole party to keep at least one eye open for the beautiful scene at our left. In the distance looms squarely up a bold and lofty mountain. In the foreground the stream rushes heedlessly on among large rocks, as if indifferent of its fate; now leaping over this, and dashing on and past that; here with a seething, there with a roaring sound; yonder bubbling and gurgling, or

"Smokin, and frothin'
Its tumult and wrath in,"

until the enchanting sight, united with its songs and performances, may tempt us to linger too long.

Half a mile farther we come to the top of a rocky promontory, and before us is presented a view that will equal, if not surpass, any we have yet seen. This is "Prospect Point." While the guide is again arranging and securing our saddles (never permit this to be omitted), preparatory to the descent of the mountain, let us realize, if we can, its ineffable grandeur. That bright and sparkling stream is the Merced (meaning "River of Mercy"). Released from its pure snowy reservoir among the tops of the Sierras, it has leaped the wonderful walls of Yo-Semite, and is hurrying on through an almost impassable cañon, to fertilize and gladden the valleys below. Three days were once spent by us in that cañon, alone, seeking to know if a home could be made in Yo-Semite during winter. In the far distance lies "Mount Bullion," the easterly boundary of the Fremont grant. In the hollow to the right is a waterfall of some eight hundred feet, made by the union of the " Big " and " Little " Cascade Creeks. Beyond that is the " Stand-point of Silence," on the old Coulterville trail ; the view from which looking up through the cañon and into the valley is inexpressibly grand.

Now with your permission we will commence the descent of the mountain. There is nothing in it to make us nervous or uneasy. Keep a moderately tight rein, and *trust to your horse.* He knows where to place his foot firmly at every step. He makes his own personal safety a study, as well as ours. There are but one or two very steep places in the entire descent. The most timid may wish to dismount and walk at those places. As they are short, that is soon accomplished. And upon the whole, although we breathe more freely when the valley is reached, it is over with almost before we know it.

The picturesque wildness of the scene on every hand ; the exciting wonders of so romantic a journey ; the difficulties surmounted ;

the dangers braved and overcome, put us in possession of one unanimous feeling of unalloyed delight; so that when we reach the foot of the mountain, and look upon the beautiful rapids of the river rolling and swelling at the side of the trail, while a forest of oaks and pines stands sentinel on its banks, or ride side by side among the trees in the valley, we congratulate each other upon looking the very picture of happiness personified.

RIVER SCENE IN THE YO-SEMITE VALLEY, NEAR THE FOOT OF THE TRAIL.

From a Photograph by C. L. Weed.

We will here remark that there are but two localities by which this valley can at present be safely entered, the one by which we have come, and the other immediately opposite the river, by way of Mariposa. Should a railroad ever enter the valley—and even now one is in contemplation—its course will, substantially, follow that of the river up the cañon.

THE RIDE UP THE VALLEY.

When nearly opposite the "Pohono" or "Bridal Veil" Fall, by noticing the second high point of the mountain west, a large head and strikingly noble features of a man in profile can easily be distinguished. This is connected with the legend of Tu-tock-ah-nu-lah, alluded to in other portions of this chapter, who is awaiting the return of his long-lost and lamented Tis-sa-ac.

Here, too, if it is evening, a strong breeze is generally noticed, first among the foliage of the trees, then by its swaying their tops and branches, and afterward by its refreshing coolness on the brow. This breeze seldom extends beyond a circumference half a mile in diameter, and probably became the origin of the Indian tradition from whence the name "Pohono" derived its significa-tion. After passing through this cool circle, gusts of warm wind are frequently felt at intervals for some two miles. Having had to ride up the valley many times after sunset, these experiences have almost always been realized.

Fatigued as we may be, every object around us has an interest as we pass this point, or watch that shadow slowly climbing those towering granite walls, when the last rays of the setting sun are quietly draping the highest peaks of this wonderful valley with a purple veil of hazy ether; or, as Mr. Greeley expresses it, in his interesting descriptive visit,—

"That first full, deliberate gaze up the opposite height! can I ever forget it? The valley is here scarcely half a mile wide while its northern wall of mainly naked, perpendicular granite, is at least four thousand feet high—probably mor. But the modicum of moonlight that fell into this awful gorge [Mr. Greele arrived in the night] gave to that precipice a vagueness of outline, an indefinite vastness, a ghostly and weird spirituality. Had the mountain spoken to me in audible voice, or begun to lean over with the purpose of burying me beneath its crushing mass, I should hardly have been surprised. Its whiteness, thrown into bold relief by the patches of trees or shrubs which fringed or flecked it wherever a few handfuls of its moss, slowly decomposed to earth, could contrive to hold on, continually suggested the presence of snow, which suggestion, with difficulty refuted, was at once renewed. And, looking up the valley, we saw just such mountain precipices, barely separated by intervening watercourses of inconsiderable depth, and only receding sufficiently to make room for a very narrow meadow inclosing the river, to the furthest limit of vision."

"POM-POM-PA-SUS," OR THE THREE BROTHERS, 4,000 FEET HIGH.
From a Photograph by C. L. Weed.

Our trail, for the most part, lies among giant pines, from two hundred to two hundred and fifty feet in height, and beneath the refreshing shade of outspreading oaks and other trees. Not a sound breaks the expressive stillness that reigns, save the occasional chirping and singing of birds as they fly to their nests, or the low, distant sighing of the breeze in the tops of the forest. Crystal streams occasionally gurgle and ripple across our path, whose sides are fringed with willows and wild flowers that are ever blossoming, and grass that is ever green. On either side of us stands almost perpendicular cliffs, to the height of thirty-five hundred feet; and on whose rugged faces, or in their uneven tops

DISTANT VIEW OF THE "POHONO," OR BRIDAL VEIL WATERFALL.
From a Photograph by C. L. Weed.

and sides, here and there a stunted pine struggles to live, and
every crag seems crowned with some shrub or tree. The bright
sheen of the river occasionally glistens from among the dense
foliage of several long vistas that continually open before us.
At every step, some new picture of great beauty presents itself,
and some new shapes and shadows from trees and mountains
form new combinations of light and shade, in this great kaleido-
scope of nature.

Shortly after passing Tu-tock-ah-nu-lah, on our left, we come
in sight of three points which the Indians know as "Pom-p·
pa-sus"—mountains playing leap-frog, but which some lacka
cal person has given the common-place name of "The Three .
Brothers," beyond which we get the first glimpse of the upper
part of the Yo-Semite waterfall.

Perhaps we ought previously to have mentioned, that the first
water-fall of any magnitude which strikes our attention on entering the valley—and, indeed, on several occasions before reaching the bottom land of the valley—is the "Pohono" (Indian

THE FERRY.
From a Photograph by C. L. Weed.

name), or " Bridal Veil " Fall, and which we shall more fully describe when we take a near view of it.

Surrounded by such scenes of loveliness and sublimity, we feel a reluctance to break the charm they throw upon us by any speech ; when some one is almost sure to cry out —" The Ferry." Here the river is about sixty feet wide, and twelve feet deep —across which we can be speedily conveyed on a good boat, at the rate of thirty-seven and a-half cents per head for men, women, and animals.

By consulting the accompanying outline map of the valley and its surroundings, it will readily be seen that a little detour to the left will enable us to avoid the delay and expense of the ferry. By taking the trail indicated, we cross " The Point of Rocks ;" from whence some charming scenes are obtained, and are on the direct course for Hutchings' Bridge, the only one in the valley,—which spans the Merced River just opposite his house, and is entirely free to the public.

As we ride along, the " Yo-Semite Fall," the " North Dome," " Royal Arches," " Washington Tower," " Clouds Rest," " South

Dome," " Sentinel," and other grand points of interest, now seen
only at a distance, impressively suggest the treat in store for us
when we obtain a closer personal interview with their matchless
wonders.

Now, notwithstanding the many objects of interest we have
passed, we venture, upon a guess, that one thought has frequently
intruded itself upon our notice, it is this—" Shall we ever come
up to that mountain ?" and the length of time consumed·in the
attempt—especially if the unaccustomed ride has brought with it
a corresponding amount of fatigue—would seem to give back the
nonchalant and unfeeling answer, " Never ! " There is, however,
no greater proof of the unrealized altitudes of these mountain-sides
than this—the time it takes to reach or pass them.

But amidst all these we can hear one ejaculation that seems to
contain more real satisfaction in it than any amount of sight-seeing just now. It is this one : " Thank goodness. Here's the Yo-
Semite Hotel. Here's Hutchings' ! "—and commending ourselves
to its most generous hospitalities—for we need them—we will dismount in the hope that a refreshing glass of pure California wine
(or something stronger, if we prefer it, as none but excellent
liquors are considered by the landlord to be worth packing in) a
good wash, and an acceptable dinner await us.

THE FIRST NIGHT IN THE VALLEY.

After the fatigue and excitement of the ride, and the novel circumstances of the past few nights, it is natural to suppose that
with a comfortable bed will come refreshing slumbers ; yet experience may prove that, weary as we are, it seems such a luxury to
lie awake and listen to the splashing, washing, roaring, surging,
hissing, seething sound of the great Yo-Semite Falls, just opposite :
or to pass quietly out of our resting-place, and look up between the
lofty pines and spreading oaks to the granite cliffs that tower up
with such majesty of form and boldness of outline against the vast
ethereal vault of heaven; or watch, in the moonlight, the ever-
changing shapes and shadows of the water, as it leaps the cloud-
draped summit of the mountain, and falls in gusty torrents on the

unyielding granite, to be dashed to an infinity of atoms. Then to return to our welcome couch and dream of some tutelary genius, of immense proportions, extending over us his protecting arms— of his admonishing the waterfall to modulate the music of its voice, that we may sleep and be refreshed.

THE FIRST DAY IN THE VALLEY.

Some time before the sun can get a good, honest look at us, deep down as we are in this awful chasm, we see him painting his rosy smiles upon the ridges, and etching lights and shadows in the furrows of the mountain's brow, as though he took a pride in showing up, to the best advantage, the wrinkles time had made upon it; but all of us feel too fatigued fully to enjoy the thrilling grandeur and beauty that surrounds us.

But little laborious effort being desired on the first day after arrival, it will be well to rest long and breakfast late. The morning can be devoted to scenes that are near the hotel, and there are enough to employ and charm us. Fortified by a morning of quiet and a substantial lunch, let us in the afternoon pay a visit to

THE LOWER YO-SEMITE FALL.

Crossing the bridge over the main stream, which is here about eighty feet in width and five in depth, we keep down the northern bank of the river for a short distance, to avoid a large portion of the valley in front of the hotel, that is probably overflowed with water.

Presently we reach one of the most beautifully picturesque scenes that eye ever saw. It is the ford. The oak, dogwood, maple, cottonwood, and other trees, form an arcade of great beauty over the sparkling, rippling, pebbly stream, and, in the background, the lower fall of the Yo-Semite is dropping its sheet of snowy sheen behind a dark middle distance of pines and firs.

As the snow rapidly melts beneath the fiery strength of a hot summer sun, a large body of water, most probably, is rushing past, forming several small streams—which, being comparatively shallow, are easily forded. When within about a hundred and fifty yards of the fall, as numerous large boulders begin to inter-

THE FORD OF THE YO-SEMITE.

From a Photograph by C. L. Weed.

cept our progress, we may as well dismount, and, after fastening
our animals to some young trees, make our way up to it on foot.

Now a change of temperature soon becomes perceptible, as we
advance; and the almost oppressive heat of the centre of the
valley is gradually changing to that of chilliness.   But up, up, we
climb, over this rock, and past that tree, until we reach the foot,
or as near as we can advance to it, of the great Yo-Semite Fall,
when a cold draught of air rushes down upon us from above,
about equal in strength to an eight knot breeze; bringing with it
a heavy shower of finely comminuted spray, that falls with sufficient force to saturate our clothing in a few moments.   From

NEAR VIEW OF THE YO-SEMITE FALLS.—2,550 FEET IN HEIGHT.

this a beautiful phenomenon is observable—inasmuch as, after striking our hats, the diamond-like mist shoots off at an angle of about thirty-five or forty degrees, and as the sun shines upon it, a number of miniature rainbows are formed all round us.

Those who have never visited this spot, must not suppose that the cloud-like spray that descends upon us is the main fall itself, broken into infinitesimal particles, and becoming nothing but a sheet of cloud. By no means; for, although this stream shoots over the margin of the mountain, nearly seven hundred feet above, it falls almost in a solid body—not in a continuous stream exactly, but having a close resemblance to an avalanche of snowy rockets that appear to be perpetually trying to overtake each other in their descent, and mingle the one into the other; the whole composing a torrent of indescribable power and beauty.

Huge boulders, and large masses of sharp, angular rocks, are scattered here and there, forming the uneven sides of an immense, and apparently ever-boiling cauldron; around, and in the interstices of which, numerous dwarf ferns, weeds, grasses, and flowers, are ever growing, where not actually washed by the falling stream.

It is beyond the power of language to describe the awe-inspiring majesty of the darkly-frowning and overhanging mountain walls of solid granite that here hem us in on every side, as though they would threaten us with instantaneous destruction, if not total annihilation, did we attempt for a moment to deny their power. If man ever feels his utter insignificance at any time, it is when looking upon such a scene of appalling grandeur as the one here presented.

The point from whence the photograph was taken from which our engraving is made—being almost underneath the fall—might lead to the supposition that the lower section, which embraces more than two-thirds of the picture, was the highest of the two seen; when, in fact, the lower one, according to the measurements of Mr. Denman, superintendent of Public Schools in San Francisco; of Mr. Peterson, the engineer of the Mariposa and Yo-Semite Water Company; and of Mr. Long, county surveyor, is about seven hundred feet above the level of the valley, while the upper fall is about one thousand four hundred and forty-eight feet, and between the two, measuring about four hundred feet, is a series of rapids rather than a fall, giving the total height of the entire fall at two thousand five hundred and forty-eight feet. *

After lingering here for several hours, with inexpressible feelings of suppressed astonishment and delight, qualified and intensified by veneration, we may take a long and reluctant last upward gaze, convinced that we shall " never look upon its like again," until we pay it another visit at some future time ; and, making the best of our way to where our horses are tied, return to the hotel.

SECOND DAY IN THE YO-SEMITE VALLEY.—RIDE TO LAKE AH-WI-YAH, OR MIRROR LAKE.

After a substantial breakfast, made palatable by that best of all sauces, a good appetite, our guide announces that the horses are ready.   As much of the beauty of the lake consists in the reflection of its glorious surroundings—mountains four thousand to between five and six thousand feet in height—it is desirable that a reasonably early start should be obtained.   Sometimes the unbroken calm of its glassy bosom is not disturbed before twelve o'clock M.   At other times the breeze has broken it up by ten o'clock A. M.   But generally the mirror is perfect until nearly noon.   On account of the early time desirable for setting out on this trip, it is better to postpone it until the second day, as a premature departure from our couch on the first morning, will generally bring on premature fatigue, and a consequent decrease in the amount of our enjoyment.   The distance is only three miles, and we can ride all the way on horseback.

* Prof. J. D. Whitney makes the height of this fall to be from 2,537 to 2,641 feet. First fall 1,500—Second 626—and Third 400.   A notice we saw upon a stump, placed there by the State Geological Survey, in 1863, gave its total height above the valley as 2,634 feet.   That we think should be the preferred measurement.

Leaving the hotel, we cross the bridge and thread our way through the far-stretching vistas of luxuriant green that open before us; the bright sunlight and somber shadows ever winking and twinkling upon the sparkling and gurgling streams that cross our trail, until we emerge on a grassy and flower-covered plateau on the north side of the valley, near the base of the great North Dome, called by the Indians "·To-coy-æ." This mountain of naked granite, with scarcely a tree or shrub growing from a single crevice, towers above you to the height of three thousand seven hundred and twenty-five feet. Its sides are nearly perpendicular for more than two thousand feet, and in which a colossal arch is formed, doubtless from the falling of several sections of the rock. This has been designated the "Royal Arch of To-coy-æ." This, we believe, has never been measured; but we should judge its altitude, from the valley to the crown of the arch, to be about one thousand seven hundred feet, and its span about two thousand feet; its depth in, from the face of the rock, is about eighty or ninety feet.

On our way up we pass the winter-quarters of Mr. Lamon on our left, and about half a mile above his cabin we can see his garden and orchard on our right. Between the two are several brushy structures in the Indian style of architecture, built by the Mono Indians for the purpose of storing acorns during the winter, in order to give them a supply of that (to them) useful edible during summer. Piñons, or pine nuts, and acorns are their staple articles of diet. When the supply of piñons fail, acorns are generally abundant, and the Indians visit Yo Semite during fall, in strings of from forty to fifty, for the purpose of packing acorns over the sierras to Mono for their winter supply. This is generally done by the women! They peel and dry them before packing. When wanted for use they are ground by being pounded on a rock. The tannin is then taken out by means of warm water; and after boiling it with hot stones dropped into water-tight baskets it resembles mush and is eaten with the fingers. There is one feature here that should not be overlooked, and that is the small streams of water that leap down over the granite walls, like falling strings of pearls and diamonds. These add much, in early spring, to the attractiveness of the scene.

Having crossed the plateau, we ride over some rocky hillocks, and among a park-like array of oak trees, until we arrive at Lake Ah-wi-yah, so named and known by the Indians, but which has

LAKE AH-WI-YAH, OR MIRROR LAKE.

been newly christened by American visitors " Lake Hiawatha," " Mirror Lake," and several others, which, though pretty enough, are equally common-place and unsuitable. But of this we shall have something to say in another place.

This lake, although a charming little sheet of crystal water of almost a couple of acres in extent, in which numerous schools of speckled trout may be seen gaily disporting themselves, would be unworthy of a notice, but for the picturesque grandeur of its surroundings. On the north and west lie immense rocks that have become detached from the tops of the mountain above ;

among these grow a large variety of trees and shrubs, many of which stand on and overhang the margin of the lake, and are reflected on its mirror-like bosom. To the north-east opens a vast gorge or cañon, down which impetuously rush the waters of the north fork of the Merced, which debouches into and supplies the lake.

On the south-east stands the majestic Mount Tis-sa-ack, or "South Dome," four thousand five hundred and ninety-three feet in altitude above the valley. Almost one-half of this immense mass, either from some convulsion of nature, or

"Time's effacing fingers,"

has fallen over, by which, most probably, the dam for this lake was first formed. Yet proudly, aye, defiantly erect, it still holds its noble head, and is not only the highest of all those around, but is the greatest attraction of the valley. Moreover, in this are centred many agreeable associations to the Indian mind; as here was once the traditionary home of the guardian spirit of the valley, the angel-like and beautiful *Tis-sa-ack*, after whom her devoted Indian worshippers named this gloriously majestic mountain. While we sit in the shade of these fine old trees, and look upon all the objects around us, mirrored on the unruffled bosom of the lake, let us relate the following interesting legend of Tu-tock-ah-nu-lah, after whom the vast perpendicular and massive projecting rock at the lower end of the valley was named, and with which is interwoven this history of Tis-sa-ack.

This legend was told in an eastern journal, by a gentleman residing here, who signs himself "Iota," and who received it from the lips of an old Indian; the relation of which, although several points of interest are omitted, will, nevertheless, prove very entertaining:

THE LEGEND OF TU-TOCK-AH-NU-LAH AND TIS-SA-ACK.

"It was in the unremembered past that the children of the sun first dwelt in Yo-Semite. Then all was happiness; for Tu-tock-ah-nu-lah sat on high in his rocky home, and cared for the people whom he loved. Leaping over the upper plains, he herded the wild deer, that the people might choose the fattest for the feast. He roused the bear from his cavern in the mountain, that the brave might hunt. From his lofty rock he prayed to the Great Spirit, and brought the soft rain upon the corn in the valley. The smoke of his pipe curled into the air, and the golden sun breathed warmly through its blue haze, and ripened the crops, that the women might gather them in. When he laughed, the face of the winding river was rippled with smiles; when he sighed, the wind swept sadly through the singing pines; if he spoke, the sound was like the deep voice of the cataract; and when he smote the far-striding bear, his whoop of triumph rang from crag to gorge—echoed from mountain to mountain. His form was straight like the arrow, and elastic like the bow. His foot was swifter than the red deer, and his eye was strong and bright like the rising sun.

"But one morning, as he roamed, a bright vision came before him, and then the soft colors of the West were in his lustrous eye. A maiden sat upon the southern granite dome that raises its gray head among the highest peaks. She was not like the dark maidens of the tribe below, for the yellow hair rolled over her dazzling form, as golden waters over silver rocks; her brow beamed with the pale beauty of the moonlight, and her blue eyes were as the far-off hills before the sun goes down. Her little foot shone like the snow-tufts on the wintry pines, and its arch was like the spring of a bow. Two cloud-like wings wavered upon her dimpled shoulders, and her voice was as the sweet, sad tone of the night-bird of the woods.

"'Tu-tock-ah-nu-lah,' she softly whispered; then gliding up the rocky dome, she vanished over its rounded top. Keen was the eye, quick was the ear, swift was the foot of the noble youth as he sped up the rugged path in pursuit; but the soft down from her snowy wings was wafted into his eyes, and he saw her no more.

"Every morning now did the enamored Tu-tock-ah-nu-lah leap the stony barriers, and wander over the mountains, to meet the lovely Tis-sa-ack. Each day he laid sweet acorns and wild flowers upon her dome. His ear caught her footstep, though it was light as the falling leaf; his eye gazed upon her beautiful form, and into her gentle eyes; but never did he speak before her, and never again did her sweet-toned voice fall upon his ear. Thus did he love the fair maid, and so strong was his thought of her that he forgot the crops of Yo-Semite, and they, without rain, wanting his tender care, quickly drooped their heads, and shrunk. The wind whistled mournfully through the wild corn, the wild bee stored no more honey in the hollow tree, for the flowers had lost their freshness, and the green leaves became brown. Tu-tock-ah-nu-lah saw none of this, for his eyes were dazzled by the shining wings of the maiden. But Tis-sa-ack looked with sorrowing eyes over the neglected valley, when early in the morning she stood upon the gray dome of the mountain; so, kneeling on the smooth, hard rock, the maiden besought the Great Spirit to bring again the bright flowers and delicate grasses, green trees, and nodding acorns.

"Then, with an awful sound, the dome of granite opened beneath her feet, and the mountain was riven asunder, while the melting snows from the Nevada gushed through the wonderful gorge. Quickly they formed a lake between the perpendicular walls of the cleft mountain, and sent a sweet murmuring river through the valley. All then was changed. The birds dashed their little bodies into the pretty pools among the grasses, and fluttering out again, sang for delight; the moisture crept silently through the parched soil; the flowers sent up a fragrant incense of thanks; the corn gracefully raised its drooping head; and the sap, with velvet footfall, ran up into the trees, giving life and energy to all. But the maid, for whom the valley had suffered, and through whom it had been again clothed with beauty, had disappeared as strangely as she came. Yet, that all might hold her memory in their hearts, she left the quiet lake, the winding river, and *yonder half-dome*, which still bears her name, '*Tis-sa-ack*.' It is said to be four thousand five hundred feet high, and every evening it catches the last rosy rays that are reflected from the snowy peaks above. As she flew away, small downy feathers were wafted from her wings, and where they fell—on the margin of the lake—you will now see thousands of little white violets.

"When Tu-tock-ah-nu-lah knew that she was gone, he left his rocky castle and wandered away in search of his lost love. But that the Yo-Semites might never forget him, with the hunting-knife in his bold hand, he carved the outlines of his noble head upon the face of the rock that bears his name. And there they still remain, three thousand feet in the air, guarding the entrance to the beautiful valley which had received his loving care

If a precautionary provision was not made in the morning for our noon repast, by this time an admonishing voice from the organs of digestion will be seductively suggestive of an early departure for the hotel. On our way we should by no means deny ourselves the gratification of a visit to Lamon's Garden. For in addition to its excellent cultivation, the variety and abundance of fine and delicious fruits, it will be an acceptable intrusion upon the owner's bachelor solitude to see so many cheery faces within it. Much of his pleasure consists in showing it to appreciative visitors, and the charge is merely nominal, only twenty-five cents each for all the fruit we can eat. He has two orchards of over five hundred fruit-trees in each. One winter he lived in Yo-Semite entirely alone, locked in by the snowy ridges and was some twenty-five miles from his nearest neighbor.

Our lunch snugly disposed of, succeeded by a good rest, let us take a delightful ride of four miles, and pay an afternoon's visit to

THE "POHONO" OR BRIDAL VEIL WATERFALL.

Visitors generally prefer paying a visit to the Pohono Fall, before undertaking those of greater difficulty at the upper end of the valley, that they may become somewhat better rested from the fatigue of the journey. Let us, therefore, not be out of the fashion, but take a quiet ride down the south side of the valley at once; and the first point of striking interest we shall notice on our left will be Sentinel Rock, a lofty and solitary peak, upon which the watch-fires of the Indians have often been lighted to

SENTINEL ROCK, 3,270 FEET HIGH.

give warning of approaching danger; and which can readily be
seen from all the principal points within and around the valley.

Further on, we see a singular group of peaks, that will resemble
almost any thing we can conjure up, according to the time of day
we may be passing, as every change in the position of the sun will
give a new set of shadows; but that which it most resembles, is
the dilapidated front of some grand old cathedral, with towers
and buttresses; and, in one place, a circle that a strong imagination can make into a clock, which will indicate the time of day to
a moment!

This passed, we come in front of the Pohono Fall. After
threading our way among trees and bushes, over rocks and watercourses, it becomes necessary that we should dismount, and tie

our animals, as the remaining distance is over a rough ascent of rocks, which will have to be accomplished on foot. As this is short, we shall thread our way among bushes and boulders, without much difficulty, until the heavy spray from the fall saturates our clothing, and the velvety softness of the moist grasses growing upon the little ridge we have climbed, reminds us that the goal of our desire is reached.

It is impossible to portray the feeling of awe, wonder, and admiration—almost amounting to adoration—that thrills our very souls as we look upon this enchanting scene. The gracefully undulating and wavy sheets of spray, that fall in gauze-like and ethereal folds; now expanding, now contracting; now glittering in the sunlight, like a veil of diamonds; now changing into one vast and many-colored cloud, that throws its misty drapery over the falling torrent, as if in very modesty, to veil its unspeakable beauty from our too eagerly admiring sight.

In order to see this to the best advantage, the eye should take in only the foot of the fall at first; then a short section upward; then higher, until, by degrees, the top is reached. In this way the majesty of the waterfall is more fully realized and appreciated.

The stream itself—about forty feet in width—resembles an avalanche of watery rockets, that shoots out over the precipice above you, at the height of nearly nine hundred feet, and then leaps down, in one unbroken train, to the immense cauldron of boulders beneath, where it surges and boils in its angry fury, throwing up large volumes of spray, over which the sun forms two or more magnificent rainbows which arch the abyss.

Like most other tributaries of the main middle fork of the Merced, this stream falls very low toward the close of the summer, but is seldom, if ever, entirely dry. When we visited the valley in July, 1855, this branch did not contain more than one-tenth the water usually seen in the month of May or June.

The river has its origin in a lake at the foot of a bold, crescent-shaped, perpendicular rock, about thirteen miles above the edge of the Pohono Fall. On this lake a strong wind is said to be continually blowing; and, as several Indians have lost their lives there and in the stream, their exceedingly acute and superstitious imaginations have made it bewitched.

An Indian woman was out gathering seeds, a short distance above these falls, when, by some mishap, she lost her balance and fell into the stream, and the force of the current carried her down with such velocity, that before any assistance could be rendered, she was swept over the precipice, and was never seen afterward.

"Pohono," from whom the stream and the waterfall received their musical Indian name, is an evil spirit, whose breath is a blighting and fatal wind, and, consequently, is to be dreaded and shunned. On this account, whenever, from necessity, the Indians have to pass it, a feeling of distress steals over them, and they fear it as much as the wandering Arab does the simooms of the African desert; they hurry past it at the height of their speed. To point at the waterfall, when travelling in the valley, to their minds, is certain death. No inducement could be offered sufficiently large to tempt them to sleep near it. In fact, they believe that they hear the voices of those that have been drowned there, perpetually warning them to shun "Pohono."

How much more desirable is it to perpetuate these expressive Indian names—many of which embody the superstitious and highly imaginative characteristics of the Indian mind—than to give them Anglicized ones, be they ever so pretty. We think the name of "Bridal Veil Fall" is not only by far the most musical and suitable of any or of all others yet given, but is the only one that is worthy of the object named; and yet, we confess that we should much prefer the beautiful and expressive Indian name of "Pohono," to that of "Bridal Veil."

The vertical, and, at some points, overhanging mountains on either side of the Pohono, possess quite as much interest as the fall itself, and add much to the grandeur and magnificence of the whole scene. A tower-shaped rock, about three thousand feet in height, standing at the south-west side of the fall, and nearly opposite "Tu-tock-ah-nu-lah," has on its top a number of projecting rocks that very much resemble canon. In order to assist in per-

NEAR VIEW OF THE "POHONO," OR BRIDAL VEIL FALL, 940 FEET HIGH.

From a Photograph by C. L. Weed.

petuating the beautiful legend before given concerning that Indian semi-deity, we shall take the liberty of christening this point Tu-tock-ah-nu-lah's Citadel.

Other wild and weird-like points of equal interest stand before us, on the summit and among the niches of every cliff; so that it is not this or that particular rock that attracts, so much as the infinite variety, all of which are so distinctly different.

As the line of shadow is rapidly climbing the mountain, we had better retrace our steps to the hotel.

As we sit in the stillness and twilight of evening, thinking over and conversing about the wondrous scenes our eyes have looked upon this day; or listen, in silence, to the deep music of the distant waterfalls, our hearts seem full to overflowing with a sense of the grandeur, wildness, beauty, and profoundness to be felt and enjoyed when communing with the glorious works of nature, which call to mind those expressive lines of Moore:—

> "The earth shall be my fragrant shrine!
> My temple, Lord! that arch of thine;
> My censer's breath, the mountain airs;
> And silent thoughts, my only prayers."

THIRD DAY IN YO-SEMITE VALLEY.

By this time it is to be hoped that all of our party have been sufficiently toughened by exercise and rest to endure the fatigue of the trip we are about to take. Fortified with a substantial lunch and other etceteras, let us now set out for

THE "PI-WY-ACK" OR VERNAL, AND YO-WI-YE, OR NEVADA, FALLS.

It is always well to start as early as we conveniently can, without hurrying ourselves too much, as by this course we obtain many advantages that need not now be enumerated; therefore, as soon as the sun has begun to wink at us from among the pine-trees on the mountain-tops, we may as well start on our visit to the Pi-wy-ack, or Vernal, and the Yo-wi-ye or Nevada, falls.

At first, we pass round the granite points that extend into the level meadow land, just above the hotel; then, as we advance, the valley gradually widens, and, with the oak-trees growing at irregular intervals of distance, reminds us of the beautiful parks of Europe, especially those of England and France.

On our right is a high wall of granite, nearly perpendicular, to the height of three thousand seven hundred and forty feet—down which several small, silvery, ribbon-like streams are leaping. Here and there, from the sides of this vast mountain, a single tree or shrub is standing alone. Surmounting one of the lower points of rock, several rugged peaks unite, and resemble an immense hospice, which has, not inappropriately, been named Mount St. Bernard.   Another has a distant kinship, in form at least, with a bear.   Another, a huge head.   In fact, you can look at the various parts of the mountain, and trace a resemblance to a hun-

RIVER SCENE JUST BELOW THE BRIDGE, LOOKING EAST.
From a Photograph by C. L. Weed.

dred different objects; and as the shadows change, when the day advances, to as many more.   On our left stand the Royal Arches, Washington Tower, North and South Domes, and other objects of absorbing interest.   Numerous majestic trees overshadow the

9

way, such as the yellow pine (*Pinus ponderosa*), the cedar (*Libo-cedrus decurrens*), the black oak (*Quercus sonomensis*), with here and there a Douglas spruce (*Abies Douglasii*), and an occasional dogwood or two. By the streams can be found the balm of Gilead (*Populous balsamifera*) and the alder (*Alnus virinis*) in considerable abundance. On the *débris* piles large numbers of the live oak (*Quercus chrysolepis*) and maples (*Acer macrophyllum*) are found. Shrubs of various kinds are abundant, among the most beautiful and most fragrant stands the white azalea (*Azalea occidentalis*); then comes the pungent-flavored and aromatic laurel (*Tetranthera Californica*),—the latter is occasionally seen six inches in diameter, and could be classed among trees,—and many others. Flowers of many kinds are abundant, such as the yellow and purple evening primroses, larkspur (*Œnothera*), and also a very pretty pink everlasting (*Spraguea*). But to give a complete list of flowers would fill a volume.

About two miles above Hutchings' we arrive at, and continue up, the southern bank of the Merced, beneath a bower of trees and shrubs, over the roughest and rockiest portion of the trail. Formerly visitors used to tie their horses here, and make the ascent on foot, but some recent improvements now induce visitors to ride nearly up to the Vernal Fall. On our left the river forms a foaming cataract to the very foot of the fall, and the thundering boom of its waters rises at times above the sound of human voices.

Presently we arrive at a stream of very respectable size, which, having made the leap of the Tu-lool-we-ack Fall, about a mile and half above, has hurried down the "South Cañon," and now runs directly across our path. If the water is not too high we can ford it with safety; but if it is, it will be inexpedient to attempt it. In the latter event we will here tie our horses, and crossing a log-formed bridge, make the remainder of the ascent on foot.

Upward and onward we climb; and, after passing a bold point, and reading some of the names inscribed on Register Rock, we obtain, suddenly, the first sight of the Pi-wy-ack, or Vernal

Fall. While gazing at its beauties, let us, now and forever, earnestly protest against the perpetuation of any other nomenclature to this wonder, than " Pi-wy-ack," the name which is given to it by the Indians, which means " a shower of sparkling crystals," while " Vernal" could, with much more appropriateness, be bestowed upon the name-giver, as the fall itself is one vast

THE " PI-WY-ACK," OR VERNAL FALL, THREE HUNDRED AND FIFTY FEET HIGH.

sheet of sparkling brightness and snowy whiteness, in which there is not the slightest approximation, even in the tint, to any thing " vernal."

Still ascending and advancing, we are soon enveloped in a sheet of heavy spray, driven down upon us with such force as to resemble a heavy storm of comminuted rain. Now, many might suppose that this would be annoying, but it is not, although the only really unpleasant part of the trip is that which we have here to take, on a steep hill-side, and through a wet, alluvial soil, from which, at every footstep, the water spirts out, much to the inconvenience and discomfort of ladies—especially of those who wear long dresses.   As the distance through this is but short, it is soon accomplished, and in a few minutes we stand at the foot of " The

THE LADDERS.

Ladders."   Beneath a large, overhanging rock at our right, is a man who takes toll for ascending the ladders, eats, and "turns in" to sleep, upon the rock.   The charge for ascending and descending is seventy-five cents; and as this includes the trail as well as the ladders, the charge is very reasonable.

Formerly there were no means of ascending or descending this perpendicular wall of rock, except with ropes fastened to an oak-tree that grows in one of the interstices; and that, too, at great personal risk and inconvenience—so that but few persons would make the dangerous attempt.

By the measurements of different gentlemen whose figures approximate, the height of this fall is given at three hundred and fifty feet   Prof. J. D. Whitney says : " Our measurements give, all the way, from 315 to 475 feet."   But as the professor ascribes the difference to the height of the water, at the various seasons, instead of, as we think, to the difference (160 feet) in the calculations, we regret our inability to concur in his conclusions.

THE "YO-WI-YE," OR NEVADA FALL.

Ascending the ladders, we reach an elevated plateau of rock, on the edge of which, and about breast high, is a natural wall of granite, that seems to have been constructed by nature for the especial benefit and convenience of people with weak nerves, enabling them to lean upon it, and look down over the precipice into the deep chasm below.

The waters of the river, which rush through a narrow gorge above, with great speed and power, here spread out to the width of about sixty-five feet, before shooting over the edge of the fall.

RIVER RUSHING THROUGH THE GORGE ABOVE THE PI-WY-ACK FALL.

Advancing gently and pleasantly, we arrive at the gorge, before alluded to, and as several large pieces of burnt timber are probably lying near, if we roll them in upon the angry bosom of the hurrying current, we shall find that they are tossed about, and borne along as though they were waifs. After working our way over a low point of rocks, we come in sight of the Yo-wi-ye Fall, the greatest, yet not the highest fall, in or near the Yo-Semite

THE "YO-WI-YE," OR NEVADA FALL, 700 FEET IN HEIGHT.

From a Photograph by C. L. Weed.

Valley, several different measurements making it about seven hundred feet in height.

When the base of this fall is reached, or as nearly so as the eddying clouds of spray will permit, it appears to be different in shape to either of the others; for, although it shoots over the precipice in a curve, and descends almost perpendicularly for four-fifths of the distance, it then strikes the smooth surface of the mountain, and spreads and forms a beautiful sheet of silvery whiteness, about one hundred and thirty feet in width.

This point is about as far as visitors generally go, although some more enthusiastic spirits work their way by the side of the smooth mountain wall—that here prevents further progress, without considerable toil and difficulty—to the top of the fall; and as we expect the courteous reader is of the latter class, we will, with his consent, make one of the party to see what we can find.

By the enterprise of the commissioners, who have constructed a rustic bridge over the gorge below, we are enabled to make the ascent to the wondrous scenes above by an easier and safer route. Let us, therefore, retrace our steps to the bridge; and, standing on its center, look for a moment into the angry stream. If the sun is brilliantly shining, the rushing waters above the bridge will be transformed below into a cascade of diamonds. As those gems are, unmistakably, of the " purest water," there would seem to be a reckless disregard for the danger "from chipping," to be apprehended from this method of transportation. But as all the chips seem to be carefully gathered and re-run, let us not linger here, but attempt

THE ASCENT OF THE CAP OF LIBERTY.

This is the name given to the striking mass of almost perpendicular rock that stands boldly out at the north side of the Nevada Fall. Its altitude above the foot of the fall is estimated at about two thousand feet. The singularity and majesty of its presence are impressed upon every beholder. Numerous aspirants, or their friends, have attempted to attach individual names to it, such as "Mount Francis," "Mount Gwin," "Bellows Butte," "Mount

Broderick," and others; but these names, however highly thought
of in the circles among which their owners lived, have not been
respected in connection with this magnificent formation.

The best route for us to take in order to reach its lofty summit,
will be on its western side. Avoiding the mouth of the precipitous ravine up which our course runs, let us strike across the first
mountain bench, and, threading our way among bushes, make for
and keep up the ravine named, until we reach a grassy meadow
at its head. Then it will be readily seen there is but one way by
which the top of the " Cap " can be gained. That followed, let
us suppose ourselves standing upon its grand old crown.

Here our first attention will be called to a group of large juniper-
trees (*Juniper occidentalis*), two of which are ten feet each in
diameter. There are also a few stunted Douglas spruce trees, and
several dwarf shrubs belonging to some variety of oak with which
we are unacquainted. How they find sustenance, or even foothold, on such an apparently barren mass of naked granite is a mystery to us. Down, deep down, in the little Yo-Semite Valley,
meanders the Merced. The tall pines, everywhere abundant,
appearing about the size of ordinary walking-canes. But, if we
have courage, let us go to its southeastern corner, and holding
firmly to the rock, look down the almost vertical precipice upon
the Nevada Fall. All will confess that this sight alone repays
us. So that the Yo-Semite Fall, the Sentinel Dome, Mount Starr
King, and above all, the apparently omnipresent South Dome,
with numerous other wonderful mountains, are all thrown into the
bargain. Descending to the meadow land at the back of the Cap,
let us take a hasty glance at the little Yo-Semite Valley and

THE COUNTRY ABOVE THE YO-WI-YE FALL.

Our course now lies up and across the numerous spurs that hem
in, or rather that almost monopolize and form the so-called valley,
with the exception, perhaps, of from a third to a half mile on the
sides of the stream. Numerous clumps of fir-trees and pines stand
here and there; some on the banks of the river, and some in moist
p'aces, that, during a short season of the year, are shallow lakes.

Numerous grouse and mountain quail whirr past us—simply, as we think, perhaps, to torment us, as on this occasion most likely we have no gun, knowing that at other times when we had, we found no use for one. By the side of every little hillock, especially at the bottom of the spurs, there are deer trails, deeply worn, and full of recent imprints of their feet; also those of the cinnamon and grizzly bear. On the limited portions of alluvial soil, a thick growth of short, fine grass is growing, resembling the buffalo grass of the plains. On the low ridges or spurs in the valley, there is also an abundance of tuft or bunch grass.

The mountains on either side of this valley, are, if possible, more singular than those of the great Yo-Semite Valley, on account of the formation being distinctly different. For instance, a large and uneven, yet sugar-loaf shaped rock, at its eastern extremity, near another waterfall, has a wide belt of reddish, fine-grained granite near its base, and which extends from the one side to the other; similar layers of rock continue, although of different kinds and colors, to the very summit of the rock, while that in the valley below is of gray granite almost exclusively. The waterfall at the head of this valley, and two and a half miles from the Yo-wi-ye, might more properly be denominated a cascade, as the main body of water forming the river rushes down an inclined plane of about 150 feet in length, at an angle of about $37°$. The mountains on either side being lofty, rugged, pine-studded, and precipitous, add much to the grandeur as well as beauty of the scene.

On reaching the top, near the edge of the fall, we find the rock very smooth and bare for many rods, with here and there a stunted tree, living on a short allowance of soil in a narrow crevice. At the back of this bare rock is a limited forest of pines and firs. Huge boulders and masses of granite lie scattered here and there. The river, for some distance above, forms a series of rapids. As a tree has lodged across the stream about a quarter of a mile from the fall, and the smooth rock to the eastward forms another barrier to our progress in that direction, let us cross to the edge of the Merced, and take one brief glance down into the gulf into which the Yo-wi-ye (Nevada) is leaping.

Lying down upon a flat and solid rock, apparently formed—like the parapet at the head of the Pi-wy-ack (or Vernal) Fall—for the purpose of enabling the beholder safely to see those wonderful sights, let us have one good look at the majesty and glory beneath us.   The fall as it daringly leaps its rocky rim, soon strikes the unvertical wall, and apparently forms into an immense mass of wavy, lacy folds, composed from top to bottom of sparkling diamonds, now swaying to this side, now draping the other.   The base—as if to make the whole scene a miniature heaven, and, if possible, convey to man some faint idea of the outer footstool of the Almighty throne—is spanned with rainbows; while the beautiful river hurries on heedlessly, the grand mountains around stand sentinel carelessly, and, as the mantle of night will soon embrace them in its sombre folds, and cover up and change it into "weird spirituality," unless we wish to take lodgings under its cold coverlet, let us up and be going.

FOURTH DAY IN THE YO-SEMITE VALLEY.

After the feast as well as the fatigues of yesterday—as we have but one life—perhaps it would be a good plan to rest to-day, and review and digest the scenes witnessed.   But, if a majority think otherwise, let us to-day pay a visit to

THE TU-LOOL-WE-ACK, OR SOUTH CAÑON FALL.

It will be remembered that, in riding up the uneven trail to the Vernal and Nevada falls, we crossed a stream of considerable volume, divided into two or three branches; this came down the Tu-lool-we-ack,* or South Cañon.   About two miles above the crossing alluded to, up the rough bed of the stream, we come to

---

* Prof. Whitney has given this fall and cañon the name of "Illilouette." Thinking, as this was a Yo-semite Indian name, that we might be in error in its proper pronunciation, we have carefully questioned the Indians concerning it; and while every one, without exception, calls it *Tu-lool-we-ack*, the name of "Illilouette" is entirely unknown among them.   The difference in the pronunciation of Indian names by Americans results from the difficulty of catching and rendering the exact pronunciation of the vowels.

another large fall, which, although but seldom seen, it will be well for us to visit.

This crossing is about three miles above Hutchings', and is the usual place of leaving animals, at which point we leave the trail and soon find that, poor as it undoubtedly is, we are prepared to accord to it any amount of excellence, in comparison with the steep, boulder-filled, and trailless cañon of the South Fork.

Here we have to stoop or creep beneath low arches; there we assist each other to climb a rock; yonder a spur shoots out from the mountain to the very margin of the stream and forces us to cross it. At such places, fortunately, the few who have preceded us have bridged the river, by felling trees over it, thus enabling us to fol-

THE SOUTH DOME AS SEEN FROM THE SOUTH CAÑON.
From a Photograph by C. L. Weed.

low in their footsteps with great advantage to ourselves. Miniature mountains of loose rocks seem to be piled on each other, still higher and higher as we advance.

About a mile and a half above the confluence of the South with the Middle Fork, we emerge from a heavy growth of timber into an open and treeless chasm, the bed of which is covered with large angular rocks, bounded on either side with vertical walls of time-worn and rain-stained granite. On the uneven tops of these, a few of the Douglass spruce-trees are struggling to weather the storms and live. From this point, we obtain a fine distant view, above the tops of the lofty pines, of the Great South Dome, and also of the Pi-wy-ack Fall.

THE TU-LOOL-WE-ACK, OR SOUTH FORK WATERFALL.
From a Photograph by C. L. Weed.

About two o'clock P. M. (if we start early) we reach the head of the cañon and the foot of the Tu-lool-we-ack Fall. This cañon here is suddenly terminated by an irregular, horse-shoe shaped end, the sides and circle of which, on the one side, are perpendicular, and on the other so much so as to be inaccessible without great danger of slipping, and consequently requiring great care.

This waterfall is about five hundred and fifty feet in height, which, after shooting over the precipice, meets with no obstacle to break its descent, until it nearly reaches the basin into which it falls. It is a fine sheet of water, of about the same volume as the Yo-Semite (four hundred gallons per second), at the time we visited and measured it. As we had no instruments for ascertaining the altitude of the Tu-lool-we-ack, of course the above is only given as its approximate height.

The engraving given of this, presents a side section only, as the distance across the cañon, opposite the fall, not being over one hundred and fifty yards, is altogether too short to allow the instrument to take in the whole front view on one picture.

Our fatiguing ascent having occupied the greater portion of the day, and the sunshine having already departed from the west side of the cañon, and as we are not prepared to pass the night here, our work and return has to be conducted with brevity and dispatch; consequently, the moment we have satisfied our minds we had better commence the descent. On our way down, we secure another good view of Tis-sa-ack (the South Dome), from the south cañon, and which, from this point, presents a singular conical shape of that mountain which is not to be seen from any other point; and arrive at our quarters at the hotel in safety just after dark, well pleased with the result of our difficult undertaking.

While discussing the viands of our much relished evening's repast (for after such a jaunt our appetites will supply the most desirable of condiments), we venture to predict that before very long the rapidly increasing travel to Yo-Semite will not only call for, but justify, the expenditure of considerable sums of money by the State, or some one else, in the making of trails to open up all such points of interest as this, so that they can be visited on horseback, and consequently with so much additional pleasure. Now, it requires a strong frame, well trained by exercise, to accomplish such fatiguing undertakings. Of the reward after success, even with the present labor, there will be no question.

FIFTH DAY IN THE YO-SEMITE VALLEY.

It is not for us to say how many days should be spent in Yo-Semite. Nor, whether there should be alternating days of activity and quiet—these must be determined by individual tastes and convenience. Experience has taught us that our capacity for enduring comfort (without complaining), united with an undying love for the beautiful, leads us occasionally to prefer luxuriating *siestas*, in the shadow of trees, day-dreaming and resting; short strolls among picturesque "little bits" of landscape; mental photograph taking of these unparalleled walls of granite; trout fishing; fruit gathering, and all such agreeable methods (as the uncontrollably active, or the unappreciative mind would suggest) of "killing time." But if the majority say let us travel—let us to-day—

RIDE TO MOUNT BEATITUDE AND INSPIRATION POINT.

We immediately concur. It is especially desirable that those who have accompanied us thus far by Big Oak Flat, and who, from whatever cause, prefer returning the same way, should be with us on this trip. For if possibly we exclude the scene from "Glacial Point," or from the summit of the "Three Brothers," there is nothing in this world known to man that can equal the views from "Mount Beatitude" and "Inspiration Point." If, however, it has been determined to return *via* the Mariposa grove of big trees and Mariposa,—and we emphatically hope that it has, inasmuch as all tourists who can, should arrive one way and depart the other,—these glorious sights can be witnessed on the route homeward, without an especial visit.

On our ride down the valley, almost immediately opposite Pompompasus (the "Three Brothers"), on our left there is upon the face of the mountain a white irregular spot, from which, although of apparently insignificant size, the *débris* covered several acres. Back of this point, high up toward the top, Mr. E. J. Muybridge, in 1868, discovered a remarkable fissure in the wall rock. " It is," he says, " one thousand feet deep, five feet wide at the top and front, and gradually growing narrower as it goes down and back into the mountain. Several stones have fallen into it, and lodged about half way down."

Near here can be seen some of the effects of the great storm of Dec. 23, 1867, when the whole valley was a broad foaming river ; and rocks weighing many tons were hurled down these mountain torrents with terrible power : the *talus* when washed down filled up ravines, as you see, and buried the base of trees from two to twenty feet high. In the meadow opposite, within eleven acres of ground, there are forty-two large pine and cedar trees piled one upon the other. We have already counted one hundred and thirty-one of those noble tenants of the valley, that were prostrated by the one single storm ;—enough, if cut into lumber, to construct all improvements wanted in the valley for many years. Others shot over the Yo-Semite Fall, and after making a surging swirl or two struck the unyielding granite, and broke into thousands of frag-mentary pieces. By evidences everywhere apparent there has been no storm to equal it during the present century.

River views ; forest openings ; rocky points ; waterfalls ; indis-tinct animals, heads of men and women outlined in projection, or shadow, or water stain upon the vertical walls of granite, with numerous other objects to attract and interest, are all the way to the very foot of the mountain. Then comes the climb. Let us travel easily, and slowly, and while the horses breathe, we can catch glimpses and foretastes of our expected reward when the goal of our desires is reached at the top.

Up, up we climb, bench after bench, stretch after stretch, with fine views all the way, until at last, we arrive at the turning off place for " Mount Beatitude." Let us now tie our horses, and while they rest, walk out about one hundred and fifty yards to the wonderful sight.

There is a truism that " Some things can be done as well as

GENERAL VIEW OF THE YO-SEMITE VALLEY.

From the Mariposa Trail.

others." In our opinion a full description of this scene is not one of them. A passage in the good book says, " Eye hath not seen, neither hath ear heard, neither hath it entered into the heart of man to conceive what there is laid up in heaven for those who love and serve God." Now, without wishing to detract from the interesting inducement there so graphically pictured and offered, we simply wish to apply the language to those who have the good fortune to see Yo-Semite from this stand-point. Is that satisfactory? We hope so, as we can only give a few plain facts and leave you to " do the sublime."

Remember we are standing on a precipice of nearly three thousand feet. The whole valley and its surroundings are unrolled before us like a map. The river below is as a ribbon of silver, seen only at intervals, winding among the trees; the trees resembling mere shrubs. The grand old sides, and proud head, of Tu-tock-ah-nu-lah loom grandly up. Ditto the " South Dome," and the " Clouds Rest," and the " Sentinel Dome," and the " Sentinel," with any number of others. In the distance are many snow-covered peaks of the sierras, visible almost to their culminating crest. In the foreground, on our left, is the " Ribbon Fall," three thousand three hundred feet above the valley; on our right is the Pohono, or " Bridal Veil Fall," nine hundred and forty feet. Above and back of that stands the " Three Graces," three thousand six hundred feet high. If the storm has been gathering, perhaps we can see it swoop down " on the wings of the wind," and drape the whole landscape in cloud. At times the entire valley is filled with them, piled layer above layer, stratum above stratum, to the very tops of the mountains, their edges sufficiently light to allow the granite walls to be dimly revealed.

Inspiration Point stands out and up at a somewhat greater altitude than Mount Beatitude, but although the view of the distant sierras is more comprehensive, that of the valley is more limited. The general characteristics of both being similar there is no necessity for any further remarks. Therefore let us enjoy the scene in peaceful reflection, and when we can say " enough," let us depart on our winding way, and dream of that we have seen.

10

Those who walk past and look up at the great Yo-Semite
Fall, as it shoots out over the precipice its four hundred gallons
every second during the early melting of the snows above; or

VIEW OF INDIAN CANON, IN FRONT OF THE HOTEL.

watch the gauzy clouds that float below its summit, feel an in-
definable longing to stand upon and look down from the top
of the mountain walls that encompass this valley; to examine

the surrounding country above, and measure the width and depth of the Yo-Semite Creek below. Accordingly, let us repair to the foot of an almost inaccessible mountain gorge, named Indian Cañon, situated about a quarter of a mile to the east of the Yo-Semite Falls, and nearly opposite to the hotel, for the purpose of making the ascent. This, also, is a fatiguing and difficult task, that few have ever undertaken.

In order the better to insure our success, we must start early in the morning. The day may prove to be very warm; yet, after fairly entering the cañon, the trees and shrubs that grow between the rocks, afford us a very grateful shelter, for a quarter of the distance up, when the almost vertical mountain side on our right throws its refreshing shadow across the ascent, for the greater portion of the remaining distance.

Thus protected, we climb over, creep beneath, or walk around, the huge boulders that form the bed of the gorge; and which, owing to their immense size, frequently compel us to make a detour in the sun to avoid them, and to seek as easy an ascent as possible in the accomplishment of this, our excessively fatiguing task.

A cascade of considerable volume is leaping over this, dashing past that, rushing between those, and gurgling among these rocks, affording us gratuitous music, and drink, as we climb. Large pine trees that fell across the cañon, during the rapid melting of the snow, have been lifted up and tossed, like a skiff by an angry sea, to the top of some huge rocks, and there left.

Onward and upward we toil, the perspiration rolling from our brows; but we are cheered and rewarded by the increasing novelty and beauty of the scenes that are momentarily opening to our view as we ascend.

About noon we can reach the summit of the mountain. It is impossible to describe the magnificent panorama that is here spread out before us. Deep, deep below, in peaceful repose, sleeps the valley; its carpet of green cut up by sheets of standing water, and small brooks that run down from every ravine and gorge, while the serpentine course of the river resembles a huge silver ribbon, as its sheen flashes in the sun. On its banks, and at the foot of the mountains around, groves of pine trees, two hundred feet in height, look like mere weeds.

All the hollows of the main chain of the Sierras, stretching to the eastward and southward, apparently but a few miles distant, are filled with snow, above and out of which sharp and bare saw-like peaks of rock rise, well defined, against the clear blue sky. The south dome from this elevation, as from the valley, is the grandest of all the objects in sight; a conical mountain beyond, and a little to the south of the south dome, is apparently as high, but few points, even of the summits of the Sierras, seem to be but little higher than it.

The bare, smooth granite top of this mountain upon which we stand, and the stunted and storm-beaten pines that struggle for existence and sustenance in the seams of the rock, with other scenes equally unprepossessing, present a view of savage sterility and dreariness that is in striking contrast with the productive fertility of the lands below, or the heavily timbered forests through which we pass on our way to the valley.

From this ridge, which most probably is not less than 3,500 feet above the valley, we descend nearly 1,000 feet, at an easy grade, to the Yo-Semite River. The current of this stream, for half a mile above the edge of the falls, runs at the rate of about eight knots an hour. Upon careful measurement with a line, we find it to be thirty-four and a half feet in width, with an average depth of twelve inches. The gray granite rock over which it runs is very hard, and as smooth as a sheet of ice; to tread which in safety great care is needed, or before one is aware of it, he will find his head where his feet should be, and the force of the current sweeping him over the falls.

When, on our return, we have reached the top of the ridge before mentioned, and again see the wonders and glories that are beyond us, all that we seem to wish or hope for is the possession of a single pound of bread, or any other edibles; and after building us a fire, by which to sleep for the night without blankets, that we may pursue our interesting explorations to a more satisfactory close on the morrow.

We must not allow this charming spot to detain us too long, however, as the descent will probably keep us busy for at least three hours; and as the uneven character of our pathless way down the cañon will be attended with both difficulty and danger after dark, a liberal allowance of time will be a good investment. Therefore, let us say, " off."

SEVENTH DAY IN YO-SEMITE.—VISIT TO THE FOOT OF THE UPPER YO-SEMITE FALL.

Every sight worth seeing, with a knowledge how to see it, should be known to every visitor. It does not follow that because each one is thus pointed out, and its attractions mentioned, that every one has the strength, or the wish, or the time to go to see it. That must be determined according to mental or bodily condition, and other contingencies. After journeying so far, all other considerations permitting, it will be well that as many scenes of beauty, or of singularity, or of majesty, should be witnessed, as may be possible. There are but few more astonishing and impressive than the one planned out for to-day. Therefore, hoping that " circumstances," over which we are supposed to have some control, are on our side, let us make the attempt.

Leaving behind all unnecessary clothing, but taking some little refreshment, let us cross the bridge, and striking out over the meadow in a northerly direction, climb the *débris* on the opposite side. Arriving at the first bench of the mountain, let us work our way along it, almost to the upper edge of the lower Yo-Semite Fall. The surging cataract at our side, and the comprehensive view into and around the valley, at this point alone, amply repay us already for our trouble. The garden, trees, bridge, river, house, and farm-buildings; the diminutive cattle and horses, and men and women, all seem smaller; while the walls that surround us appear larger and higher, and more weird-like and wonderful.

Let us not linger, however, too long; but, threading our way upward, among stunted live oaks and manzanita bushes that grow in a gently-ascending crevice of the mountain, and give us foothold and protection, until we have surmounted its top, and stand, awed, in the immediate presence of such untold and bewildering majesty as that now rewarding our toil. Alas! who can describe it? Who tell of its glories, its wonders, its beauties? A simple, realizing idea merely, is almost next to impossible.

The fall, very naturally, first attracts our attention. That it is an avalanche of water about to bury us up, or sweep us into the abyss beneath, is the apparently irresistible first impression. By degrees we take courage, and, climbing the watery mass with our eye, discern its remarkable changes and forms. Now it would seem that numerous bands of fun-loving fairies have undisputed possession, each of whom had set out for a frolic; and, assuming the shape of a watery rocket, have entered the fall; and, after making the leap, are now playing "Hide-and-Seek" with each other; now chasing, now catching; then, with retreating surprises, disappearing from view, and re-forming, or changing, shoot again into sight. While the wind, as if shocked at such playful irreverence, takes hold of the white diamond mass, and lifts it aside like a curtain; when each rocket-formed fairy, leaping down from its folds, disappears from our eyes and becomes lost among rainbows and clouds.

The first great vertical leap of this fall is sixteen hundred feet— the highest in any portion of the globe yet known to man. The wall of granite at its back, although less than half the height of Tu-tock-ah-nu-lah, is scarcely less impressive when we stand almost immediately beneath it. The pine-tree that grows at the top of the shrubby point, east of the stream, although apparently but a mere speck, is one hundred and twenty-five feet in height.

During the winter large quantities of ice form each night at the sides of the fall, and being immediately opposite the east, the rays of the morning sun soon loosen them, when they fall with a loud boom, and the opposite walls catch and re-echo the sound until the whole valley seems filled with its reverberating peals.

This is not all. The descending water, by displacing the air around it, creates an immense vacuum, and the atmosphere above, for a large circumference, rushing in to fill it, makes almost a tornado in its immediate circle. The result is, that when snow is falling, it is drawn from quite a distance into this vacuum, and uniting with the ice deposited at the foot of the fall, forms an immense depth of congealed snow and ice, of from three hundred to four hundred feet. When the spring thaw commences in good earnest, the large stream played from above upon that mass of ice, soon wears out a funnel-shaped hollow, into which it falls, and, after striking, rebounds upward from five to seven hundred feet, filling the whole space at the left with heavy clouds of spray. The sun, shining upon these, paints them with all the colors of the rainbow ; and when one gust of spray drives stronger than another into this beautiful mass, the colors are made to run and intermix, until the whole scene is beyond description one of the most gorgeous and overpowering.

Beneath the upper fall, there is a cave, of some thirty-five or forty feet in depth, from its face. Some few persons, more venturesome than prudent, have run into this when the wind has lifted the entire body of falling water to one side. But it is a "risky" experiment ; for, in addition to the danger of its return to its vertical position, thus cutting off all chances of retreat, the whole cave is densely filled with comminuted spray, which renders breathing almost impossible.

The top of the fall can be reached by the steep cañon on the west, when the waters of Yo-Semite are low enough to permit crossing. But owing to a dense growth of shrubbery, bent forward and downward by winter snows, its ascent would be attended with difficulty, and perhaps with sundry rendings of the garments.

Still this has been several times successfully accomplished by enterprising tourists ; when, after crossing Yo-Semite above the fall, they have returned to the valley by Indian Cañon.

EIGHTH DAY IN YO-SEMITE.—CLIMB TO THE TOP OF GLACIAL POINT AND SENTINEL DOME.

Supposing that exercise is toughening us into the endurance of almost any reasonable amount of physical fatigue, and that the

great sights witnessed much more than compensate us for the toil
expended in reaching them, let us set out at once for the new
points above indicated—at least in imagination :—for if any of us
wish to see Yo-Semite in its glory, from a precipice of nearly four
thousand feet, and, by climbing to the top of the Sentinel Dome
look upon nearly every prominent peak of the sierras for a distance of fifty miles, we had better not stay behind. Leaving the
hotel, we take the same course for about a mile that we did when
on our way to the Vernal and Nevada falls.

As our feet fall on the flower-covered and beautiful, though not
very fertile bottom-lands of the upper part of the valley, and we
thread our way through a labyrinth of oak, pine, maple, cottonwood, and other trees, the mountain walls on either side throw
their awe-inspiring and heavy shadows over us, and make our
hearts to leap with wild emotion and new pleasure, as though we
stood upon enchanted ground, and all the scenes upon which we
look are the magical creations of some wonder-working genii.

VIEW OF NORTH AND SOUTH DOMES, "TO-COY Æ" AND "TIS-SA-ACK," FROM THE VALLEY.

"A thin mist is lying," as Mr. Tirrel so beautifully remarks, "upon the valley, and stealing up the mountain sides. The cliffs upon our left are all in deep shadow, the outline of their summits cutting darkly and strongly against the brilliant light of the unclouded sky. Great streams of sunlight come pouring through the openings in the cliffs, illuminating long, radiating belts of mist, which extend clear across the valley, and are lost among the confusion of rock and foliage forming the *débris* on the opposite side. Directly in front of us, and about three miles distant, is the South Dome, the highest mountain in the valley, as well as the boldest and most beautiful in outline. Its base is shrouded in the hazy mystery which envelops every thing in the valley. Numerous little white clouds, becoming detached from this misty curtain, are sailing up the mountain side. Dodging about among the projecting spurs, intruding their beautiful forms slowly into the dark caverns, puffed out again in a hurry by the eddying winds which hold possession of these gloomy recesses, and then resume their upward flight, each following the other with the precision and regularity of a fleet of white-winged yachts rounding a stake-boat, and each eaten up by the sun with astonishing rapidity, as they sail slowly past the angle of shadow cast across the lower half of the mountain. High above all this, in the clear, bright sunshine, towers the lofty summit. Every projection and indentation, weather and water stain, fern, vine, and lichen, so clearly defined that one can almost seem to touch it."

Turn where we may, objects of interest seem inexhaustible. Every new point passed, by rock or by river, has some new beauty to attract and charm us; so that even when we have left the comparatively level bottom-lands of the valley, and ascended the *débris* to a considerable height, views of the opposite walls over the tops of the trees reward us at every step. Ferns, mosses, flowers, and flowering shrubs, are at our side. The "shadow of a great rock" is on our left hand, giving us its refreshing shelter. Then, turning past a bold, jutting promontory of rock, from whence views of great majesty are unfolded to us, our course is up the rocky bed of a ravine, somewhat steep, but perfectly safe to the very top. By sitting down frequently, to rest and look about us, we are constantly receiving our reward.

Reaching a shrub and tree covered plateau, we strike eastwardly, and soon arrive at the summit of Glacial Point. Before looking down, let us call attention to a somewhat noticeable projecting point, that, seen from the valley, apparently extends out some three or four feet, but which we find, when standing by it, is over thirty feet beyond the nearly vertical wall. Watkins, the photographer, once ran out to the very point of this rock, and from it took one of the finest views of the South Dome and the country beyond ever obtained.

Now let us advance to the margin of the precipice. We can steady ourselves by pressing against the large rock at our side; or we can lie down, and, having some one to take hold of our feet, slide out like a snake to its utmost edge. It may make us a little nervous, perhaps, but, taking all necessary precautions, we shall find it unaccompanied with any real danger, and we shall certainly never regret that our courage was equal to the task of one good look into such an awful abyss.

The greatest of artists have almost invariably failed in portraying *depth* from a high stand-point; and we know of no writer, living or dead, who has been any more successful than the artist. We wish, for the sake of our friends who cannot see this with their own eyes, that "the coming man" had arrived—he who would prove the exception to the rule. But, alas, he has not, as yet, made his appearance. No "trumpet of fame" announces the gratifying fact of his approach. "Under these distressing circumstances," as the pathetic novelist would say, "we are prepared to wait;" and looking down with our own common-place eyes, "see what we shall see."

Large trees, two hundred feet high, are dwarfed to utter insignificance. The little checker-board like spot first noticed is Lamon's apple-orchard of four acres, and which contains over five hundred trees, each of which are twenty feet apart. The other cultivated point beyond, formed by the junction of Tenieya Creek with the Merced River, is Lamon's other orchard, and fruit and vegetable garden. The bright speck which throws out its silvery sheen in that deep, tree-dotted cañon, is Mirror Lake. While the South Dome, apparently forever omnipresent in any scene near or within the valley, overshadows and eclipses every lesser wonder by monopolizing a large share of our admiration and attention. Elsewhere, the North Dome, Cloud's Rest, Cap of Liberty, Mount Starr King, Yo-Semite, and other prominent objects here visible, would have their due effect; but, although at this altitude and position they differ altogether in outline and conformation, the South Dome stands, pre-eminently, king over all.

On the right of this " monarch," in the deep gorge of the river, the magnificent Nevada Fall, Diamond Flume and Apron, Vernal Fall, and the foaming cataract of the Merced, all flash out their silvery sheen most gloriously, while mountains piled on mountains in every conceivable shape, stand guard on every side. But to see these, and other points, to advantage, let us ascend the now easily reached Sentinel Dome.

Had this lofty dome, been " scalped " by some tornado it could have scarcely shown less vegetation; for, with the exception of one or two stunted and deformed storm-beaten pines, whose solitary and exposed condition almost excite our sympathy, there is scarcely a vestige of a living thing upon it; but almost every failing has some virtue to counterbalance it, and often among the meanest of men. It is thus with this point; for if it has no trees to clothe and to beautify, it certainly has none to obstruct or circumscribe the limit of our vision.

Before us lies the very backbone—so to speak—of the Sierra Nevadas; and, although some thirty miles distant, and every prominent peak distinctly visible for fifty miles, it seems almost near enough for us to stretch our hands and touch it. Its vertebræ, however, besides being very uneven, has altitudes upon it exceeding thirteen thousand feet above the sea; and in its sheltered hollows immense banks of snow are eternally sleeping. The following are some of the most noteworthy mountains seen from this stand-point: Mt. Hoffman, 10,872 feet high; Cathedral Peak, 11,000; Mt. Dana, 13,227; Mt. Lyell, 12,270; Castle Peak,

12,500; Gothic Peak, 10,850; Mount Starr King, 9,600; South Dome, 10,000 feet. There are numerous others visible which, although both high and prominent, are as yet nameless.

Did time permit us we might profitably tarry here for hours, or even days, as new beauties would be opening, and strange forms made manifest on every side. Before leaving, however, let us look once more down into the valley, as the haze-draped vertical walls of Tu-tock-ah-nu-lah can be seen from base to summit. The Yo-Semite too, with the country above it through which it runs, before making its wonderful leap,—its bare ridges, singular groups of rocks, forest-clothed heads of ravines, up to its source at Mount Hoffman, are all spread beneath us—for, remember, we are over one thousand feet above the Yo-Semite Fall. Stretching far away to the west we can look upon the broad valleys of the San Joaquin and Sacramento, and distinctly see the Coast Range near the Golden Gate. But, the rapidly declining sun admonishes us to return; so, let us not tempt the danger that will lurk in our path, if we have to descend any portion of the way in the dark.

How many days—or weeks, or even months—could be well spent in Yo-Semite it would be difficult to determine. Hurried visits like those we are making only give glimpses and foretastes of a few of its wonderful sights. Quiet, rest-giving rides, with intervals of physical toil, should give us all time to *feel* as well as to see, its infinite glories, and beauties, and wonders.

As yet our feet have not trod the tops of such mountains as Tu-tock-ah-nu-lah (El Capitan), Pom-pom-pa-sus (Three Brothers), North Dome, and Mount Hoffman, on the north side of the valley; while on the south side there would be the fissure, one thousand feet deep, the Clouds' Rest, and others' equally worthy. But in order to see all of such points to advantage, and with real enjoyment, camping-out parties should be organized, properly provided with suitable outfits and servants, and the "round trip" be made from Tamarack Flat to Tuolumne Valley, by Cathedral Valley and Lake Tenieya; and returning by the Mountain Meadows on the Mariposa side.

The time will come when such glorious scenes as could be witnessed on such an excursion will be one of the great charms in visiting Yo-Semite. The health-giving properties of such a journey too, would in untold instances renew the apparently short lease of life vouchsafed to many. The comfortably bracing atmosphere and the pure delicious water, united with the sublime scenery would be the magical genii of their cure.

Charles Brace, in his valuable work "The New West," thus graphically writes:—

"From this hotel [the Yo-Semite] there are excursions enough to occupy one for weeks, among the beautiful scenes of the valley. Each morning the guide saddles the horses—which had been turned loose in the mountain pasture—and fastens them in front of the house; and after lunch has been packed, we set off in different directions, to see the famous points and objects. One of the most enjoyable features of the excursion is simply cantering up and down the valley, getting the new aspects which open freshly every half-mile, and are different every hour of the day. The wonderful thing about the cañon, which will hereafter draw many an invalid here from distant lands, is its divine atmosphere. To me, just recovering from a tedious fever, it seemed the very elixir of life—cool, clear, stimulating, and filled with light and glory from the sun of the south, which here never seems in summer to have a cloud. The nights are cool, but midday would be too warm were it not for the delicious sea-breeze which every day at eleven, blows in from the Golden Gate, a hundred and fifty miles away. The gorge is fortunately east and west just about opposite to San Francisco, and about midway between the two flanks of the sierras—here some seventy miles in width. Were it a north and south valley, even at its altitude (4,000 feet), it would be almost intolerable. Now nothing can surpass its mild, invigorating climate, and harmonious atmosphere. Life seems to have a new spring and hope under it. The charm of the wonderful valley is its cheerfulness and joy. Even the awe-inspiring grandeur and majesty of its features do not overwhelm the sense of its exquisite beauty, its wonderful delicacy, and color, and life, and joy.

"As I recall those rides in the fresh morning or the dreamy noon, that scene of unequalled grandeur and beauty is forever stamped on my memory, to remain when all other scenes of earth have passed from remembrance—the pearly-gray and purple precipices, awful in mass, far above one, with deep shadows on their rugged surfaces, dark lines of gigantic archways or fantastic images drawn clearly upon them, the bright white water dashing over the distant gray tops seen against the dark blue of the unfathomable sky, the heavy shadows over the valley from the mighty peaks, the winding stream, and peaceful greensward with gay wild-flowers below, the snowy summits of the sierras far away, the atmosphere of glory illuminating all, and the eternal voice of many waters wherever you walk or rest! This is the Yo-Semite in memory!

"I have been thinking much of scenes in Norway, Tyrol, and Switzerland, with which to compare this. Switzerland, as a whole, is much superior in combinations and variety of features to the sierra region. But there is no one scene in Switzerland, or the other parts of mountainous Europe, which can at all equal this Californian valley. The Swiss scene has the advantage in the superb glaciers which flow into the upper end of the valley, but it is inferior in grandeur, and even in life, to the Californian. The latter having immensely grander precipices, and, instead of one waterfall—the Staubbach—a dozen on a much grander scale."

An English gentleman, a member of the celebrated Alpine Club, spent seventeen days in Yo-Semite, and upon leaving he remarked to the writer. "I never left a place with so much pleasurable regret in my life. I have several times visited all the noted places in Europe, and many that are out of the ordinary tourist's round. I have crossed the Andes in three different places, and been conducted to the sights considered most remarkable—I have been among the charming scenery of the Sandwich Islands, and the mountain districts of Australia, but never have I seen so much of sublime grandeur relieved by so much beauty, as that which I have witnessed in Yo-Semite."

COMPARISON BETWEEN THE YO-SEMITE VALLEY AND SOME PARTS OF
SWITZERLAND.

A love for the beautiful, in nature or art, is not only a magnet
of attraction to persons of kindred tastes, but, dispelling all
national prejudices and social ceremonies, becomes a bond of
individual friendship between men of different countries, habits,
and peculiarities. Especially is this remarkable in those who
travel much; for, without being offensively obtrusive, they have
learned to accept and bestow kindnesses promptly, as matters of
natural courtesy; and to ask or answer questions, sometimes in
partial anticipation of the wishes and pleasures of a fellow-
traveller, without any apparent obligation to or from either, and
which places them upon terms of intimacy and friendliness to
each other.

Through such a medium, by the kindness of Rev. P. V. Veeder,
of Napa, we are favored with the following notes of comparison
between the scenery of the Yo-Semite Valley, and that of some
parts of Switzerland:

"The Alps of Switzerland and Savoy may be compared to a
vast shield or buckler, lying on the bosom of the earth, and extending one hundred and fifty miles from the borders of France
to the Alps of the Tyrol, and one hundred miles from the plains of
Piedmont to the broad valley between the Alps and the Jura
Mountains. From this rough-seamed surface, there rise three immense bosses, or projecting points—three radiating centres, sending
off lofty chains of mountains toward each other, and into the
plains of France, Italy, and Switzerland, at their feet. The loftiest
of these bosses or centres is Mont Blanc in Savoy, the height of
which is fifteen thousand seven hundred and forty-four feet; the
next in height is Monte Rosa, fifteen thousand two hundred feet
high; and the third is the Bernese Alps, the culminating point of
which is the Finster-aarhorn, fourteen thousand one hundred feet
high. These three grand centres are about sixty miles apart, and
each has a scenery peculiar to itself. They are alike vast, rugged,
mountain masses, towering six thousand feet into the region of

perpetual snow; but Mont Blanc has its "aiguilles" or needles;
Monte Rosa, its wonderful neighbor, Mont Cervin; and the Bernese Alps have their beautiful valley of misty waterfalls, leaping
over perpendicular cliffs. The traveller who visits Yo-Semite
Valley after seeing the Alps, will be reminded of each of these
three grand centres. He will see the aiguilles of Mont Blanc in
the 'Sentinel,' or 'Castle Rock,' rising, as straight as a needle,
to the height of three thousand two hundred feet above the valley,
and in several other pointed rocks of the same kind. He will be
reminded of the sublimest object in the vicinity of Monte Rosa,
the Materhorn, or Mont Cervin, the summit of which is a dark
obelisk of porphyry, rising, from a sea of snow, to the height of
four thousand five hundred feet. The 'South Dome,' at Yo-
Semite Falls, is a similar obelisk, four thousand five hundred and
ninety-three feet in height.

"But, above all, the general shape, the size, and the waterfalls
of Yo-Semite Valley give it the closest resemblence to the famous
valley of Lauterbrunnen, at the base of the Jungfrau, in the
Bernese Alps. No part of Switzerland is more admired and
visited. To me, its chief charm is not so much its sublime precipices, and its lofty waterfalls, which give the valley its name,
'Lauterbrunnen,' meaning 'sounding-brooks,' as the magnificent
mountain summits, towering up beyond the precipices, and the
unearthly beauty and purity of the glistening snows on the bosom
of the Jungfrau, and the mountains at the head of the valley.
But these summits are not the peculiar characteristic features of
Lauterbrunnen Valley. These are the waterfalls, the perpendicular precipices, and the beautiful grassy and vine-clad vale
between. And these are the grand features of Yo-Semite Valley.
Here you stand in a level valley of about the same dimensions as
the Lauterbrunnen—from eight to ten miles long, and a little
more than a mile wide—covered here with a magnificent pine
forest, the trees averaging two hundred feet in height; there, with
a growth of noble oaks; and elsewhere opening into broad, grassy
fields. These natural features almost equal in beauty the vineyards, gardens, and cultivated fields of Lauterbrunnen.

"But look now at the waterfalls: only one of them in the Swiss valley has a European celebrity—the Staubbach, or 'Dust-Brook'—known as the highest cascade in Europe. It falls at one leap, nine hundred and twenty-five feet. Long before it reaches the ground it becomes a veil of vapor, beclouding acres of fertile soil at its foot. It is worthy of all the admiration and enthusiasm it excites in the beholder. But the 'Bridal Veil' (Pohono) Fall in Yo-Semite Valley is higher, being nine hundred and forty feet in altitude; leaps out of a smoother channel, in a clear, symmetrical arch of indescribable beauty; has a larger body of water, and is surrounded by far loftier and grander precipices.

"When we come to the 'Yo-Semite Falls' proper, we behold an object which has no parallel anywhere in the Alps. The upper part is the highest waterfall in the world, as yet discovered, being fifteen hundred feet in height. It reminds me of nothing in the Alps but the avalanches seen falling at intervals down the precipices of the Jungfrau. It is, indeed, a perpetual avalanche of water comminuted as finely as snow, and spreading, as it descends, into a transparent veil, like the train of the great comet of 1858. As you look at it from the valley beneath, a thousand feet below, it is not unlike a snowy comet, perpetually climbing, not the heavens, but the glorious cliffs which tower up three thousand feet into the zenith above, not unlike a firmament of rock.

"The lower section of the Yo-Semite Falls has its parallel in Switzerland, the Handeck, but is much higher. The scenery around the 'Vernal' (Pi-wy-ack) Falls—which resemble a section of the American Falls at Niagara—is like that of the Devil's Bridge, in the great St. Gothard road, which is, perhaps, the wildest and most savage spot in Switzerland, unless we except that wonderful gorge of the Rhine—the Videllala. But when you climb through blinding spray, and up 'The Ladders,' to the top of the Vernal Falls, and follow the foaming river to the foot of the 'Nevada' (Yo-wi-ye) Falls, all comparison fails to convey an idea of the wildness and sublimity of the scene. The Swiss traveller must climb the rugged sides of Mont Blanc, cross the Mer de Glace, and, stationing himself on the broken rocks of the

11

Gardin, imagine a river falling in a snowy avalanche over the shoulder of one of the sharp aiguilles, or needle-shaped peaks around him.   There are no glaciers at the foot of the Nevada Falls, but every other feature of the scene has an unearthly wildness, to be *equalled* only near Alpine summits.

"To return again to the comparison of the sister valleys—the Yo-Semite and the Lauterbrunnen.   The third peculiar feature of the Swiss valley is the parallel precipices on each side, rising perpendicularly from one thousand to fifteen hundred feet.   They are, indeed, sublime, and where the cliff projects, in a rounded form, like the bastions of some huge castle, you might imagine that you beheld one of the strongholds of the fabled Titans of old.   But what are they, compared with such a giant as Tu-tock-ah-nu-lah, lifting up his square, granite forehead, three thousand and ninety feet above the grassy plain at his feet, a rounded, curving cliff, as smooth, as symmetrical to the eye, and absolutely as vertical, for the upper fifteen hundred feet, as any Corinthian pillar on earth!   What shall we say, when, standing in the middle of a valley more than a mile wide, you know that if these granite walls should fall toward each other, they would smite their foreheads together hundreds of feet above the valley!   What magnificent domes are those, scarcely a mile apart—the one three thousand eight hundred feet, and the other four thousand five hundred and ninety-three feet in height!   When you stand in the valley of Lauterbrunnen, and look at the snowy summit of Jungfrau, or 'Virgin,' you behold an object eleven thousand feet above you; but your map will tell you that it is five miles distant, and, by a little calculation, you will find that you raise your eyes at an angle of only twenty-three degrees.   So at Chamounix, you look up at the snowy dome of Mont Blanc, rising twelve thousand three hundred and thirty feet above you; but you must remember that it is six and one-half miles distant from you, and the angle at which you view it is only twenty degrees, while the very sharpest angle at which you can view it is twenty-five degrees.   But at Yo-Semite you need but climb a few rods up the rocks at the base of that granite wall, and, leaning up against it, you may look up—if your nerves are steady enough to withstand the impression that the cliffs are falling over upon you—and see the summits above you, at an angle of nearly ninety degrees; in other words, you will behold a mountain top three thousand feet above you *in the zenith.* I have seen the stupendous declivity of the Italian side of Monte Rosa—a steep, continuous precipice of nine thousand feet; but it is nothing like Tu-tock-ah-nu-lah, being nowhere absolutely perpendicular."

ATTEMPTS TO ASCEND THE GREAT SOUTH DOME, MOUNT TIS-SA-ACK.

As no footsteps have ever trod the hazy summit of the dome-crowned mountain of granite, named Tis-sa-ack, that stands at the head of the Yo-Semite Valley; and no eye has ever looked into the purple depth and misty distance that stretches far away across the valley of the San Joaquin, from its lofty top; and, as we had long desired to explore all of its unknown and mysterious surroundings, it is very natural that we should feel an earnest yearning to gaze upon the wonders, beauty, and majesty, that may be visible from so bold and so high a stand-point,—as there can be but little doubt of its being at least a mile in perpendicular height above the valley.*

"If you feel like making the attempt to climb it," said two excellent and companionable friends, "we are ready to accompany you, and will take you by the Indian trail up the mountain; but it is a very difficult and fatiguing undertaking, we assure you, accompanied with some danger." The chances were accepted.

On, on we march, in Indian file, until we are nearly on the margin of the river. When we reach it, we find that a small, yet tall tree has fallen across to form a bridge, over which we walk, while the thundering water splashes and surges as it sweeps against the rocks, much to the discomposure of the nervous system of some, knowing that we have to follow suit, or stay behind.

This accomplished, we soon begin the ascent of the mountain over loose fragments of *débris,* and among huge masses of fallen

---

* Measurements of this mountain have differed very materially; several engineers having made it from 4,700 to 5,500. Prof. Brewer informed the writer in 1865, that from observations made by him, at about the same altitude, and with the South Dome in full sight, its summit was 10,000 feet above the sea, and 6,000 above the valley

rocks, lying at the side of the mountain, and in the bed of a small but very deep cañon; but these are soon left behind, and we have to commence climbing around and over points of rocks, walking on narrow edges, or feeling our way past some projecting point, or tree, or shrub; steadying ourselves by a twig, or crevice, or

THE "INDIAN TRAIL" UP THE MOUNTAIN.

jutting rock; or holding on with our feet, as well as our hands, knowing that a slip will send us down several hundred feet, into the deep abyss that yawns beneath.

In some places, where the ledges of rock are high and smooth, broken branches of trees have been placed, so as to enable the Indians to climb above them; and then, by removing the means of their ascent, cut off the pursuit of any advancing foe. These, although risky places to travel over, and in no way inviting to a nervous man, are of considerable assistance in the accomplishment of our task.

After an exciting and fatiguing exercise, of about three hours, we reach a large projecting rock, that forms a cave. Here we take a rest of a few minutes, and then renew our efforts to reach the top of the mountain. A little before noon this is accomplished.

To our great comfort and satisfaction, a cool and refreshing breeze is blowing upon us as soon as we reach the summit; and this is especially welcome, as the heat, on the sheltered side, by which we have ascended, has been very oppressive, pouring down upon us from a hot sun, without the slightest breeze to fan, or shadow to shelter us, as we climb.

The reader must not anticipate our narrative, by supposing that the difficult task of ascending the Great Dome is now accomplished, far from it; for, although we have reached the top of the elevated plateau, or mountain ridge, to the height of about three thousand seven hundred feet above the valley, the great, bald-headed object of our aspirations is still lifting its proud summit more than a thousand feet above us.

While advancing toward Tis-sa-ack, looking out for some point where the ascent can be the most successfully attempted, we come upon the projecting margin of the immense granite wall of rock seen from below; and, as we stand upon it, looking down into the far off and misty depths of the valley beneath, with the river winding hither and thither, no language can describe the appalling grandeur and frightful profoundness of the scene.

Steadying ourselves against a stunted pine tree, that has been toughened and strengthened by its perpetual struggles with the tempests and storms of many a year, and which is growing from a narrow crevice in the granite mass on either side, we roll several large, round rocks, that lie temptingly near the edge of the precipice, into the abyss beneath; when we are surprised to find that many seconds elapse before they are heard to strike on the bare rock below. It is our opinion that this precipice cannot be less than two thousand seven hundred feet in perpendicular altitude. Here we are enabled to find some flowers of a genus but recently known to botanists, and, consequently, new.

Without lingering too long, we again start on our enterprise, and find that on this, the south side of the Dome, it is utterly impossible to climb up; so we work our way through a dense, though comparatively dwarfish growth of manzanita bushes, growing at the base of the Dome (which makes sad havoc in broadcloth unmentionables), and about two o'clock p. m. reach the foot of a low, flattish, dome-shaped point of rock, that lies at the back or eastern side of the great Tis-sa-ack, and which is not seen from the valley.

As we have not found a single drop of water to assuage our thirst, since we left the river, and the day and the exercise alike provocative of it, our gratification is strong at the sight of a snow bank, snugly ensconced in the shade, on the north side of the Dome. We now quicken our footsteps, and soon find ourselves sitting comfortably beside it, taking lunch. An abundance of good water being found issuing from a crevice in the rock, a short distance down the mountain, we repair thither to finish our repast, and take a good, hearty draught, before attempting the ascent. Here we find several new varieties of flowering shrubs, in addition to some bulbous roots, and very pretty mosses.

The inner man being satisfied, the rapidly descending sun admonishes us to make the best of daylight to accomplish the task we have set ourselves. Accordingly, we repair to the Lower Dome, which is one immense spur of granite, belonging to the Great Dome; and, as its surface, by time and the elements, is made tolerably rough, there is found comparatively but little difficulty in climbing it, especially with a little assistance.

In some of the fissures or seams of this rock, some low, stunted shrubs are growing. When we reach the top of the Lower Dome, which is, perhaps, about four hundred and fifty feet above the average level of the main ridge, to our dismay and disappointment, we find that not only is the gently rounding surface of the Great Dome itself at an angle of about sixty-eight or seventy degrees, but is overlaid and overlapped, so to speak, with vast circular granite shingles—as smooth as glass—about eighteen inches in thickness, and extending around the Dome as far as our

ASCENDING THE LOWER DOME.

eyes can reach. These put every hope to flight, of our feet, or those of any other visitors, ever treading upon the lofty crown of this dome, without extensive artificial adjuncts to aid in its accomplishment. On the top of this immense mountain of smooth rock, one solitary pine is growing; and although it is barely discernible from the valley (and not at all from the Lower Dome, where we are standing), by the aid of the telescope, it is seen to be a tree of goodly size.

Much disappointed at the failure of the principal object of the enterprise, we will place our national banner upon the highest point attainable, in the hope that the day is not far distant when the number of visitors who shall annually come to worship at this sublime temple of nature, may create the necessity for the construction of a strong iron staircase to the very summit of Mount Tis-sa-ack; and, that from the topmost crown of her noble head, the stars and stripes may wave triumphantly, as from this elevation the whole surrounding country can be seen afar off, and a thousand times fully reward the perseverance and fatigue of the ascent.

SUMMARY.

The Yo-Semite Valley (pronounced Yo-Sem'-i-ty) is about 150 miles nearly due east from San Francisco, and by the routes travelled it is, to Stockton, by rail 93 miles, by steamboat 120 miles; add to those distances from Stockton, *via* the Calaveras Big Tree Grove, 168 miles (157 by stage and 11 by horseback); *via* Big Oak Flat direct, 109 miles (98 by stage and 11 by horseback); *via* Mariposa 152 miles (107 by stage and 45 by horseback).

The altitude of Yo-Semite above the sea, as given by the State Geological Survey, is 4,060 feet. It is about seven miles long, by from half a mile to one and a quarter miles in width; surrounded by walls (in many places nearly vertical) from three thousand to six thousand feet in height. Its general course is northeasterly and southwesterly. From one end to the other there is a fall of about fifty feet, the total area within the walls of the valley, as given by the Commissioner of the General Land Office, Washington, is 8,480 acres, 3,109 of which are meadow land, the entire grant comprising 36,111 acres. The main Merced River about eighty feet in width, and perfectly clear, runs through it. Trout in reasonable abundance can be seen at almost any point of the river.

Numerous kinds of deciduous and evergreen trees and shrubs are interspersed entirely through it. Ferns, flowers, and grasses grow in almost endless quantities and varieties. Several fine chalybeate springs have been discovered there. The atmosphere is very temperate, bracing, and healthy both summer and winter, the thermometer seldom running above 80° in the summer, or more than 16 below freezing point in the winter. A cooling breeze from the northwest in the day-time, and from the southeast at night, keeps the valley in summer at a very comfortable temperature. Floods sweep through it in the early spring, and in the late fall, sometimes doing considerable damage. Snow falls in winter to the depth of from two and a half to five feet. The sun rises on Hutchings' Hotel during the short days about half-past one o'clock in the afternoon, and sets about half-past three.

On this account a comfortable cabin was built on the sunny and north side of the valley. Rain or snow generally comes from the south. The heavy snows on the mountains crossed by the trails, shut out all personal intercourse between the inhabitants and the great world outside for about six months out of twelve. An Indian mail-carrier brings us letters, papers, books, and magazines once in three months, during winter, and if the weather is favorable twice in that time.

TABLE OF ALTITUDES AT YO-SEMITE VALLEY.

WATERFALLS.

Indian Name.	Signification.	American Name.	Feet above Valley.
Pohono	Spirit of the Evil Wind	Bridal Veil Fall	940
Lung-oo-too-koo-ya	Long and slender	Ribbon Fall	3,300
Yo-Sem-i-te	Large Grizzly Bear	Yo-Semite Fall	2,034

First fall, 1,600 feet; second fall (or cataract), 434 feet; third fall, 600 feet.

Pi-wy-ack	Cataract of Diamonds	Vernal Fall	350
Yo-wi-ye	Meandering	Nevada Fall	700
Tu-lool-we-ack		South Cañon Fall (above base)	600
Loya	A Medicinal Shrub	Sentinel (cataract)	3,850
To-coy-æ	Shade to Baby Cradle-Basket	Royal Arch Fall	2,000

The two latter streams, with numerous smaller ones, run only in the early spring.

MOUNTAINS.

Tis-sa-ack	Goddess of the Valley	South Dome	6,000
		Cloud's Rest	6,450
To-coy-æ	Shade to Baby Cradle-Basket	North Dome	3,725
Hunto	Watching Eye	Washington Tower	2,200
Mah-tah	Martyr, or Suicide, Mountain	Cap of Liberty (above foot Nevada Falls)	2,000
See-wah-lam		Mount Starr King	5,000
Er-na-ting Law-oo-too	Bear Skin	Glacier Point	3,705
Loya	A Medicinal Shrub	Sentinel	3,270
Poo-see-nah Chuck-ka	Large Acorn Storehouse	Cathedral Spires	2,400
Ko-soo-kong		Three Graces	3,750
		Cathedral Rock	2,670
		Inspiration Point	3,200
		Mount Beatitude	2,900
Tu-tock-ah-nu-lah	Semi-Deity and Great Chief of Valley	The Captain	3,300
Pom-pom-pa-sus	Mountains playing Leap-Frog	Three Brothers	4,000
Hum-moo	Lost Arrow	Point East of Yo-Semite	3,100

VIEW DOWN THE VALLEY, TO "CATHEDRAL ROCKS."

DEPARTURE FROM THE VALLEY.

It is much to be regretted that the tourist should allow himself so brief a period in this wonderful valley,—generally about four days only, when it should have been fourteen,—for, after he has left its sublime solitudes, its numerous waterfalls and brooklets, its picturesque river scenes, its groups of shrubs and trees, its endless variety of wild flowers, its bold, rugged, awe-inspiring, pine-studded, and snow-covered mountain heights, with all their ever-changing shadows and curious shapes, and its health-giving and invigorating air, with its thousand of unmentioned charms, that would have given pleasurable occupation and grateful variety to every class and condition, both of body and mind, for months, he contrasts that which he saw with that he might have seen, and becomes dissatisfied with his course in spending so much time, as well as money, in travelling there, and then riding off without seeing more than a limited portion of such remarkable scenes.

Wishing all a safe and joyous return, with none but pleasant memories forever of their Yo-Semite trip, we bid each agreeable companion a reluctant "good-bye," in the hope of soon welcoming them again to the beauty and majesty of the landscapes, and the invigorating air and pure waters of our unparalleled Yo-Sem'-i-te.

SCENE IN THE FREZNO GROVE OF MAMMOTH TREES.

CHAPTER V.

THE MAMMOTH TREES OF MARIPOSA AND FREZNO.

"Go abroad
Upon the paths of Nature, and, when all
Its voices whisper, and its silent things
Are breathing the deep beauty of the world,
Kneel at its simple altar, and the God
Who hath the living waters shall be there."—N. P. WILLIS.

THE DISCOVERERS OF THESE GROVES.

FOR several years after the discovery of the mammoth trees of
Calaveras county had astonished the world, that group of trees

was supposed to be the only one of the kind in existence. But, during the latter part of July or the beginning of August, 1855, Mr. Hogg, a hunter, in the employ of the South Fork Merced Canal Company, while in the pursuit of his calling, saw one or more trees, of the same variety and genus as those of Calaveras, growing on one of the tributaries of Big Creek, and related the fact to Mr. Galen Clark, and other acquaintances. Late in September, or early in October ensuing, Mr. J. E. Clayton, civil engineer, residing in Mariposa, while running a line of survey for Colonel J. C. Fremont, across some of the upper branches of the Frezno River, discovered other trees of the same class, but, like Mr. Hogg, passed on without further examination or exploration.

About the 1st of June, Mr. Milton Mann and Mr. Clark were conversing together on the subject, at Clark's Ranche on the South Fork of the Merced, when they mutually agreed to go out on a hunting excursion in the direction indicated by Mr. Hogg and Mr. Clayton, for the purpose of ascertaining definitely the locality, size, and number of the trees mentioned.

Well mounted, they left Clark's Ranche, and proceeded up the divide between the South Fork of the Merced and Big Creek, in a south-eastern course, with the intention of making a circuit of several miles, if not at first successful—this plan being the most suggestive of their rediscovery.

When on the summit of the mountain, about four miles from Clark's, they saw the broad and towering tops of the mammoth trees—since known as the "Mariposa Grove"—and shortly afterward were walking among their immense trunks. A partial examination revealed the fact, that a second grove of trees had been found, that was far more extensive than that of Calaveras, and many of the trees fully as large as those belonging to that world-renowned group.

Early the following spring, Mr. Clark discovered two smaller groves of large trees, of the same class and variety, each not exceeding a quarter of a mile in distance from the other.

About the end of July of the same year, he discovered another large grove upon the head waters of the Frezno; and two days afterward, Mr. L. A. Holmes, of the *Mariposa Gazette*, and Judge Fitzhugh, while on a hunting excursion, saw the tracks of Mr. Clark's mule as they passed the same group; and as both these parties were very thirsty at the time, and near the top of the ridge at sundown, without water for themselves and animals, they were anxious to find this luxury and a good camping-place before dark. Consequently, they did not deem it best then to tarry to explore it, intending to pay this grove a visit at some early time of leisure in the future. This interesting task, however, seemed to be reserved for the writer and Mr. Clark, on the 2d and 3d of July, 1859.

With this short epitome of the discovery of these additional wonders, we shall now give a brief narrative of a visit paid them.

THE MARIPOSA GROVES OF MAMMOTH TREES.

Arriving at Clark's Ranche (situated about half-way between the Great Valley and Mariposa), Mr. Galen Clark, the proprietor of the ranche, very kindly offered not only to guide us through the Mariposa Grove of mammoth trees, but also to conduct us to the Frezno Grove; observing that, although the latter had been discovered by himself the previous year, it had not yet been examined or explored by any one. Of course, as the reader may guess, this offer was too generous, and too much in accordance with our wishes, to be declined. Our preparations completed, and when about to mount into the saddle, we both stood waiting. "Are you ready?" asked our guide. "Quite," was the prompt rejoinder; "but haven't you forgotten your hat, Mr. Clark?" "Oh, no," he replied, "I never have been able to wear a hat since I had the fever some years ago, and I like to go without now, better than I did then to wear one." So much for habit.*

With our fire-arms across our shoulders, and our blankets and a couple of days' provisions at the back of our saddles, we proceeded for a short distance through the thick, heavy grass of the ranche, and commenced the gradual ascent of a well-timbered side-hill, on the edge of the valley, and up and over numerous low ridges, all of which were more or less covered with wild flowers,

* Mr. C. has since been able to abandon this habit.

on our way to the Mariposa Grove. Although the trail was well
worn and good, yet, on account of the long ascent to the summit
of the ridge, it was with no small pleasure that we found ourselves
in the vicinity of the grove.

THE "TWINS," IN THE MARIPOSA GROVE.
Sketched from nature, by G. Tirrel.

Who can picture, in language, or on canvas, all the sublime
depths of wonder that flow to the soul in thrilling and intense
surprise, when the eye looks upon these great marvels? Long
vistas of forest shades, formed by immense trunks of trees, extending hither and thither : now arched by the overhanging branches
of the lofty taxodiums, then by the drooping boughs of the white-
blossomed dogwood ; while the high, moaning sweep of the pines,
and the low whispering swell of the firs, sung awe-inspiring anthems to their great Planter.

The Indians, in years that are past, have, with Vandal hands,
set portions of this magnificent forest on fire; so that burnt stumps
of trees and blackened underbrush frown upon you from several
points.   Indeed, many of the largest and noblest looking are
badly deformed from this cause. Still, beautiful clumps of from

three to ten trees in each, and others standing alone, are numerous, sound, and well formed.

"Passing up the ravine, or basin," says Mr. J. Lamson, who kindly sent us the sketch from which this engraving is made, "we came to a large stem, whose top had been stripped of its branches, giving it somewhat the resemblance of an immense spear, and forcibly reminding one of Milton's description of Satan's weapon of that name:

'To equal which, the tallest pine,
Hewn on Norwegian hills to be the mast
Of some great ammiral, were but a wand.'

Believing this to be far greater than any tree Milton ever dreamed

SATAN'S SPEAR.

of, and fully equal to the wants of any reasonable Prince of Darkness, in compliment to the poet and his hero, we named it 'Satan's Spear.' Its circumference is seventy-eight feet.

"Several rods to the left of this, is another large trunk, with a dilapidated top, presenting the appearance of a tower, and is called 'The Giant's Tower;' seventy feet in circumference. Beyond this, stand two double trees, which have been named 'The Twin Sisters.' Still further on, is a tree with a straight and slender body, and a profusion of beautiful foliage; near which, frowned a savage-looking monster, with a scarred and knotted trunk, and gnarled and broken branches, bringing to one's recollection the story of 'Beauty and the Beast.' Crossing the ravine near 'Satan's Spear,' there are many fine trees upon the side and summit of the ridge. One of the finest, whose circumference is sixty feet, and whose top consists of a mass of foliage of exceeding beauty, is called 'The Queen of the Forest.' Above these, stands 'The Artist's Encampment,' seventy-seven feet in circumference, though so large a portion of its trunk has decayed or been burned away to a height of thirty feet, as materially to lessen its dimensions."

As the size of the principal trees was ascertained by Mr. Clark, and Colonel Warren, editor of the *California Farmer*, in which journal it first appeared, and as their measurements doubtless approximated to correctness, we give them below:

"The first tree was 'The Rambler,' and measuring it three and a half feet from the ground, we found it eighty feet in circumference; close at the ground, one hundred and two feet; and, carefully surveyed, two hundred and fifty feet high. Tree No. 2, nearly fifty feet in circumference. No. 3 (at the spring), ninety feet, three and a half feet from the ground; one hundred and two at the ground; and three hundred feet high. Nos. 4 and 5 ('The Sisters') measured eighty-two and eighty-seven feet in circumference, and two hundred and twenty-five feet high. Many of the trees had lost portions of their tops, by the storms that had swept over them.

"The whole number measured, was one hundred and fifty-five, and these comprise but about half the group, which we estimate

12

cover about two to three hundred acres, and lie in a triangular form. Some of the trees first meet your view in the vale of the mountain ; thence rise southeasterly and northwesterly, till you find yourself gazing upon the neighboring points, some ten miles from you, whose tops are still covered with their winter snows. The following are the numbers and measurement of the trees :*

1 tree, 102 feet in circumference.	1 tree, 40 feet in circumference.	
1 tree, 97 feet	do	1 tree, 35 feet	do
1 tree, 92 feet	do	2 trees, 36 feet each	do
3 trees, 76 feet each	do	2 trees, 32 feet each	do
1 tree, 72 feet	do	1 tree, 28 feet	do
3 trees, 70 feet each	do	2 trees, 100 feet each	do
1 tree, 68 feet	do	1 tree, 82 feet	do
1 tree, 66 feet	do	1 tree, 80 feet	do
1 tree, 63 feet	do	2 trees, 77 feet each	do
3 trees, 63 feet each	do	1 tree, 76 feet	do
2 trees, 60 feet each	do	3 trees, 75 feet each	do
1 tree, 59 feet	do	1 tree, 64 feet	do
1 tree, 58 feet	do	4 trees, 65 feet each	do
3 trees, 57 feet each	do	2 trees, 63 feet each	do
1 tree, 56 feet	do	1 tree, 61 feet	do
3 trees, 55 feet each	do	10 trees, 60 feet each	do
2 trees, 54 feet each	do	3 trees, 59 feet each	do
1 tree, 53 feet	do	2 trees, 51 feet each	do
1 tree, 51 feet	do	6 trees, 50 feet each	do
4 trees, 50 feet each	do	1 tree, 49 feet .	do
6 trees, 49 feet each	do	1 tree, 47 feet	do
5 trees, 48 feet each	do	1 tree, 46 feet	do
2 trees, 47 feet each	do	2 trees, 45 feet each	do
3 trees, 46 feet each	do	1 tree, 43 feet	do
2 trees, 45 feet each	do	7 trees, 44 feet each	do
1 tree, 44 feet	do	4 trees, 42 feet each	do
2 trees, 43 feet each	do	3 trees, 41 feet each	do
2 trees, 42 feet each	do	8 trees, 40 feet each	do

"Some of these were in groups of three, four, and even five, seeming to spring from the seeds of one cone. Several of these glorious trees we have, in association with our friend, named. The one near the spring we call the Fountain Tree, as it is used as the source of the refreshment. Two trees, measuring ninety and ninety-seven feet in circumference, were named the Two Friends.

* Prof. Whitney gives the total number of trees here at 365, of a diameter of one foot or over; and 125 trees, over 40 feet in circumference.

The groups of trees consisted of many of peculiar beauty and interest. One of those, which measured one hundred feet in circumference, was of exceeding gigantic proportions, and towered up three hundred feet ; yet a portion of its top, where it apparently was ten feet in diameter, had been swept off by storms. While we were measuring this tree, a large eagle came and perched upon it, emblematical of the grandeur of this forest as well as that of our country.

" Near by it stood a smaller tree, that seemed a child to it, yet it measured forty-seven feet in circumference. Not far from it was a group of four splendid trees, two hundred and fifty feet high, which we named the " Four Pillars," each over fifty feet in circumference. Two gigantic trees, seventy-five and seventy-seven feet in circumference, were named " Washington" and " Lafayette ;" these were noble trees. Another group we called "The Graces," from their peculiar beauty. One mighty tree that had fallen by fire and burned out, into which we walked for a long distance, we found to be the abode of the grizzly ; there he had made his nest, and it excited the nerves to enter so dark an abode. Yet it was a fitting place for a grizzly. Another tree, measuring eighty feet, and standing aloof, was called the Lone Giant ; it went heavenward some three hundred feet. One monster tree that had fallen and been burned hollow, has been recently tried, by a party of our friends, riding, as they fashionably do, in the saddle, through the tunnel of the tree. These friends rode through this tree, a distance of one hundred and fifty-three feet. The tree had been long fallen, and measured, ere its bark was gone and its sides charred, over one hundred feet in circumference, and probably three hundred and fifty feet in height.

" The mightiest tree that has yet been found, now lies upon the ground, and, fallen as it lies, it is a wonder still ; it is charred, and time has stripped it of its heavy bark, and yet across the butt of the tree as it lay upturned, it measured thirty-three feet without its bark ; there can be no question that in its vigor, with its bark on, it was forty feet in diameter, or one hundred and twenty feet in circumference. Only about one hundred and fifty feet of the trunk remains, yet the cavity where it fell is still a large hollow beyond the portion burned off; and, upon pacing it, measuring from the root one hundred and twenty paces, and estimating the branches, this tree must have been four hundred feet high. We believe it to be the largest tree yet discovered."

This grove of mammoth trees consists of about three hundred, more or less. It must not be supposed that these large taxodiums monopolize the one mile by a quarter of a mile of ground over which they are scattered ; as some of the tallest, largest, and most graceful of sugar pines and Douglass firs we ever saw, add their beauty of form and foliage to the group, and contribute much to the imposing grandeur of the effect.

THE SOUTH GROVE.

Crossing a low ridge to the south-westward of the large grove, is another small one, before alluded to, in which there are many fine trees. We measured one sturdy, gnarled old fellow, which, although badly burned, and the bark almost gone, so that a large portion of its original size was lost, is, nevertheless, still ninety feet in circumference, and which we took the liberty of naming the "Grizzled Giant."

An immense trunk lay stretched upon the ground, that measured two hundred and sixty-four feet in length, although a considerable portion of its crown has been burned away. This was named by Mrs. J. C. Fremont, "King Arthur, the Prostrate Monarch."

VISIT TO THE FREZNO GROVE.

Leaving the "South Grove," we struck across Big Creek and its branches, in a course almost due south, as near as the rugged, rock-bound mountain spurs would permit, in the direction of the Frezno group, some of whose majestic and feathery tops could be seen from the ridge we had left behind.

Apparently, these trees were not more than six miles distant from the Mariposa Grove; but which, owing to the trailless course we had to take, down and across the spurs of Big Creek, were not

THE GRIZZLED GIANT.
From Nature, by G. Tirrel.

less than ten miles. About six o'clock P. M., we arrived at the foot of some of the mammoth trees, that stood on the ridge, like sentinel guards to the grove. These were from fifty to sixty feet, only, in circumference.

As the sun was fast sinking, we deemed it the most prudent course to look out for a good camping-ground. Fortunately, we discovered at first the only patch of grass to be found for several miles; and, as we were making our way through the forest, feeling that most probably we were the first whites who had ever broken its profound solitudes, we heard a splashing sound, proceeding from the direction of the bright green we had seen. This, with the rustling of bushes, reminded us that we were invading the secluded home of the grizzly bear, and that good sport or danger would soon give variety to our employments.

Hastily dismounting, and unsaddling our animals, we picketed them in the swampy grass-plat, still wet with the recent spirtings of several bears' feet that had hurriedly left it; then kindling a fire, to indicate by its smoke the direction of our camp, we started quietly out on a bear hunt.

Cautiously peering over a low ridge but a few yards from camp, we saw two large bears slowly moving away, when a slight sound from us arrested their attention and progress. Mr. Clark was about raising his rifle to fire, when we whispered—"Hold, Mr. C., if you please—let us have the first shot at that immense fellow there." "With pleasure," was the prompt response, and, at a distance of twenty-five yards, a heavy charge of pistol balls, from an excellent shot-gun, was poured into his body just behind the shoulder, when he made a plunge of a few feet, and, wheeling round, stood for a few moments as though debating in his own mind whether he should return the attack or retreat; but a ball from the unerring rifle of our obliging guide determined him upon the latter course. The other had preceded him.

We immediately started in pursuit; and although their course could readily be followed by blood dropping from the wounds, a dense mass of chaparal prevented us from getting sight of either again, although we walked around upon the look-out until the darkness compelled us to return to camp, where, after supper, we were soon soundly sleeping. Early the next morning we followed up the *divertissement* for a few hours; but meeting with no game larger than grouse, we commenced the exploration of the grove.

This consists of about five hundred trees of the taxodium family, on about as many acres of dense forest land, gently undulating. The two largest we could find measured eighty-one feet each in circumference, well formed, and straight from the ground to the top. The others, equally sound and straight, were from fifty-one feet to seventy-five feet in circumference. The sugar pines (*Pinus lambertiana*) were remarkably large; one that was prostrate near our camp measured twenty-nine feet and six inches in circumference, and two hundred and thirty-seven feet in length.

It ought here to be remarked, that Mr. L. A. Holmes and Judge Fitzhugh saw an extensive grove of much larger trees than these on the head-waters of the San Joaquin River, about twelve miles east of those on the Frezno; but it has never been explored.

All of these trees are precisely of the same genus and variety as those of Calaveras, and will abundantly reward visitors who spend a day or two here, on their way to the Yo-Semite Valley.

There are no less than ten groves of these remarkable trees (*Sequoia gigantea*) already discovered in California. The Calaveras, containing about one hundred trees; the great South Grove, having one thousand three hundred and eighty; the South Tuolumne grove, thirty-one; one unnamed, on the south side of the dividing ridge between the Tuolumne and Merced rivers, below Crane Flat, forty-two trees; the Mariposa groves numbering three hundred and sixty-five; the Frezno, about five hundred; the San Joaquin (estimated at) seven hundred; the Kings and Kaweah River, belt of big trees extending for some ten miles, thought to contain thousands; the North Tule River, and the South Tule River, the trees of which are scattered over several square miles. These last-named groves were discovered by Mr. D' Heureuse, of the State Geological Survey, in 1867.

METAL YARD AND ENTRANCE TO THE ALMADEN MINE.

CHAPTER VI.

THE QUICKSILVER MINES OF NEW ALMADEN AND HENRIQUITA.

THE ROUTE TO NEW ALMADEN.

SIXTY-FIVE miles south of San Francisco, near the head of the beautiful and fertile valley of San José, and in an eastern spur of the Coast Range of mountains, is the quicksilver mine of New Almaden.

With your permission, kind reader, we will enter the railway train waiting in San Francisco,—and, as the clock strikes eight, start at once on our journey. Lucky for us, it is a fine, bright morning, as the fog has cleared off, and left us (on a dew-making excursion, no doubt, up the country), and as we are to be fellow-travellers, at least in imagination, and wish to enjoy ourselves; let us say good-bye to our cares, as we did to our friends, and leave them with the city behind us.

How refreshing to the brow is the breeze, and grateful to the eye is the beautiful green of the gardens, as we pass them, in the suburbs of the city, on our way. Even the hills in the distance are dotted with the dark green of the live oaks, and are beautiful by contrast.

On, on, we go, shooting among hills, travelling through the valley, passing farms and way-side houses, until we reach the flourishing old Mission of Santa Clara. Here we long to linger, and as we look upon the orchards laden with fruit, we wish to buy, beg, or steal, those cherry-cheeked and luscious-looking pears; or take a walk amid the shadows of the old Mission church. But, leaving the railway, we here take the omnibus, when the signal, "all aboard," hurries us to our seats, and we soon enter an avenue of old willow and poplar trees, that extends from Santa Clara to San José, a distance of three miles, and which was planted by and for the convenience of the two Missions. What good, thoughtful souls those old padres were. We fear that due credit is not given them for the amount of civilization they introduced. On either side of this avenue, at intervals, there are tasteful cottages, flourishing farms, nurseries, and gardens, which are well supplied with water from artesian wells.

Arriving in San José we find a neat and pleasant agricultural city, with all the temptations of fruit and flowers in great variety, and a brisk business activity observable in each department of business in the streets. One thing may impress us unfavorably here, viz.: the large number of members of the legal profession (thirty-seven, we believe) in so small a city.

This fact brought to mind—

AN OLD SAW.

"An upper mill, and lower mill,
　Fell out about the water;
To war they went, that is to law,
　Resolved to give no quarter.

"A lawyer was by each engaged,
　And hotly they contended;
When fees grew scant, the war they waged,—
　They judged, 'twere better ended.

"The heavy costs remaining still,
　Were settled without pother—
One lawyer took the upper mill,
　The lower mill the other."

—and it set us to ruminating. But let us jump into the easy coach in waiting, and we shall forget all that, and have a very pleasant ride of fourteen miles upon a good road, through an evergreen grove of live oaks, and past the broad shading branches of the sycamore trees, and in a couple of hours find ourselves drinking heartily of the delicious waters of the fine cool soda spring, at the romantic village of New Almaden. As we have passed through enough for one day, let us wait until morning, before climbing the hill to examine the mines.

THE DISCOVERY AND OWNERSHIP OF THE NEW ALMADEN MINE.

This mine has been known for ages by the Indians, who worked it for the vermilion paint that it contained, with which they ornamented their persons, and on that account had become a valuable article of exchange with other Indians, from the Gulf of California to the Columbia River. Its existence was also known among the early settlers of California, although none could estimate the character or value of the metal.

In 1845 a captain of cavalry in the Mexican service, named Castillero, having met a tribe of Indians near Bodega, and seeing their faces painted with vermilion, obtained from them, for a reward, the necessary information of its locality, when he visited it, and having made many very interesting experiments, and deter-

SAN JOSE, SANTA CLARA COUNTY, CALIFORNIA.

mined the character of the metal, he registered it in accordance with the Mexican custom, about the close of that year.

A company was immediately formed, and the mine divided into twenty-four shares, when the company immediately commenced working it on a small scale; but, being unable to carry it on for want of capital, in 1846 it was leased out to an English and Mexican company for the term of sixteen years; the original company to receive one-quarter of the gross products for that time. In March, 1847, the new company commenced operations on a large scale, but finding that to pay one-fourth of the proceeds, and yet to bear all the expenses of working the mine, would incur a considerable loss, they eventually purchased out most of the original shareholders.

In June, 1850, this company had expended *three hundred and*

GENERAL VIEW OF THE QUICKSILVER WORKS AT NEW ALMADEN.

eighty-seven thousand eight hundred dollars over and above all their receipts.   During that year, a new process of smelting the ore was introduced by a blacksmith, named Baker, which succeeded so well, that fourteen smelting furnaces have been erected by the company upon the same principle.

PROCESS OF EXTRACTING THE QUICKSILVER FROM CINNABAR.

The process of extracting the quicksilver from the cinnabar is very simple.   The *ore chamber*, B. is filled with cinnabar, and covered securely up; a fire is then kindled in the furnace at A, from which, through a perforated wall of brick, the heat enters the ore chamber and permeates the mass of ore, from which arises the quicksilver, in the shape of vapor, and, passing through the perforated wall on the opposite side, enters the condensing chambers at C, rising to the top of one, and falling to the bottom of the other, as indicated by the arrows, and as it passes through the condensing chambers (thirteen in number), it cools and becomes quicksilver.   Should any vapor escape the last condensing chamber, it passes over a cistern of cold water at D, where, from an enclosed pipe, water is scattered

SECTION OF THE SMELTING FURNACE.

over a sieve, and falls upon and cools the vapor as it passes into the chimney, or funnel chamber, at E.

The quicksilver then runs to the lower end of each condensing chamber, thence through a small pipe into a trough that extends from one end of the building to the other, where it enters a large circular caldron, from which it is weighed into flasks, in quantities

MEXICANS WEIGHING QUICKSILVER.

of seventy-five pounds. To save time, one set of furnaces is generally cooling and being filled, while the other is burning.

Now, let us gradually ascend to the *patio*, or yard, in front of
the mine, a visit to which has been so truthfully and beautifully
described by Mrs. S. A. Downer, that we are tempted to introduce
the reader to such good company.

THE ROAD TO THE MINE.

"At the right, was a deep ravine, through which flowed a
brook, supplied by springs in the mountains, and which, in places,
was completely hid by tangled masses of wild-wood, among which
we discerned willows along its edge, with oak, sycamore, and
buckeye. Although late in the summer, roses and convolvuli,
with several varieties of floss, were in blossom; with sweet-brier,
honeysuckle, and various plants, many of which were unknown
to us, not then in bloom, and which Nature, with prodigal hand,
has strewn in bounteous profusion over every acre of the land.
To the left of the mountain side, the wild gooseberry grows in
abundance. The fruit is large and of good flavor, though of rough
exterior. Wild oats, diversified with shrubs and live-oak, spread

around us, till we reach the *patio*, nine hundred and forty feet above the base of the mountain. The road is something over a mile, although there are few persons who have travelled it on foot, under a burning sun, but would be willing to make their affidavits it was near five.

"Let us pause and look around us. For a distance of many miles, nothing is seen but the tops of successive mountains; then appears the beautiful valley of San Juan, while the Coast Range is lost in distance. The *patio* is an area of more than an acre in extent; and still above us, but not directly in view, is a Mexican settlement, composed of the families and lodging-cabins of the miners. There is a store, and provisions are carried up on pack-mules, for retail among the miners, who may truly be said to live from hand to mouth. This point had been the resort of the aborigines, not only of this State, but from as far as the Columbia River, to obtain the paint (vermilion) found in the cinnabar, and which they used in the decoration of their persons. How long this had been known to them, cannot be ascertained; probably a long time, for they had worked into the mountain some fifty or sixty feet, with what implements can only be conjectured. [Stones and pointed sticks.—ED.] A quantity of round stones, evidently from the brook, were found in a passage, with a number of skeletons; the destruction of life having been caused, undoubtedly, by a sudden caving in of the earth, burying the unskilled savages in the midst of their labors. It had been supposed for some time that the ore possibly contained the precious metals, but no regular assay was made till 1845; a gentleman now largely interested, procured a retort, not doubting that gold, or at least silver, would crown his efforts. Its real character was made known by its pernicious effects upon the system of the experimenter. The discovery was instantly communicated to a brother, a member of a wealthy firm in Mexico, who, with others, purchased the property, consisting of two leagues, held under a Spanish title, of the original owner. For some years but little was done. The ore proved both abundant and rich, but required the outlay of a vast amount of capital to be worked to advantage; and while Nature, with more than her usual liberality, had furnished in the mountain itself all the accessories for the successful prosecution of her favors, man was too timid to avail himself of her gifts.

PROCESS OF WORKING THE MINE.

"In 1850, a tunnel was commenced in the side of the mountain, in a line with the *patio*, and which has already been carried to the distance of one thousand one hundred feet by ten-feet wide, and ten feet high to the crown of the arch, which is strongly roofed with heavy timber throughout its whole length. Through this the rail-track passes; the car receiving the ore as it is brought on the backs of the carriers (*tenateros*) from the depths below, or from the heights above. The track being free, we will now take a seat on the car and enter the dark space. Not an object is visible save the faint torch-light at the extreme end; and a chilling dampness seizes on the frame, so suddenly bereft of warmth and sunshine. This sensation does not continue as we descend

SHRINE OF SENORA DE GUADALUPE.

into the subterranean caverns below; and now commence the wonders as well as the dangers of the undertaking. By the light of a torch we pass through a damp passage of some length, a sudden turn bringing us into a sort of vestibule, where, in a niche at one side, is placed a rude shrine of the tutelary saint, or protectress of the mine—*Nuestra Señora de Guadalupe*, before which lighted candles are kept constantly burning, and before entering upon the labors of the day or night, each man visits this shrine in devotion. You descend a perpendicular ladder, formed by notches cut into a solid log, perhaps twelve feet;

then turn and pass a narrow corner, where a frightful gulf seems yawning to receive you. Carefully threading your way over the very narrowest of footholds, you turn into another passage black as night, to descend into a flight of steps formed in the side of the cave, tread over some loose stones, turn around, step over arches, down into another passage that leads into many dark and intricate windings and descendings, or chambers supported by but a column of earth ; now stepping this way, then that, twisting and turning, all tending down, down to where, through the darkness of midnight, one can discern the faint glimmer, which shines like Shakspeare's ' good deed in a naughty world,' and which it seems impossible one can ever reach. We were shown a map giving the subterranean topography of this mine; and truly, the crossings and recrossings, the windings and intricacies of the labyrinthine passages, could only be compared to the streets of a dense city, while nothing short of the clue furnished Theseus by Ariadne, would insure the safe return, into day, of the unfortunate pilgrim who should enter without a guide.

"The miners have named the different passages after their saints, and run them off as readily as we do the streets of a city; and after exhausting the names of all the saints in the calendar, have commenced on different animals, one of which is not inaptly called *El Elefante*. Some idea of the extent and number of these passages may be formed, when we state, that sixty pounds of candles are used by the workmen in the twenty-four hours. Another turn brings us upon some men at work. One stands upon a single plank placed high above us in an arch, and he is drilling into the rock above him for the purpose of placing a charge of powder. It appears very dangerous, yet we are told that no lives have ever been lost, and no more serious accidents have occurred than the bruising of a hand or limb, from carelessness in blasting. How he can maintain his equilibrium is a mystery to us, while with every thrust of the drill his strong chest heaves, and he gives utterance to a sound something between a grunt and a groan, which is supposed by them to facilitate their labor. Some six or eight men working in one spot, each keeping up his agonizing

18

sound, awaken a keen sympathy. Were it only a cheerful sing-song, one could stand it; but in that dismal place, their wizard-like forms and appearance, relieved but by the light of a single tallow candle stuck in the side of the rock, just sufficient to make 'darkness visible,' is like opening to us the shades of Tartarus; and the throes elicited from over-wrought human bone and muscle, sound like the anguish wrung from infernal spirits, who hope for no escape.

MINEROS AT WORK IN THE MINE.

"These men work in companies, one set by night, another by day, alternating week about. We inquired the average duration of life of the men who work under ground, and found that it did not exceed that of forty-five years, and the diseases to which they are mostly subject are those of the chest; showing conclusively how essential light and air are to animal, as well as vegetable life. With a sigh and a shudder we step aside to allow another set of laborers to pass. There they come; up and up, from almost interminable depths, each one as he passes panting, puffing, and wheezing, like a high pressure steamboat, as with straining nerve

TENATEROS CARRYING THE ORE FROM THE MINE.

and quivering muscle he staggers under the load, which nearly bends him double. These are the *tenateros*, carrying the ore from the mine to deposit it in the cars; and, like the miners, they are burdened with no superfluous clothing. A shirt and trowsers, or the trowsers without a shirt, a pair of leathern sandals fastened at the ankle, with a felt cap, or the crown of an old hat, completes their costume.

"The ore is placed in a flat leather bag (*talégo*) with a band two inches wide that passes around the forehead, the weight resting along the shoulders and spine. Two hundred pounds of rough ore are thus borne up, flight after flight, of perpendicular steps;

now winding through deep caverns, or threading the most tortuous passages; again ascending over earth and loose stones, and up places that have not even an apology for steps, all the while lost in Cimmerian darkness, but for a torch borne aloft, which flings its sickly rays over the dismal abysm, showing that one unwary step would plunge him beyond any possibility of human aid or succor. Not always, however, do they ascend; they sometimes come from above; yet we should judge the toil and danger to be nearly as great in one case as in the other. Thirty trips will these men make in one day, from the lowest depths.

"For once we were disposed to quarrel with the long, loose skirts, that not only impeded our progress, but prevented our attempt to ascend to the summit, and enjoy from thence a prospect of great beauty and extent. But one woman, we believe, has ever accomplished this feat, which severely tasks the strength of manhood.

"We will now follow the *tenateros*, as they load the car with the contents of their sacks, and run after it into the open air. There they go, with shouts of laughter; and really, as one emerges into the warm sunshine, the change is most inspiriting. They have reached the end of the track, and throw off the great lumps of ore without an effort, as if they were mere cabbages. What capacious chests, and how gaily they work! Such gleeful activity we never before beheld. The large lumps deposited, they now seize shovels, and jumping on the cars, the small lumps mixed with earth are cleared off with the most astonishing celerity. Do but behold that fellow of Doric build, with brawny muscles, and who is a perfect *fac simile* of Hercules, as he stood engraved with his club, as we remember him in Bell or Tooke's Pantheon!

"The ore deposited on the *patio*, another set of laborers engage in separating the large lumps and reducing them to the size of common paving stones, which are placed by themselves. The smaller pieces are put in a separate pile, while the earth (*tierra*) is sifted through coarse sieves for the purpose of being made into *adobes*. There is also a blacksmith's shop for making and repairing implements. The miner is not paid by the day, but receives pay for the ore he extracts. They usually work in parties of from two to ten; half the number work during the day, the other half by night, and in this manner serve as checks upon each other. Should a drone get into the number, complaint is made to the engineer, who has to settle such matters, which he generally does by placing him with a set nearer his capacity, or sometimes by a discharge. The price of the ore is settled by agreement for each week. Should the passage be more than commonly laborious, they do not earn much; or if, on the contrary, it proves to be easy and of great richness, the gain is theirs; it being not infrequent for them to make from thirty to forty dollars a week a-piece, and seldom less than fifteen. In those parts of the mine where the ore is worthless, but still has to be extracted in order to reach that which will pay, or to promote ventilation, they are paid by the square *vara*,* at a stipulated price. They do nothing with getting the ore to the *patio;* this is done by the *tenateros* at the company's expense, as is also the separating, sifting, and weighing. Each party have their ore kept separate; it is weighed twice a week and an account taken. They select one of their party who receives the pay and divides it among his fellows.

"'The *tenateros* receive three dollars per diem; the sifters and weighers, two dollars and a half; blacksmiths and bricklayers, five and six; while carpenters are paid the city price of eight dollars a day. These wages seem to be very just and liberal, yet, such is their improvidence, that no matter how much they earn, the miners are not one *peso* better off at the end of the month than they were at its beginning. No provision being made for sickness or age, when that time comes, as come it will, there is nothing for them to do but, like some worn-out old charger, lie down and die. This has reference exclusively to the Mexicans; and it is a pity that a Savings Bank could not be established, and made popular among them. They number between two and three hundred in all; but they are, perhaps, the most impracticable people in the world, going on as their fathers did before them, firmly believing in the axiom, that 'sufficient unto the day is the evil thereof.'"

* A *vara* is thirty-three and one-third inches.

For some time this mine was closed by an injunction from the United States Court, but the difficulties being adjusted, it is now being worked with great success.

THE HENRIQUITA QUICKSILVER MINE,

Is the name of a newly opened quicksilver mine, situated in a beautiful and romantic valley on Guadalupe Creek, at the extreme western point of the same range of hills as that of New Almaden, and about four and a half miles from it. This mine was discovered in 1847, but was not attempted to be worked till 1850, when a company was formed and operations commenced ; but, owing to the high price of labor and supplies, and the company running short of funds, after a few months, were suspended. In 1855, a new company was formed and incorporated by charter, from the legislature of Maryland, under the title of the " Santa Clara Mining Association, of Baltimore," with a sufficient working capital to open the mine. erect the necessary smelting works, and carry them on.

"Veins of quicksilver," writes a friend, " were long since known to exist in these hills, but, owing to the difficulty of finding sufficient quantities of ore to render mining remunerative, nothing of importance was attempted. In November, 1858, Mr. Laurencel employed a party of Irish and Mexican miners to prospect it more thoroughly, and several places were found to be of good promise, and opened. One was called the Providentia Mine, another was placed under the protection of Saint Patrick, and at length, in January, 1859, the present Henriquita mine was found and immediately opened. During the winter and spring quite a limited number of men carried on the work, but the labors of these few were sufficient to prove that there existed a large deposit. In the beginning of June the work was advanced upon a larger scale, and preparations were made to put up the proper machinery for reducing the ore. Every thing was done with dispatch, and on the spot where stood a forest in June, we saw now an establishment so far advanced as to promise to go into operation, producing quicksilver, early in September; good proof of the energy and activity of our California miners.

"The system adopted for the reduction of ores is, I understand, the same that was employed by Dr. Ure, many years since, at the mines of Obermoschel, in the Bavarian Rhein Kreis, and which has proved to be much superior to the systems in practice at the Almaden mine in Spain, and the Idria mine of Austria.

"What the production of this mine will be, is impossible to foresee; but quite a little mountain of ore, already taken out, and what we saw in our descent into the mine, looks well for the future prospect. A large number of Mexican miners were at work, and as we passed their different parties, I broke from the rocky walls a number of pieces, which, on coming to the light of day, proved to be rich ore.

"The location of the Henriquita mine is one of considerable beauty. A picturesque valley below, with the winding stream of the Capitancillos, and pleasant groves of oaks and sycamores, looks up on one hand to the hill where the mine is perched, some three hundred and forty or fifty feet above, and on the other to the rugged mountain, rising to the height of between three and four thousand feet. The mine employs about one hundred laborers of all classes; the families added would make a total population already of about four hundred persons. A little village has sprung up near the works, containing many neat cottages, a hotel, and several stores. Two lines of stages run daily between the mine and the city of San José.

"While here I visited also another spot of considerable interest —a gigantic oak, standing upon a prominent spur of the mountains on the south. It measures some thirty-six feet in circumference, and is, I doubt not, the largest of its family in California. From its commanding position and size, it is visible at a great distance, still towering high, when all the trees around it are dwarfed into the appearance of mere underbrush.

"In leaving the Henriquita mine, I was more than ever reminded of the immense mineral resources of our State, and of the industry

of our people. The works of years in older countries, were here
the labor of a few short months only.

· "The county of Santa Clara will find in this mine a new source
of wealth, and must rejoice at the diligent prosecution of an enterprise so important. As an old miner, I was gratified at what I
saw. What the California miner needs is cheap quicksilver; but,
as long as its supply is limited, it is kept up at exorbitant prices.
With an increased production and a healthy competition, we may
expect·soon to see it at such a·price as will render it hereafter a
small item only in the working of the quartz mines, so important
a source of wealth and prosperity to California.

DEDICATORY CEREMONY OF BLESSING THE MINE.

"The interesting dedicatory ceremonial of Blessing the Mine is a
custom of long standing in many Catholic countries, where mining
is carried on, especially among those people who speak the Spanish
language. Without it, workmen would feel a religious dread, and
consequently a timid reluctance to enter upon their daily labors,
lest some accidental mishap should overtake them from such an
omission. After this has been duly performed, great care is taken
to erect a shrine, be it ever so rude, at some convenient point
within the mine, to some favorite tutelary saint or protectress,
whose benediction they evoke. Before this shrine, each workman
devoutly kneels, crosses himself, and repeats his Ave Maria, or
Paternoster, prior to entering upon the duties and engagements
of the day. At this spot, candles are kept burning, both by day
and night, and the place is one of sacred awe to all good Catholics.
The blessing and dedication of a mine is, consequently, an era of
importance, and one not to be lightly passed over, or indifferently
celebrated.

" On the morning of the day set apart for this ceremony, at the
Henriquita or San Antonio quicksilver mine, the Mexican and
Chilian señors and señoras began to flock into the little village at ·
the foot of the cañon, from all the surrounding country, in anticipation of a general holiday, at an early hour.

" Of course, at such a time, the proprietor sends out invitations to those guests he is particularly desirous should be present to do honor to the event; but no such form is needed among the workmen and their friends or acquaintances, as they understand that the ceremony itself is a general invitation to all, and they avail themselves of it accordingly.

"Arriving in procession at the entrance to the mine, Father Goetz, the Catholic curate of San José, performed mass, and

THE HENRIQUITA QUICKSILVER MINE, ON THE MORNING OF DEDICATION.

formally blessed the mine, and all persons present, and all those who might work in it; during which service a band of musicians was playing a number of airs. At the close, fire-crackers and the boom of a gun cut in the ground, announced the conclusion of the ceremony on the outside; when they all repaired to the inside, where the Father proceeded to sprinkle holy water, and to bless it.

"These duly performed, they repaired to the village, near which is the beautiful residence of Mr. Laurencel, its proprietor, where, in a lovely grove of sycamores, several tables were erected and bounteously covered with good things for the inner man. Here were feasted nearly two hundred guests, of both sexes, with choice viands, in magnificent profusion, while native wines, and other light potables, flowed in abundance. A large number of specially invited guests were at the same time hospitably and courteously entertained within the house by Mr. Laurencel, his lady, and her household. After dinner, there was music and dancing upon the green, exhibitions of skilful horsemanship, and a variety of amusements, which were participated in by the assembled company with the utmost zest, and were kept up, we understand, until a late hour. The day chosen for this festival was the day of San Antonio, the patron saint of the mine, and the birthday of the little Henriquita, Mr. Laurencel's daughter, the more immediate patroness of the same."

VIEW OF MOUNT SHASTA, THIRTY MILES DISTANT.

CHAPTER VII.

MOUNT SHASTA.

THIS isolated and lofty volcanic mountain is located in latitude 41° 30′, and is the head and main source of the Sacramento, Shasta, and other streams. For many years it was considered the highest in California, and was estimated at 18,000 feet; more recent measurements, however, make it only about 13,000 feet. Being alone, and unconnected with any great mountain chains of the State, it seems to be the culminating crest or starting point of an independent range.

Covered with snow at all seasons of the year—the only one in the State that can be so considered—it is one of those glorious and awe-inspiring scenes which greet the traveller's eye, and fill his mind with wondering admiration, as he journeys among the bold and beautiful mountains of our own California. One almost wishes to kneel in worship as he gazes at the magnificent, snow-covered head and pine-girded base of this "monarch of mountains;" and even as you ascend the valley of the Sacramento, Mount Shasta appears to you like a huge mountain of snow just beyond the purple hills of the horizon; and is a constant land-mark upon which to look, and which one unconsciously feels himself constrained to notice, as something even more remarkable and inviting than the green and flower-covered valley beside him.

ASCENT OF MOUNT SHASTA ALONE.

As we are favored with the following graphic sketch of an ascent —alone—by Israel S. Diehl, we shall allow him, without comment, to relate his interesting narrative:

"The morning of the ninth of October, 1855, opened beautiful and bright; the earth had been cooled by refreshing showers which had copiously fallen during the night, as I took up my line of march from Yreka to Mount Shasta, to make its ascent, if possible. Notwithstanding the extensive arrangements by way of *talk* and *promises*, that were made by the company contemplating the same visit (alas! for California pleasure parties), when the eventful day came, I was reluctantly compelled to start on my journey alone, dependent upon circumstances for the social pleasures that add so much to such a romantic trip. No equipped and noted travellers, officers, literati, or blooming lively belles, whose merry, joyful laugh and bright countenances could add so much of interest, were my attendants; and thus 'solitary and alone,' and somewhat fearful because of the stupendous and unknown undertaking, by any *single traveller*, I slowly, yet determinedly, set out upon my journey.

"From the western side of Shasta Valley, Mount Shasta was in full view before me, in all its beauty and glory, as it reared its majestic head some seventeen thousand feet into the heavens, while its sides were covered with the deep-driven snow of ages, adding so much antiquity to the inspiring awe, as if to say, 'I am the mighty monarch and sentinel of this western coast,' and almost steadily did my unweary, wondering eyes gaze admiringly upon the scene before me—hundreds of peaked little hillocks dotted the Shasta Valley for twenty-five miles around, like so many attendants (evidently all lesser volcanic formations), while the Shasta River, and other smaller streams, clear as crystal, and icy cold, sprang from its side.

"For a day and a half did I ride steadily on and around it, to make its ascent; all the time with the mountain in full view, and apparently but a little way off, deceiving even the best eye on calculation.

"For two nights, ere my ascent, did I watch the setting sun, with its purple rays lingering and playing for twenty or thirty minutes around its brow, when, to all other mountains, the sun had set. That scene was beautiful beyond description.

"By the noon of the second day, I had rounded the Mount to its south side, and fed my weary horse and self at the beautiful Strawberry Valley Ranche, or Gordon's, after which, with indefinite and unsatisfactory directions, I bade adieu to every hope of seeing another person ere my fate became decided. Fearful accounts and warnings were given of grizzlies, California lions, avalanches, falling rocks and stones, with deep cañon crevices, by and in which I might perish, and have no burial or resurrection until the 'Resurrection Morn;' but, unwilling to give up, and trusting in God, with a good horse, and a bag of provisions, I commenced the ascent.

"For twelve or fifteen miles, I followed a blind snow trail through bushes of manzanita, and other obstacles, which almost threw me from my horse; and would surely have torn my garments had I not been equipped with a good new suit of buckskin. After an arduous journey, I reached the upper edge of the belt of trees, and of the horse trail, but not until the sun had set. Night came on, rendering it too dark to find water for myself and animal until ten o'clock at night.

"After much difficulty, a fire was kindled, (as the last matches were being used) to keep off the grizzlies and lions, but, unfortunately, from the scarcity of trees and the amount of dead wood lying around, I set fire to all about me. This drove me out, and excluded me altogether: so, making a shelter of my saddle and mochila, and wrapping myself in my saddle-blanket, I crept underneath them, covering my head and feet, saying, "Mr. Grizzly, you must take saddle and all, or none." Between shivering with cold, dozing, fearing, and dreaming, I awoke, and awaited the dawn of day. At last it came—gladly to me—when, after feeding my horse and bidding him adieu, I commenced the ascent.

"On the east side of the west spur, and the south side of the mountain, there were vast quantities of clink and volcanic stones, and for four weary hours I never set my foot off broken stone, but up, up, up, over rocks and stones, till I reached the base of an almost perpendicular ledge of rocks, the so-called Red Bluffs, which I found to be indurated clay, colored by the peroxyd of iron. Through a little ravine I struggled on, on, climbing for one more painful hour, while large masses of rock, becoming loosened, went bounding to the awful abyss below.

"After reaching what I thought the desired summit, imagine my surprise to look over fields of lava, scoria, snow, and fearful glaciers. I now had to cross ravines or fissures, from fifty to one hundred feet deep, and from one hundred to three hundred feet wide, and worn through a solid mass of conglomerates, and sometimes half filled with snow and ice, the ice lying in perfect ridges, resembling the waves on the ocean, and were both sharp and dangerous to cross. I slipped and fell several times, once coming near being dashed thousands of feet below. After ascending for another hour, among this strangely mingled mass, hoping again to have reached the long desired summit, I was both disappointed and pleased to see the table-land of snow from one-fourth to one-half mile in diameter, where it lay from one hundred to probably one thousand and more feet deep, as I could look down into fissures where it had sagged apart, for a fearful depth, and from this field, a few hundred feet from the summit, the Sacramento River takes its rise; running through the deep gorges, sometimes on top, then hidden, then appearing at the summit of hills, then concealed for miles, it breaks forth in magnificent springs and miniature rivers, with sulphur and soda springs intermixed.

"After crossing the field of ice with great difficulty, on account of the sun melting the snow from the east and south, while the wind and cold froze it from the west and north, thus rendering it dangerous, I reached another perfect mountain of loose and coarse lava, ashes, and other volcanic matter, through which I waded, although a foot in depth, for some distance; and as I ascended, I caught a full and first view of the actual summit, which I imagine is not seen from below, as it is a perfectly bare crag or comb of rocks, while the sides and top around are so covered as to hide the real summit. Across another field of snow, and I was evidently upon the original and main crater, a concavity covering several acres, almost hemmed in by a considerable rim of rocks, and here I came upon the long sought hot and sulphur springs; and here, free from wind and snow, finding it warm and comfortable after being nearly benumbed with cold, I warmed, and took a hasty meal; and in my haste to warm my fingers, nearly lost them by awfully scalding them.

"I spent nearly an hour here, contemplating and watching this wonderful view. A hundred little boiling springs were gurgling and bubbling up through a bed of sulphur, and emitting steam enough to drive a small factory (if well applied), while all around lay the everlasting snow.

"After resting, I made the final summit, a few hundred feet above, composed of a perfect edge or comb of rocks, running nearly north and south, and from this summit, perhaps the highest, variously estimated at from sixteen thousand five hundred, to seventeen thousand five hundred feet, and decidedly the most magnificent of our Union, if not of the continent, I could look around and see ' all the kingdoms of this lower world,' [Did you tempt any one, Mr. Diehl?]

"Looking to the westward, far beyond the Scott, Trinity, Siskiyou, and Coast Range of mountains, I imagined I saw the proud

Pacific. Northward, looking far over into Oregon, one could see her peaks, her vallies, and lakes, to the Dalles, and what I took to be Mount Hood. East, far over the Sierras into Utah, and the deserts, while beautiful lakes lay like bright meadows, far in the distance. South, I could trace the Sacramento and Pitt Rivers, far below Shasta, where they were lost in the smoke and haze, but on the south-west I could clearly see Mount Linn, Mount St. John, and Ripley, and above the haze, could distinctly see the Marysville Buttes, if not the top of Mount Diablo (as I have clearly seen Mount Shasta from the summit of Mount Diablo). South-east, I could trail the Sierras by the Lassen, Spanish, Pilot, Seventy-six, Downieville, and other peaks, to the range below Lake Bigler, or to Carson Valley.

"I contemplated the unsurpassed scenery presented to my eye, for hours. The day was clear and beautiful, after our first October rains, while the scenery was delightful beyond description. And upon that peak I planted the temperance banner, side by side with the American flag (placed there in 1852, by Captain Prince), deposited some California papers and documents in the rocks, for safe keeping, as the papers carried up in 1852 were unharmed, and fresh as ever. Then, with a great reluctance, notwithstanding the wind, cold, loneliness, and coming night, I was compelled to beat a descent.

"The sun was fast declining. My watch told three P. M., when I collected my minerals, sulphurs, and all objects of interest, for a future and fuller description, and bidding adieu to the magnificent sights, with a promise of a return some day, I commenced the descent, and in three hours' running, jumping, tumbling, sliding on the snow, from one-fourth to one-half a mile at a time, in a few moments—having a glorious time, easier by far, and fuller of enjoyment than the ascent—I found my horse, mounted, and hastened away; and after a concatenation of circumstances, lost and bewildered, at twelve at night, dismounted, unsaddled and loosed my horse; weary and exhausted, nature gave way, sleep conquered, and until dawn of day, I knew no trouble save the piercing cold, and woke to find my trusty horse missing, giving me a half day's hunt to recapture him, when, by perils by river, land, and Indians, I followed the Sacramento down one hundred miles to Shasta, to spend the Sabbath, after six days' labor—much better and happier for my ascent of Mount Shasta."

14

THE SOUTH FARALLONE ISLAND, FROM THE BIG ROOKERY, LOOKING EAST.

CHAPTER VIII.

THE FARALLONE ISLANDS.

This is the name of a small group of rocky islands, lying in the Pacific Ocean, about twenty-seven miles west of the Golden Gate, and thirty-five miles from San Francisco. These islands have become of some importance, and of considerable interest, on account of the vast quantity of eggs that are there annually gathered, for the California market; these eggs having become an almost indispensable article of spring and summer consumption, to many persons.

By the courtesy of the Farallone Egg Company, through their President, Captain Richardson, the schooner Louise, Captain Harlow, was placed at our service, for the purpose of visiting them; and, in company with a small party of friends, we were soon upon the deep green brine, ploughing our way to the "Isles of the Ocean."

Bright and beautiful slept the morning, as a light breeze, blowing gently from the mountains, filled our sails, and sped us on our way through

THE GOLDEN GATE.

There are probably but few persons, comparatively, who have ever passed through this entrance to the fine Bay of San Francisco, that are familiar with the origin and meaning of the name, the popular idea being that its name was suggested by the staple mineral of the country—gold. This is incorrect, as it was called "The Golden Gate" before the precious metal was discovered; and the first time that it was used, most probably, was in a work entitled "A Geographical Review of California," with a relative map, published in New York, in the month of February, 1848, by Colonel J. C. Fremont; and as gold was discovered on the 19th of January preceding, in those days it would have been next to impossible for the news to have reached the office of publication of that work, in time for the name to be given, from such a cause.

The real origin of the name was from the excessively fertile lands of the interior—especially of those adjacent to the Bay of San Francisco. There may have been some "Spiritual Telegrams" sent from California (!) to the parent of the name, telling him of the glorious dawn of a Golden Day that had broke upon the world at Sutter's Mill, Coloma, and that such a name would be the magic charm to millions of men and women in every quarter of the world, in the Golden Age about to be inaugurated. We do not say that it was so. We do not wish the reader to believe it, as our opinion, that it was thus originated; but in this age of spiritual darkness—we allude to the limited knowledge of mental phenomena—we start the supposition, in hope that it may stir up the spirit of inquiry.   This one thing is certain, that from whatever source the name "Golden Gate" may have originated, it was most happily suggestive in its character.   Having dwelt at some length upon the *name*, we will now more briefly describe the spot.

That it is the gateway or entrance to the magnificent harbor of San Francisco, every one is well aware.   The centre of this entrance is in longitude 122° 30′ W. from Greenwich.   On the south of the entrance, is Point Lobos (Wolves' Point), on the top of which is a telegraph station, from whence the tidings of the arrival of steamers and sailing vessels are sent to the city.   On the north side, is Point Bonita (Beautiful Point), readily recognized by a strip of land running out toward the bar, on the top of which is a light-house, that is seen far out to sea, on a clear day,

CLIPPER SHIP CROSSING THE BAR OUTSIDE THE ENTRANCE OF THE BAY OF SAN FRANCISCO.

but seldom before that on the Farallone Islands, some twenty-seven miles west of Point Bonita.

In front of the entrance is a low, circular sand-bar, almost seven miles in length, but on which is sufficient water, even at low tide, to admit of the largest class of ships crossing it in safety—except, possibly, when the wind is blowing from the north-west, west, or south-east; at such a time, it is scarcely safe for a very large vessel to cross it at low tide.

From Point Bonita to Point Lobos, the distance is about three and a half miles; and between Fort Point and Lime Point (just opposite each other), the narrowest part of the channel, and "The Golden Gate" proper, it is one thousand seven hundred and seventy-seven yards. Here the tide ebbs and flows at the rate of about six knots an hour.

CROSSING THE BAR.

To the dwellers of a seaport city, there is music in the ever restless waves, as they murmur and break upon the shore; but to sail upon the broad, heaving bosom of the ocean, gives an impression of profoundness and majesty, that, by contrast, becomes a source of peaceful pleasure; as *change* becomes *rest* to the weary. There is a vastness, around, above, beneath you, as wave after wave, and swell after swell, lifts your tiny vessel upon its seething surface, as though it were a feather—a floating atom upon the broad expanse of waters. Then, to look into its shadowy depth, and feel the sublime language of the Psalmist: "O Lord, how manifold are thy works! in wisdom hast Thou made them all: the earth is full of thy riches. So is this great and wide sea, wherein are things creeping innumerable, both small and great beasts. These wait all upon Thee: that Thou mayest give them their meat in due season. Thou openest thy hand, they are filled with good. Thou hidest thy face, they are troubled." "They that go down to the sea in ships, that do business in great waters: these see the works of the Lord, and his wonders in the deep. He commandeth, and raiseth the stormy wind, which lifteth up the waves thereof. He maketh the storm a calm, so that the waves thereof are still."

"Oh, that men would praise the Lord for his goodness, for his wonderful works to the children of men!"

Object after object became distant and less, as we left them far, far behind us.

"Yonder blows a whale!" cries one.

"Where?"

"Just off our larboard bow."

"Oh! I see it—but"——

"But! what's the matter?"

"Oh! I feel so sea-sick."

"Well, never mind that; look up, and don't think about it."

"Oh—I can't—I must"——

Reader, were you ever sea-sick? If your experience enables you to answer in the affirmative, you will sympathize somewhat with the poor subject of it. Yonder may be this beauty, and that

ENCHANTED WITH THE DELIGHTFUL PROSPECT OFF THE BAR.

wonder, but a "don't-care*ishness*" comes over you, and if all the remarkable scenes in creation were just before you, "I don't care" is written upon the face, as you beseechingly seem to say: "*Pray don't trouble me—my hands are full.*" Whales, sea-gulls, porpoises, and even the white, foamy spray, that is curling over Duxbury Reef, are alike unheeded.

"How are you now?" kindly asks our good-natured captain, of the one and the other.

"Ah! thank you; I am better."

"Here, take a cup of nice hot coffee."

"No; I thank you."

The mere mention of any thing to eat or drink is only the signal for a renewal of the sickness.

"Thank goodness! I feel better," says one, after a long spell of sickness and quiet.

"So do I," says another; and, just as the "Farallones" are in sight, fortunately, all are better.

SOUTH-EAST VIEW OF THE FARALLONE ISLANDS.

Now the air is literally filled with birds—birds floating above us, and birds all around us, like bees that are swarming, we thought the whole group of islands must have been deserted, and that they had poured down in myriads, on purpose to intercept our landing, or "bluff us off;" but, as the dark, weather-beaten furrows, and the wave-washed chasms, and the wind-swept masses of rock, rose more defined and distinct before us as we approached, we concluded that they must have abandoned the undertaking—for upon every peak sat a bird, and in every hollow a thousand; but, looking around us again, the number, apparently, had increased rather than diminished, and the more there seemed to be upon the islands the greater the increase round about us—so that we concluded *our fears* to be entirely unfounded.

The anchor is dropped in a mass of floating foam, on the southeast and sheltered side of the islands, and in a small boat we reach the shore, thankful, after this short voyage, to feel our feet standing firmly on *terra firma*.

ARRIVAL AT THE FARALLONE ISLANDS.

Looking at the wonders on every side, we were astonished that we had heard so little about them, and that a group of islands like these should lie within a few hours' sail of San Francisco, yet not be the resort of nearly every seeker of pleasure, and every lover of the wonderful.

It is like one vast menagerie. Upon the rocks adjacent to the sea repose in easy indifference, thousands—yes, thousands—of *sea lions* (one species of the seal), that weigh from *two to five thousand pounds each*. As these made the loudest noise, and to us were the most curious, we paid them the first visit. When we were within a few yards of them the majority took to the water, while two or three of the oldest and largest remained upon the rock, "standing guard" over the young calves, that were either at play with each other, or asleep at their side. As we advanced, these masses of "blubber" moved slowly and clumsily toward us, with their mouths open, and showing two large tusks that were standing out from their lower jaw, by which they gave us to understand that we had better not disturb the repose of the juvenile "lions," nor approach too near, or we might receive more harm than we expected or wished. But the moment we threw at them a stone, they would scamper off, and leave the young lions to the mercy of their enemies. We advanced and took hold of one, to try if the sight of their young being taken away would tempt them

to come to the rescue; but, although they roared and kept swimming close to the rock, they evidently thought their own safety of the most importance. One old warrior, whose head and front bore scars of many a hard-fought battle—for they fight fearfully among themselves—could not be driven from the field, and neither rocks nor shouting moved him in the least, except to meet the enemy, as he doubtless considered us.

All of these animals are very jealous of their particular rock, where, in the sun, they take their *siesta*, and although we remained upon some of these spots for a considerable length of time, while their usual tenants were swimming in the sea, and perhaps had

become somewhat uneasy, they were not allowed to land on the
territory of another.

SEA LIONS AND THEIR YOUNG.

They keep up an incessant short, moaning cry, that sounds like
yoi hoey, yoi hoey, in about the same key as the bray of a mule.

Most of these young seals are of a dark mouse color, but the old
ones are of a light and brightish brown about the head, and gradually become darker toward the extremities, which are about the
same color as the young calves. Most of the male and young female seals leave these islands during the months of October or

November—and generally all go at once—returning in April or May the following spring, while the older females remain here nearly alone throughout the winter—a rather ungallant proceeding on the part of the males.

THE HAIR SEAL.

There are several different kinds of seal that pay a short visit here at different seasons of the year, one of the most beautiful of which is the hair seal of the Pacific (*Phoco jubata*).

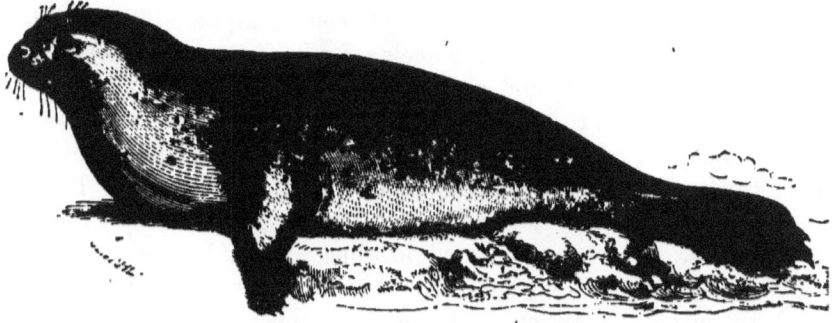

THE HAIR SEAL OF THE PACIFIC.

This seal, with which the coast of California abounds, is by no means rare, as almost all the coasts in high southern and northern latitudes abound with it. "To the Laplander, it is meat, drink, clothing, etc. To the Indians of Behring's Straits and Kamschatka it is most valuable; in fact, they could hardly exist without it. Far away in those inhospitable regions, where winter reigns three-fourths of the year, no timber can be obtained sufficiently large to build a canoe; but with a few seal-skins and a little whale-bone, the Indian will construct one of the most perfect life-boats in the world. In this he will fearlessly venture miles from land to catch fish and seals, aye, and even the whale. These canoes are difficult to manage to those who are unacquainted with them. It requires no small degree of practice, even to the Kamschatkan, in a rough sea, to keep such a boat alive. He is not allowed to marry unless he have the ability of so making and guiding them. Indeed, his canoe is all to him—his house, his clothes, his furniture, his food—for without it, his shores, prolific in fish, would be useless.

"Its countenance bears the impress of great sagacity; its full, round, beautiful eye indicates even an intelligence rarely to be found in any other inhabitant of the waters. This was remarked by the ancient historian, Pliny. He gives an amusing account of one that was easily taught to perform certain tricks. It would salute visitors freely, and would answer to its name when called. F. Cuvier narrates of one that he saw that was made to stand erect on its tail, and hold a staff between its flippers like a sentinel on duty. It would tumble heels over head when desired, give a flipper to be shaken, and present its lips for its keeper's kiss.

"Captain Russell, the assiduous traveller and explorer of the seaboard resources of California, informed us that it is most amusing sometimes to see their contests with the Coast Indians. These fellows skulk behind the rocks adjacent to some gently-sloping sand-banks, and when the shoal has become dry by the receding tide, they front the body and interpose their return to the water, each selecting as his prey the biggest and most powerful. Catching hold of the tail-flipper, the animal scuffles along the sand, dragging along after him the Indian, who, with a tight grip, follows, until, by ploughing a deep furrow with his feet, leaning back, and with all his strength resisting the powerful progress of the animal, until both come to a dead stand; the animal's side-flippers are then tied by another party, and the poor beast thus easily becomes his prey. He often, he says, remonstrated in vain against their barbarous cruelty of preparing them for food, or for blubber. A huge fire is made in a large flat hole in the ground, and the poor beasts are hurled in and roasted alive. "We have no other way," said they, "of singeing or scorching off the hair. If they were put in dead, we should have to get in the fire ourselves to turn them, but being alive, they spare us the trouble, and turn themselves, when one side is singed sufficiently."

"The whole tribe possesses remarkable peculiarities of respiration and circulation of blood. The interval between their respirations is very long. A full-grown animal can remain under water, without requiring a fresh inspiration, for upwards of half an hour. They can open and close at pleasure, for these purposes, their valvular nostrils in a surprising degree, eating their food all the time under water with perfect enjoyment. Their breathing is remarkably slow, and very irregular. After opening the nostrils and making a long expiration, the creature inhales air by a long inspiration, and just before diving, closes its nostrils as tight as any mechanical valve. In confinement, they have been observed to remain asleep, with the head under water, for an hour at each time, without any fresh inhalation of air. Naturalists account for this power by the animal's possessing a great venous canal in its liver, which assists it in diving, so that their respiration is somewhat independent of the circulation of the blood.

"One of these animals was exhibited in Adams' Museum, San Francisco, and was in excellent condition, exceedingly tame, and very submissive to its keeper. It seemed to enjoy the music, appearing to listen to it with some pleasure. This is not to be wondered at, as the hearing of this class of animals is very acute; and well attested instances are by no means rare, of many, even in a wild state, being attracted by the sound of a flute, or a horn; rising up to the surface to enjoy it the more, and sinking immediately the sounds are discontinued. The brain in the seal is very large, and its whiskers are connected with nerves of immense size, serving almost every purpose of sensation."

The Russians formerly visited these islands, for the purpose of obtaining oil and skins, and several places can be yet seen where the skins were stretched and dried.

BIRDS ON THE FARALLONES.

The birds which are by far the most numerous, and, on account of their eggs, the most important, are the *Murre, or Foolish Guillemot*, which are found here in myriads, surmounting every rocky peak, and occupying every small and partially level spot upon the islands. Here it lays its egg, upon the bare rock, and never leaves it, unless driven off, until it is hatched; the male taking its turn, at incubation, with the female—although the latter is most assid-

THE MURRE, OR FOOLISH GUILLEMOT.

uous. One reason why this may be the case, perhaps, is from the fact that the *gull* is watching every opportunity to steal its egg and eat it. The "eggers" say that when they are on their way to any part of the island, the gulls call to each other, and hover around until the murre is disturbed by them, and before they can pick up the egg, the gull sweeps down upon it, and carries it off.

When the young are old enough to emigrate, the murres take them away in the night, lest the gulls should eat them; and as soon as the young reach the water, they swim at once. Some idea may be formed of the number of these birds, by the Farallone Egg Company having, since 1850, brought to the San Francisco market between three and four millions of eggs.

On this coast these birds are numerous, in certain localities, from Panama to the Russian possessions. On the Atlantic, they are found from Boston to the coast of Labrador; differing but very little in color, shape, or size.

THE MURRE'S EGG—FULL SIZE.

It is a clumsy bird, almost helpless on land, but is at home on the sea, and is an excellent swimmer and diver, and is very strong in the wings. Their eggs are unaccountably large, for the size of the bird, and "afford excellent food, being highly nutritive and palatable—whether boiled, roasted, poached, or in omelets." No two eggs are in color alike.

THE TUFTED PUFFIN.

The bird of most varied and beautiful plumage, on the islands, is the *Mormon Cirrhatus*, or *Tufted Puffin ;* and, although they are rather numerous on this coast, they are very scarce elsewhere.

In addition to the *murre, puffin,* and *gull,* already mentioned, there are *pigeons, hawks, shag, coots,* etc., which visit here during the summer, but, with the exception of the *gull* and *shag,* do not remain through the winter.

The *horned-billed guillemot* has been seen and caught here, but it is exceedingly rare.

Now, with the reader's permission, we will leave the birds and animals—at least if we can—and take a walk up to the lighthouse, at the top of the island, three hundred and fifty-seven feet above the sea. A good pathway has been made, so that we can ascend with ease. If you find that we have not left the birds, nor the birds left us, but that, at every step we take, we disturb some, and pass others, and that thousands are flying all around us, never mind—when we reach the top we shall forget them, at least for a few moments, to strain our eyes in looking toward the horizon, and seeking to catch a glimpse of some distant object. Yonder, some eight miles distant, are the "North Farallones," a very small group of rocks, and not exceeding three acres in extent— but, like this, they are covered with birds.

Now let us enter the lighthouse, and, under the guidance of Mr. Wines, the superintendent, we shall find our time well spent in looking at the best lighthouse on the Pacific coast. Every thing is bright and clean, its machinery in beautiful order, and working as regular in its movements as a chronometer.

The wind blows fresh outside, and secretly you hope the lighthouse will not blow over before you get out. Here, too, you can see the shape of the island upon which you stand, mapped out upon the sea below.

Let us descend, wend our way to the "West End," and pass through the living masses of birds, that stand, like regiments of white-breasted miniature soldiers, on every hand—and it might be well to take the precautionary measure of closing our ears to the perpetual roaring, and loud moaning of the *sea lions,* for their noise is almost deafening. A caravan of wild beasts is nothing, in noise, to these.

Let us be careful, too, in every step that we take, or we shall place our foot upon a nest of young *gulls*, or break eggs by. the dozen, for they are everywhere around us. We soon reach the side of the " Jordan," as a small inlet is called, and across which we can step at low tide, but which is thirty feet wide at high water. To cross it, however, a rope and pulley is your mode of conveyance; so hold tight by your hands, and you'll soon get across. Safely over, let us make our way for a glimpse of the *West End View, looking East.*

VIEW FROM WEST END, LOOKING EAST.

This is a wild and beautiful scene. The sharp-pointed rocks are standing boldly out against the sky, and covered with birds and sea lions. A heavy surf is rolling in, with thundering hoarseness, and as the wild waters break upon the shore, they resemble the low, booming sound of distant thunder; while the white spray curls over, and falls with a hissing splash upon the rocks, and then returns again to its native brine; while, swimming

15

in the boiling sea, amid the foam and rocks, just peering above the water, are the heads of scores of sea lions. Let us watch them for a moment. Here comes one noble looking old fellow, who rises from the water, and works his way, slowly and clumsily, toward the young which lie high and dry, sleeping in the sun, or are engaged lazily scratching themselves with their hind claws; and, although we are very near them, they lie quite unconcerned, and innocent of danger. Not so the old *gentleman,* who has just taken his position before us, as sentry. Experience has doubtless taught him that such looking animals as we are behave no better than we should do, and he knows it!

There are water-washed caves, and deep fissures between the rocks, just at our right; and in the distance is a large arch, not less than sixty feet in height, its top and sides completely covered with birds. Through the arch, you can see a ship, which is just passing.

Now let us go to the "Big Rookery," lying on the north-west side of the island.

This locality derives its name from the island here forming a hollow, well protected from the winds; and being less abrupt than other places, is on that account a favorite resort of myriads of sea fowl, who make this their place of abode, and where vast numbers of young are raised. If you walk among them, thousands immediately rise, and for a few moments darken the air, as though a heavy cloud had just crossed and obscured the sunlight upon your path. But few persons who have not seen them can realize the vast numbers that make this their home, and which are here, there, and everywhere, flying, sitting, and even swimming, upon the boiling and white-topped surge among the seals.

Here, as elsewhere, there are thousands of seals, some are suckling their calves, some are lazily sleeping in the sun, others are fishing, some are quarrelling, others are disputing possession, and yonder, just before us, two large and fierce old fellows are engaged in direful combat with each other—now the long tusks of the one are moving upward to try to make an entrance beneath the jaw of the other—now they are below—now there is a scattering among the swimming group that have merely been looking on to see the sport, for the largest has just come up among them, and they are afraid of him. Now appears his antagonist, his eyes rolling with maddened frenzy, they again meet—now under, now over—fierce wages the war, hard goes the battle, but at last the owner of the head, already covered with scales, has conquered, and his discomfitted enemy makes his way to the nearest rock, and there lies panting and bleeding; but he may not rest here, for the owner of that claim is at home and has possession, and without any sympathy for his suffering and unfortunate brother, he orders him off, although "only a squatter," and he again takes to the sea in search of other quarters.

From this point we get an excellent view of the lighthouse, and the residence of the keepers. Everywhere there is beauty, wildness, sublimity. Let us not linger too long here, although weeks could be profitably spent in looking at the wonders around us, but let us take a hasty glance at the *View from the North Landing*.

VIEW FROM THE NORTH LANDING, LOOKING NORTH.

Here there is a fine estuary, where, with a little improvement, small schooners can enter at any season of the year, and where the oil and other supplies are landed for the lighthouse. Like the other views, it is singular and wild—each eminence covered with birds, each sea-washed rock occupied by seals, and the air almost darkened by the sea gulls skimming backward and forward, like swallows, and by the rapid and apparently difficult flight of the murres.

From this point we can get an excellent view of the *North Farallones*, that, in the dim and shadowy distance, are looming up their dull peaks just above the restless and swelling waves. From the sugar-loaf shaped peak, and the singularly high arch, and bold, rugged outlines of the other rocks, this view has become a favorite one with the " eggers."

Upon these islands, of three hundred and fifty acres, there is not a single tree or shrub to relieve the eye by contrast, or give change to the barrenness of the landscape. A few weeds and sprigs of wild mustard are the only signs of vegetable life to be seen upon them. To those who reside here it must be monotonous and dull; but to those who visit it, there is a variety of wild wonders that amply repays them for their trouble.

Some Italian fishermen having supplied our cook with excellent fish, let us hasten aboard and make sail for home.

Before saying " good-bye" to our kind entertainers, and again leaving them to the solitary loneliness of a " life near the sea," we will congratulate them upon their useful employment, and ask them to remember the comforting joy they must give to the tempest-tossed mariner, who sees, in the " light afar," the welcome sentinel, ever standing near the gate of entrance to the long wished and hoped-for port, where, for a time, in enjoyment and rest, he can recover from the hardships and forget the perils of the sea.

On our left, and but a few yards from shore, is an isle called *Seal Rock*, where the sea lions have possession, and are waving their lubberly bodies to and fro upon its very summit, and from whence the echoes of their low howling moans are heard across the sea, long after distance has hidden them from our sight.

After a pleasant run of five hours, without any sea-sickness, we are again walking the streets of San Francisco, abundantly satisfied that our trip was exceedingly pleasant and instructive.

SOUTH VIEW OF FORT POINT AND THE GOLDEN GATE.

From a Photograph by Hamilton & Co.

CHAPTER IX.

IN AND AROUND SAN FRANCISCO.

San Francisco,* approached from the sea or from the northern portion of the bay, does not present an attractive appearance to the stranger. At night, to be sure, when the broken heights are dotted with sparkling lights, and the mysterious and vague enchantment of mingled darkness and light is cast over the picture,

* For most of this chapter we are indebted to the kindness of Noah Brooks, Esq., of San Francisco.

there is something to charm the eager tourist in the vagueness and indistinctness of the glimpse which he has of the far-famed city. But by day, when the pitiless sun pours its broad rays upon the rough, sandy promontory on which San Francisco lies rudely scattered, the picture is unpleasing and almost invariably disappointing. The hills are sandy and dry, and are dotted or covered with houses, not always neat, and seldom elegant. That part of the city which is first seen as one approaches it from the Golden Gate, or from the north, is ragged with straggling wooden structures, destitute of foliage and forbidding in the extreme. It is not until one reaches the city front and gains some near views of the more tasteful architecture of the business part of the city, that the impression of newness and raggedness is removed. During the dry season the hills which surround the bay are brown and tawny, the sky is staring in its utter blue cloudlessness, and the general aspect of the scene is uninviting.

Closer acquaintance with the city, with its pleasant homes, its lovely gardens, and its really elegant private residences removes much of this unfavorable first impression, but the main facts of its roughly repelling appearance remain. As above intimated, there are many attractive homes in San Francisco, and the mildness of the climate is attested by the perennial flowering of many delicate shrubs and plants, almost unknown in the eastern States. Geraniums, fuschias, heliotropes, verbenas, passion-flowers, jessamines, roses, and a wealth of flowers which bloom only with reluctance and during a short interval in most of the older States, are here found in constant perfection, and the city conceals among the sandy hills, which the traveller by sea views disgustfully from the sea, many gardens which are emphatically "gardens of delight,"—these make San Francisco attractive.

THE CLIFF HOUSE AND SEAL ROCKS.

On the seaward side of the promontory of San Francisco, at the base of a bold cliff, are the famous Seal Rocks; as this locality is one of the very first to which the favored stranger is taken by his hospitable friends, one may be pardoned for placing it at

the head of the brief list of sights to be seen in and around San
Francisco. There are several roads leading to the sea beach, and
the Rocks, but the most frequented is the turnpike which forms
an extension of Geary Street, passing out between Lone Mountain,
and Laurel Hill Cemetery. On the right is the cemetery where
rest the ashes of most of the dead of San Francisco, their monu-
ments gleaming white in the sun. Conspicuous among these is
the tall obelisk which marks the grave of Broderick ; of Thomas
Starr King ; the monumental work erected at the burial-place of
Baker—General, Senator, and Orator—is near this point : besides
those of many others whose life and labors were a blessing to the
State. On the left of the road rises the conical peak of Lone
Mountain, surmounted by a cross, which is seen far out at sea ;
and scattered near the base are several cemeteries in charge of
benevolent associations, and Calvary Cemetery, the largest of all,
stretches well up its slope. The road is firm, hard, and smooth as
a floor, with gen le undulations whose successive rises enable the
tourist and pleasure-seeker to catch occasional glimpses of the
bay and of the Golden Gate. Half-way out from Lone Mountain is a fine view of this opening toward the sea, with the bold
precipitous cliffs which line the northward side of the Gate, just
veiled enough by the dimness of the distance to cover the bare-
ness of their seamed faces ; and beyond these rise the rounded
outlines of the hills which lead to Tamal Pais, whose sharp peak,
bristling with pines is sharply projected against the sky beyond.

The road is filled with vehicles of every description, on every
pleasant day, especially on Saturdays, when the half-holiday
which most business men take is well improved. The invigorating air, the excitement of the drive, and the mere absence from
the dusty city, all serve to make this brisk trot along the well-
kept road, a pleasure worth enjoying and remembering. Here
are conveyances of every description, from the showy equipage
of some prosperous citizen, to the humble light-wagon of less pretentious people, who, with children and family, are out for a sniff
of pure air, a look at the sea-lions and a sight at the stream of
people who come and go ; for a drive to " the cliff" is one of the

institutions of San Francisco, which all must see, whether he go in carriage, hack, omnibus, wagon, or afoot.

On rising the last of the slight hills over which the turnpike is laid, one has a fine view of the broad Pacific, stretching in an unbroken line along the horizon, and washing the beach which skirts this side of the promontory. At the right is the outer side of the Golden Gate, its broad waves ever open to the ingress or egress of the snowy sails which dot the shining blue expanse, while beyond and stretching northward into the dim vagueness of cloudland are the dim outlines of the Bolinas Mésa at the base of Duxbury Reef and Point Reyes. To the left and southward lies the long sandy beach on which the surf ever breaks mournfully or thunders threateningly; and beyond this the bold rocky shore is pushed far seaward in blue and purple peaks which melt in the distance; the vast ocean, sparkling like sapphires in the sun, or gray under passing clouds, lies all along the horizon, and at one point in its wavy line we mark the dot-like peaks of the Farallone Islands.

The road descends to the brink of an abrupt cliff overhanging the sea, and commanding a view of three or four groups of rocky islets, which rise sharply from the turbulent waves. These are the famous "seal rocks," and their sole tenants are the seals or sea-lions, which bask in the sunshine on their ledges, and the sea-birds which light in flocks upon the peaks. The seals are perpetually climbing up the rocks, their sleek coats streaming with water, or plunging into the wave again, sporting in the liquid tide as if keenly enjoying their mere existence. Here and there on the higher pinnacles of the rocks are a few solitary ambitious animals, who, having climbed far above their companions, are soundly sleeping in the sun, enjoying a long and profound nap. But for the most part, seals tumble in and out of water, over and over each other, or crawl awkwardly on the lower rocks, continually keeping up their peculiar grunt or bark, the noise of which is occasionally drowned by the thunder of the waves as they break against the cliff. With a good field-glass, one can watch every motion of the uncouth and ungainly beasts, and it is a source of endless amusement for those who are curious in the study of their habits to note their peculiar motions and changes from place to place. By a State law they are protected from slaughter, and so they increase, multiply, and possess their place of abode with as much freedom from fear of man as though they were leagues away from any inhabited country.

On the summit of the cliff is the Cliff House, kept by Captain Foster, who provides ample shelter and entertainment for pleasure-seekers and their horses and carriages! From the rear of the hotel on a broad veranda, overhanging the sea, one obtains a grand view of the panorama and of the rocks which form the principal attraction of the locality. Here are seats for the weary, protection from sun and rain, and cozy little rooms for the repasts which may be needed by those who come to " make a day of it."

THE DRIVE ALONG THE BEACH.

From the hotel a winding carriage-way, blasted out of solid rock, and guarded by a stone parapet, leads to the beach below.

THE DRIVE ALONG THE BEACH.

And along this level beach, for six or seven miles, one has a glorious drive when the tide is at its ebb.   The firm, elastic sand
makes an easy road, and the combing waves, the wide expanse of
sea, the distant or nearer sails gliding across the watery floor, the
hazy landscape in the distance, all combine to form the most
agreeable surroundings imaginable.

There is a never-ceasing pleasure to a refined mind in looking
upon, or listening to, the hoarse, murmuring roar of the sea ; an
unexplainable charm in the music of its waves, as, with a seething
sound, they curl and gently break upon a sandy shore, during a
calm, or dash in all their majesty and fury, with thundering
voices, upon the unheeding rocks in a storm.   This is sublimity.
Besides, every shell, and pebble, and marine plant, from the
smallest fragment of sea-moss to the largest weed that germinates
within the caverns of the deep, has an architectural perfection and
beauty that ever attracts the wondering admiration of the
thoughtful.

THE OCEAN HOUSE.

This beach extends continuously from Seal Rock to Muscle
Rock, about seven miles.   Near the last-named place is a soda
spring, and several veins of bituminous coal, to obtain which,
shafts have been sunk to the depth of one hundred and twenty-
four feet, in which the coal was found to grow better as they descended; but, like many similar enterprises, when means to work
it failed, it was abandoned.   Other minerals are also found in this
chain of hills.

At the lower end of the beach the road turns into the hills again, and passing up among the sand dunes, the Ocean House is reached, another hotel having been passed just before leaving the sea-side. From this point the road, a well-kept macadamized turnpike winds over the hills and reaches the city by the way of the old Mission Dolores.

THE MISSION DOLORES.

This part of San Francisco, still called "The Mission," is newly built, for the most part, and the few ancient relics of the early Spanish occupation of the country, look strangely amidst the garish display and rude vigor of the new suburb of the city. Here, sheltered from ocean winds by the hills, which also detain the cold sea-fogs, was the religious settlement of the Spanish Fathers.

THE OLD MISSION CHURCH AND OUT-BUILDINGS.
From a Photograph by Hamilton & Co.

The old-fashioned, tile-covered adobe church and buildings attached, part of which are still in use by the Mission, and a part is converted into saloons and a store. This edifice was erected in 1775–6, and was completed and dedicated August 1, 1776, and was formerly called San Francisco, in honor of the patron saint, Saint Francis, the name given to the bay by its discoverer, Junipero Serra, in October, 1769.

The visitor will notice a number of old adobe buildings scattered here and there, in different directions; these were erected for the use of the Indians, one part being used for boys, and the other for girls, and in which they resided until they were about seventeen years of age, when they were allowed to marry, after which other apartments were assigned them, more in accordance with their condition.

As late as 1849 there were two large boilers in the buildings back of the church; and as meat was almost the only article of food, an ox was killed and boiled, wholesale, at which time the Indians would gather around and eat until they were satisfied. Of course, most of our readers are aware that Catholics are not allowed to eat meat on Friday, but, owing to this being the only article of diet to the Indians and native Californians around the Mission, they were not required to abstain from it, even on that day.

According to Mr. Forbes, a very careful and accurate writer, who published a work in 1835, entitled the "History of Lower and Upper California," the number of black cattle belonging to this Mission in 1831, was five thousand six hundred and ten; horses, four hundred and seventy; mules, forty; while only two hundred and thirty-three fanegas (a fanega is about two and a half bushels) of wheat, seventy of Indian corn, and forty of small beans, were raised altogether. At that time, however, the Missions had lost much of their former glory; for, in 1825, only six years before, that of Dolores, alone, is said to have had seventy-six thousand head of cattle, nine hundred and fifty tame horses, two thousand breeding mares, eighty-four stud of choice breed, eight hundred and twenty mules, seventy-nine thousand sheep, two thousand hogs, and four hundred and fifty-six yoke of working oxen; and raised eighteen thousand bushels of wheat and barley. Besides, in 1802, according to Baron Humboldt, there were of males, in this Mission, four hundred and thirty-three; of females, three hundred and eighty-one; total, eight hundred and fourteen. And yet, according to Mr. Forbes, in 1831, there were but one hundred and twenty-four males, and eighty-five females; and now, there are—none. Truly, "the glory has departed."

At that time, the Indians and native Californians, for many miles around, would congregate at the Mission Dolores, about three times a year, bringing with them cattle enough to kill while they remained, which was generally about a week, and have a good holiday time with each other.

Before the discovery of gold, it was the custom here to keep a tabular record of all the men, women, and children ; members of the church ; marriages, births, and deaths; the number of live stock ; and amounts of produce, in all their business details ; but, since then, every thing has changed for the worse. Even the lands devoted to, and set apart for, the use of the Mission, have, nearly all, been squatted upon, so that now but a few hundred varas remain intact ; and, as to where the stock of all kinds have gone, " deponent saith not."

GENERAL VIEW OF THE MISSION DOLORES, FROM THE POTRERO.

One feels quite a pleasurable curiosity in examining the old Spanish manuscript books still extant at this Mission, and looking upon their sheepskin covered lids and buckskin clasps. Besides these, there are about six hundred printed volumes, in Spanish, on religious subjects ; but, being in a foreign language, they are seldom or never read.

The priests who taught, supported, and educated these simple-minded people are all gone, and a feeling of sadness must prevail in one's mind as he contemplates the scene, so changed, so utterly denuded of almost every thing that would serve as a remembrance of the peaceful and devoted lives of the early missionaries of the cross.

The great point of attraction here to visitors from the city, is its quiet green graveyard, which, but for its being so negligently tended, and slovenly kept, would be one of the prettiest places near the city of San Francisco.

It seems as though we could never weary in looking upon these interesting scenes; but as we have further to go, and, we trust, many more to look upon, let us again set out on our jaunt and visit this spot at our leisure.

From the Mission into the city there lead several routes, but by taking that by Howard Street, one is brought nearest to one of the few suburban resorts of San Francisco,—

WOODWARD'S GARDENS.

These may be justly called suburban. Once a dwelling-house, surrounded by ample pleasure-grounds, this place is now a small museum in the midst of a beautiful park. In the museum is a good collection of curiosities; and, scattered throughout the grounds, are many curious birds and animals. Aviaries, picture-galleries, conservatories, and zoological inclosures give variety to the scene, and, in pleasant weather, a most enjoyable day can be spent here among the trees, or inspecting the curiosities of the place. San Francisco has no public park as yet, and this result of the enterprise of a private citizen is the only substitute for what the city should have.

THE CITY OF SAN FRANCISCO.

Not much can be offered the stranger in the way of objects of architectural taste and skill in San Francisco. The city is now (1870) gradually improving, and, although its general appearance is not noble, there are a few public buildings which exhibit considerable artistic merit, and are costly enough to present a better appearance than they do. Art is yet young in San Francisco, and the only boast of its citizens is that they have done so much in so short a time. It is a perpetually recurring theme of gratulation that the city has so much to be proud of, and that its triumphs are so great—for San Francisco.

Among the most prominent public buildings may be mentioned the following, which are costly and attractive in appearance: the Grand Hotel, corner of Market and New Montgomery streets; the Mercantile Library Building, an elegant structure, opposite the Cosmopolitan Hotel, on Bush Street; the California Theatre,

SAN FRANCISCO INDUSTRIAL SCHOOL.

with an unpretending exterior, but with an admirably arranged and handsome interior and stage; the Bank of California, with probably the most artistically designed exterior of any building in the State, on the corner of California and Sansome streets; the building of the Young Men's Christian Association, on Sutter Street, above Kearney; this structure, like the bank building, is of an easily-worked and agreeably-tinted stone which is quarried from Angel Island, in the bay of San Francisco. To these might be added one or two handsome private residences, most of which, with the best churches, however, are more noticeable for elegantly-finished and furnished interiors than for any architectural beauty which would command the eye of the passer-by. There are several public institutions to which a visit would be profitable; and though they do not differ much from similar institutions elsewhere, the Protestant Orphan Asylum, the Industrial School, and several other such places are evidences of liberality, beneficence, and care for the needy and unfortunate.

VIEWS FROM THE BAY OF SAN FRANCISCO.

An excursion on the bay is one of the pleasures which a tourist ought to secure by all means, if possible. If no other way presents itself, a trip can be made on the government steamers which ply among the fortifications of the harbor. Of these public works, Fort Point is the first which attracts the notice of the voyager who enters the Golden Gate. The fort is of brick and commands the narrow entrance to the bay and harbor; its battery is formidable, but the changes which have been made in modern enginery render its brick walls any thing but impregnable. This point was first occupied by the Americans in March, 1847, when it was taken possession of by Major Hardie, of Colonel Stevenson's regiment. Here was a small battery which had been left by the Mexicans, and here was begun in 1854, the present structure, the frowning walls of which are faced by the rocky galleries of Lime Point, just across the Gate, where formidable cannon virtually sweep the entire entrance of the Golden Gate.

The light-house, adjoining the fort, can be seen for from ten to twelve miles, and is an important addition to the mercantile interests of California, although we regret to say the lantern, known as the "Fresnel Light," is only of the fifth order, and is the smallest on the coast; it is fifty-two feet above sea level. Two men are employed to attend it. Connected with this is a fog bell, weighing one thousand one hundred pounds, and worked by machinery, that strikes every ten seconds for five taps—then has an intermission of thirty-four seconds, and recommences the ten-second strike. This is kept constantly running during foggy weather.

On the same side of the harbor (the southern) as Fort Point, is the Presidio, once the place of official residence of the Spanish and Mexican commandante, and the rendezvous of the small

10

military force which was kept here. The old adobe buildings have long since disappeared, and in their place is quite a compact village of soldiers' barracks, officers' houses, mess-rooms, store-houses, etc., the whole being situated on a military reservation which stretches down to and incloses Fort Point. The number

VIEW OF THE PRESIDIO.

of troops kept here varies constantly, but the majority of those stationed in the harbor are at Camp Reynolds and the other posts on Angel Island, one of the fortified islands in the northwestern part of the bay, near Raccoon Straits; and south of this is Yerba Buena, or Goat Island, also a government reservation and military post. In the centre of that part of the bay nearest San Francisco is the island of Alcatraz (known in the government documents as Alcatraces), on which is an immense fortification, a miniature Gibraltar. The island is well nigh inaccessible, save at a single point, and the defensive and offensive works on the island, which is a mass of precipitous rock, are very complete in their design and finish.

VIEWS FROM TELEGRAPH HILL.

From Telegraph Hill, one of the most northerly of the many eminences on which San Francisco is built, one can secure the best

view of the city and bay anywhere to be found.   There is actually
no single point from which a full general view of San Francisco can
be obtained, situated as it is among the hills and straggling off
into the more level spaces which form the southern base of the
promontory.   But the most correct idea of the shape of the magnificent bay, its extent, and the position of the city is had after a
view of the wonderful panorama which is seen from the top of
Telegraph Hill.

Seaward, one looks through the Gate upon the sky line of the
ocean ; turning northward, is the range of hills which culminates
in Mount Tamal Pais ; nearer, in the same direction, is Fort Alcatraz, and, still turning northward, one sees the approaches to
Carquinez Straits, the gateway of the Sacramento and San Joaquin
rivers ; eastward, as the observer turns, are the Contra Costa hills,
brown and purple in the dry months, or gold and green in the
early spring ; due eastward is Oakland, dotting the plain and
creeping up the slopes beyond, above which rises the rounded
peak of Mount Diablo ; and southward, where the blue waters of
the land-locked bay seem to stretch interminably, are the hills
which encircle the ancient mission of San José, and still beyond
are the snowy peaks of the Coast Range.   It is a noble view, and
well worth the climb it costs.

EXCURSION TO TAMAL PAIS.

A pleasant excursion may be made to the summit of Tamal Pais,
a peak of the broken Coast Range, in Marin county, on the blunt
peninsula which is washed by the Pacific on the outer side and
the waters of the bay within.   Mount Tamal Pais is 2,597 feet high,
and from its summit a very extensive panorama of ocean, bay,
forest, and hill is seen.   Good trails lead up to the top of the
mountain from San Rafael, which town is reached by steamer
from San Francisco, though a longer but more picturesque route
from Saucelito, also reached by steamboat, is often used by tourists.
On a clear day, the view from the peak of Tamal Pais is extensive
and striking ; and even when the fogs are rolling in, the observer
will obtain some most singular and remarkable effects of light and

shade, the rolling wreaths of cloud, the broken sunlight, and the fleecy curtain of fog which shuts down over sea and mountain range, forming a moving panorama, constantly changing and most fascinating. A trip to Tamal Pais, though somewhat fatiguing, certainly includes some of the most novel sights around San Francisco.

CHAPTER X.

THE CALIFORNIA GEYSERS.

SAILING FROM THE WHARF.

S the fine little steamer "Rambler" was sounding her last whistle, we received a parting injunction—writes an esteemed acquaintance*- from friends on the Broadway street wharf, San Francisco, "to keep well aft," and stepped on board.

It was one of the chilliest, dreariest, most disagreeable of San Francisco's summer mornings. A dense fog, fresh from the great factory out on the Pacific, was roll-

THE WITCHES' CAULDRON.

Sketched from nature by George Tirrell.

* Mr. George Tirrell, designer and painter of the Panorama of California.

ing in over the hills at the back of the city, and hurrying across the bay before a stiff north-west wind. The waves, as they rolled along the sides of the shipping, or splashed among the piles, seemed to be playing a most melancholy march, to which the great army of fog-clouds moved across the cheerless water, and their commanding officer—the wind—seemed to be continually saying "forward," as it whistled through the rigging of the ships.

The individual who is always just too late, made his appearance, as usual, as the steamer's fasts were cast off, and her wheels commenced their lively though monotonous ditty in the water.

Two or three Whitehall boatmen, who were lying off the wharf, evidently expecting such a "fare," gave their lazily playing skulls a vigorous pull, which sent their beautiful little craft darting into the wharf. The boy with the basket of oranges hastened to offer the would-be-traveller "three for two bits," by way of consolation, and as he slowly proceeded up the dock again, the other boy with the papers and magazines called his attention to the last "Harper's," or "Overland Monthly."

The ten thousand voices of the city became blended into a continuous roar, as we glided out into the stream; the long drawn "go-o-o ahead," or "hi-i-gh," of the stevedores at their work, discharging the stately clippers, being about the only intelligible sounds to be distinguished above the mass.

CROSSING THE BAY.

Soon the outermost ship, on board of which a disconsolate looking "jolly tar" was riding down one of the head stays, giving it a "lick" of tar as he went, was passed, and we struck the strong current of wind which was blowing in at the Golden Gate (carelessly left open, as usual). The young giant of a city had become swallowed up in the gloom of the fog, and its thousands of busy people ceased to exist, except in our imaginations. After passing Angel Island, the fog began to lift; we were approaching the edge of the bank; and soon the sun appeared, hard at work at his apparently hopeless task of devouring the intruding fog, which had dared to interpose its cold billows between him and the bay, upon which he loves to shine.

The course of the boat was along the western side of Pablo Bay, close enough to the shore to give the passengers a fine view of it, as well as of the inland country, and the more distant mountains of the coast range. Large masses of misty clouds, which had become detached from the main fog bank, still partially obscured the sunlight, casting enormous shadows along the hill sides and across the plains, heightening, by contrast, the golden tinge of the wild oats, and giving additional beauty to the varied tints of the cultivated fields. Beyond, *Tamal Pais*, and other and lesser peaks of the Coast Range, piled their wealth of purple light and misty shadows, against the brightness of the western sky.

I wonder that our artists, in their search for the picturesque, have overlooked the splendid scene which Tamal Pais and the adjacent mountains present from the vicinity of Red Rock, or from the eastern shore of the straits. It is certainly one of the most picturesque scenes anywhere in the vicinity of San Francisco, especially toward sunset, when the long streaks of sunlight come streaming down the ravines, piercing with their golden light the hazy mystery which envelops the mountains, and brilliantly illuminating the intervening plains and hill-sides. From the familiarity of the view, a good picture would, without doubt, be much sought after.

NAVIGATION OF PETALUMA CREEK.

The seamanship of the pilot was much exercised while navigating the "Rambler" up Petaluma Creek. The creek is merely a long, narrow, ditch-like indentation, which makes up into the flat tule plains at the northern side of Pablo Bay, and into which the tide ebbs and flows. Its course very much resembles the track of a man who has spent half an hour hunting for a lost pocket-book in a field. If, after gazing awhile at the creek, the eye should be suddenly turned to a ram's horn or a manzanita stick, the latter would appear perfectly straight, by comparison. First we go toward the north star awhile, then we come to a short bend where an immense amount of backing, and stopping, and going ahead occurs, which all results in running the boat hard and fast ashore. Then the pilot, perspiring freely from his violent exertions at the wheel, thrusts his head out of the window, and, after taking a survey of the state of affairs, sets himself to ringing the signal bells again. Then the crew get out a long pole, and planting one end in the bank, apply their united strength to the other. No movement! Then the captain heroically rushes ashore in the mud and tules, and calls for volunteers to help him push. Human

strength and steam triumph in the end, and the "Rambler," with one side all besmeared with mud, goes paddling off toward Cape Horn. After progressing a short distance in this direction, another bend is reached, when more superhuman exertion on the part of the pilot ensues, and plump we go ashore again. Then the captain gives utterance to a vigorous exclamation (but as the expletive does no good, it is hardly necessary to repeat it here), and then he jumps into the mud again. Half the passengers follow suit, the crew go through with their pole exercise, pilot plays another tune on the bells, engineer gets bothered, and finally off we start in the direction of Japan, leaving the captain and his shore party standing in the mud. Upon backing up for them to get on board, the boat becomes fast again. This is a fair specimen of the navigation of Petaluma Creek above the city (of one house), called the "Haystack."

Before reaching Petaluma, we met a little steamer coming down with a load of wood. She resembled an immense pile of wood with a smoke-stack in the centre, floating down the stream, and appeared to take up the whole width of the creek, when our passengers began to wonder how we were to get by. It was a tight fit. There was not room enough left between the two boats to insert this sheet of paper. The "Rambler" puffed, and from the depths of the wood pile was heard a sort of wheezing, as if half a dozen people with bad colds were down there somewhere, all trying to cough at once, and couldn't. The captain gave utterance to a few more expletives, as the rough ends of the wood defaced the new paint on our boat; but the skipper of the wood-pile only laughed; yet, as the "Rambler," in passing, scraped off two or three cords of his cargo, it then became our turn to laugh.

PETALUMA, AND THE RUSSIAN RIVER VALLEY.

Petaluma was reached at last, and the passengers for Healdsburg found a stage in waiting. Jumping in, we were soon whizzing across the plains behind a couple of fine colts. The road lay directly up the Petaluma and Russian River Valleys. Past the ranches—along the sides of interminable fields of corn and grain—through the splendid park-like groves—sometimes across the open plain, at others winding around the base of the hills, which make up from the eastern side of the valley.

Santa Rosa was reached by sunset. Our arrival was hailed by the ringing of a great number and variety of bells. How singular it is that the arrival of a stage-coach in a country town always sets the dinner-bells to ringing, especially if the occurrence happens about meal time.

By the time supper was despatched, and a pair of sober old

stagers put to in the place of our frisky young colts, the moon had risen over the mountains, and was flooding the valley with her glorious sheen, tipping the fine old oaks with a silvery fringe of light, and laying their solemn shadows along the grass and across the road. A pleasant ride of two hours carried us to the end of our first day's journey, Healdsburg.

On the following morning, we were recommended to apply at the stable opposite the hotel for horses. Having selected one warranted not to kick up nor stand on his hind legs, nor jump stiff-legged, nor play any other pranks, he was saddled and bridled at once. Our portfolio (which, for want of a better covering, was carried in an old barley sack) was slung on one side, and our wardrobe depended at the other. A whip was added to complete the outfit, accompanied by the observation that as "Old Pete" was apt to "soger," "we might find it useful."

Then the stable man attempted to describe the road to Ray's Ranche. First, we should come to a bridge; a mile beyond that, see a house, to which we were to pay no attention, but look out for a haystack. Having found the haystack, we were to turn to the left, and would soon come to a long lane, that would lead us to another house, where we were either to turn to the right, or keep straight ahead, he had forgotten which. At this point of the description, a bystander interposed, saying that we must turn to the left; upon this, an argument sprung up between the two, which nearly led to a fight.

Finding that there was not much information to be elicited from those witnesses, "Old Pete" received a touch and started, with our head buzzing with right and left hand roads, while a regiment of ranches, lanes, and haystacks, seemed to be a "bobbing round" just ahead of the horse's nose. We found the bridge, and saw the house, to which we were to pay no attention; there was no need of looking out for *a* haystack, for a dozen were in sight; so, selecting the biggest one, we turned to the left, according to the chart.

We rode along about a mile, and came to a fence which barred any further progress in that direction; then kept along the fence until we came to a lane which took us to a pair of bars. Let down the obstruction, traversed another lane, and at the end of it found ourselves in somebody's dooryard. It was evident that we had taken the wrong road.

We now obtained fresh directions at the farm-house, but as three or four attempted at the same time to tell us the way—all talking at once, and each insisting upon his favorite route so that we speedily became mixed up again with another labyrinth of fences, lanes, and haystacks—we began to doubt the existence of such a place as "Ray's Ranche." It seemed forever retreating as we advanced, like the mythical crock of gold, buried at the foot of a rainbow, which we remembered starting in search of once, when a youngster.

But the ranche was found at last, and a very fine one it is, too. The house is situated a little way up in the foot-hills, and commands a splendid view of Russian River Valley, the Coast Range, Mount St. Helens, etc. The ranche itself, garden, orchards, and fields of wheat and corn, is situated in a valley, just below the house, which makes up between the steep mountain sides. A

RAY'S RANCHE AND RUSSIAN RIVER VALLEY.

brook winds through the whole length of the little valley, affording capital facilities for irrigation.

We had the good luck here to fall in with Mr. G——, one of

the proprietors of the Geysers, who was also on the way up. From the accounts which have been published, we expected to find the road from here a rough one. But it is nothing of the sort. It is a very good mountain trail, wide enough for a wagon to pass along its whole length. Buggies have been clear through, and could go again, were a few days' work to be expended upon the trail. It is quite steep, in many places, as a matter of course; but from the fact that Mr. G—— (who was mounted upon a young colt, that had never before been ridden, and had simply a piece of rope by way of bridle) *trotted* down most of the declivities, it may be inferred that the grade is not so very steep.

The first three or four miles beyond Ray's, to the summit of the first ridge, is all up hill; nearly 1,700 feet in altitude being gained in that distance, or 2,317 feet above the level of the sea, Ray's being 617.

VIEW FROM GODWIN'S PEAK.

There are few places in all California where a more magnificent view can be obtained, than the one seen from this ridge. The whole valley of Russian River lies like a map at your feet, extending from the south-east and south, where it joins Petaluma Valley, clear round to the north-west. The course of the river can be traced for miles, far away, alternately sweeping its great curves of rippling silver out into the opening plain, or disappearing behind the dark masses of timber. From one end of the valley to the other, the golden yellow of the plain is diversified by the darker tints of the noble oaks. In some places they stand in great crowds; then an open space will occur, with perhaps a few scattered trees, which serve to conduct the eye to where a long line of them appears, like an army drawn up for review, with a few single trees in front by way of officers; and in the rear a confused crowd of stragglers to represent the baggage train and camp followers. Here and there, among the oaks, the vivid green foliage and bright red stems of the graceful madrone, and on the banks of the river can be seen the silvery willows and the dusky sycamores.

The beauty of the plain is still more enhanced by the numerous ranches, with their widely extending fields of ripe grain and verdant corn.

Beyond the valley is the long extending line of the Coast Mountains. The slanting rays of the declining sun were overspreading the mysterious blue and purple of their shadowy sides with a glorious golden haze, through whose gauzy splendor could be traced the summits only of the different ranges—towering one above the other, each succeeding fainter than the last, until the indescribably fine outline of the highest peaks, but one remove, in color, from the sky itself, bounded the prospect.

Toward the south-east, we could see Mount St. Helen's, and the upper part of Napa Valley. St. Helen's is certainly the most beautiful mountain in California. It is far from being as lofty as its more pretentious brethren of the Sierra Nevada, and by the side of the great Shasta Butte it would be dwarfed to a molehill; but its chaste and graceful outline is the very ideal of mountain form. There is said to be a copper plate, bearing an inscription, on the summit of this mountain, placed there by the Russians many years ago.

Away off, toward the south, we could discern that same old fog, still resting, like a huge incubus, upon San Francisco bay. Its fleecy billows were constantly in motion—now obscuring, now revealing the summits of different peaks, which rose like islands out of the sea of clouds. Above, and far beyond the fog, the view terminated with the long, level line of the blue Pacific, sixty or seventy miles distant.

From the point where we have stopped to take this extended view (too much extended, on paper, perhaps the reader will think), the horses climbed slowly up the steep ascent, leading to a plateau, on the northern side of a mountain, which has received no less than three different names. As it is a difficult matter, among so many titles, to fix upon the proper one, we will enumerate them all, and the reader can take his choice. The mountain was first called "Godwin's Peak," in honor of—there, G——, the cat's out of the bag! your name has got into print, in spite of our endeavors to keep it out. With characteristic modesty, Mr.

G—— declined the honor which the name conferred upon him, and it was changed by somebody or other to "Geyser Peak;" but, for some unknown reason, this name also failed to stick, and somebody else came along and called it "Sulphur Peak." Both the latter names are inappropriate, for there are no Geysers nor no sulphur within five miles of the mountain. G., we are afraid you will have to endure your honors, and stand godfather to it.

The "Peak" rises to the height of three thousand four hundred and seventy-one feet above the level of the sea, and its sides are covered, clear to the summit, with a thick growth of tangled chaparal. From here, the trail runs along the narrow ridge of the mountains, forming the divide between "Sulphur Creek" (an odious name for a beautiful trout stream) and Pluton River. The ridge is called the "Hog's Back"—still another name, as inappropriate as it is homely. The ridge much more resembles the back of a horse which has just crossed the plains, or has dieted for some time on shavings, than that of a plump porker. From the end of this ridge the trail is quite level, as far as the top of the hill, which pitches sharply down to the river, and at the foot of which the Geysers are situated.

ARRIVAL AT THE GEYSERS.

When about two-thirds of the way down the hill, the rushing noise of the escaping steam of the Great Geyser can be heard; but, unless the stranger's attention was called to it, he would mistake the sound for the roaring of the river. About this time, too, is recognized the sulphurous smell with which the air is impregnated.

Just as the traveller begins seriously to think that the hill has no bottom, the white gable end of the hotel, looking strangely out of place among its wild surroundings, comes unexpectedly into sight.

Upon awakening, on the following morning, it was a difficult matter to convince ourselves that we had not been transported, while asleep, to the close vicinity of some of the wharves in San Francisco, there was such a *powerful* smell of what seemed to be

GEYSER SPRINGS HOTEL.

ancient dock mud. It was the sulphur. The smell is a trifle unpleasant at first, but one soon becomes accustomed to it, and rather
likes it than otherwise.

The view of the Geysers, from the hotel, is a very striking one,
more especially in the morning, when the steam can be plainly
seen, issuing from the earth in a hundred different places; the
numerous columns uniting at some distance above the earth, and
forming an immense cloud, which overhangs the whole cañon.

As the sun advances above the hills, this cloud is speedily
" eaten up," and the different columns of steam, with the exception of those from the Steamboat Geyser, the Witches' Cauldron,
and a few others, become invisible, being evaporated as fast as
they issue from the ground.

Breakfast disposed of, Mr. G. kindly offered to conduct us to the different springs. The trail descends abruptly from the house, among the tangled undergrowth of the steep mountain side, to the river, some ninety feet below. We passed on the way the long row of bathing-houses, the water for which is conveyed across the river in a lead pipe, from a hot sulphur spring on the opposite side.

The unearthly-looking cañon, in which most of the springs are situated, makes up into the mountains directly from the river. A small stream of water, which rises at the head of the cañon, flows through its whole length. The stream is pure and cold at its source, but gradually becomes heated, and its purity sadly sullied, as it receives the waters of the numerous springs along its banks.

GEYSER CAÑON.

Hot springs and cold springs; white, red, and black sulphur springs; iron, soda, and boiling alum springs; and the deuce only knows what other kind of springs, all pour their medicated waters into the little stream, until its once pure and limpid water—like a human patient made sick by over-doctoring—becomes pale, and has a wheyish, sickly, unnatural look, as it feverishly tosses and tumbles over its rocky bed.

A short distance up the cañon there is a deep, shady pool, which receives the united waters of all the springs above it. By the time the stream reaches here, its medicated waters become cooled to the temperature of a warm summer day, and the basin forms, perhaps, the most luxurious bath to be found in the world.

A few feet from this, there is a warm alum and iron spring, whose water is more thoroughly impregnated than any of the others.

PROSERPINE'S GROTTO.

A little way further up is "Proserpine's Grotto," an enchanting retreat among the wild rocks, completely surrounded and enclosed by the fantastic roots and twisted branches of the bay trees, and

17

roofed over by their wide-spreading foliage.   Glimpses of the narrow gorge above, with its numerous cascades, can be obtained through the openings of the trees ; the whole forming one of the finest " little bits," as an artist would call it, to be found in the country.

As we proceeded up the cañon the springs became more numerous.   They were bubbling and boiling in every direction.   We hardly dared to move for fear of putting our feet into a spring of boiling alum, or red sulphur, or some other infernal concoction. The water of the stream, too, was now scalding hot, and the rocks, and the crumbling, porous earth, were nearly as hot as the water. We took good care to literally "follow in the footsteps of our illustrious predecessor," as he hopped about from boulder to boulder, or rambled along in (as we thought) dangerous proximity to the boiling waters.   Every moment he would pick up a handful of magnesia, or alum, or sulphur, or tartaric acid, or Epsom salts, or some other nasty stuff, plenty of which encrusted all the rocks and earth in the vicinity, and invite us to taste them.   From frequent nibblings at the different deposits, our mouths became so puckered up, that all taste was lost for any thing else.

In addition to these strange and unnatural sights, the ear was saluted by a great variety of startling sounds.   Every spring had a voice.   Some hissed and sputtered like water poured upon red hot iron ; others reminded one of the singing of a tea-kettle, or the purring of a cat ; and others seethed and bubbled like so many cauldrons of boiling oil.   One sounded precisely like the machinery of a grist mill in motion (it is called "The Devil's Grist Mill"), and another like the propeller of a steamer.

High above all these sounds was the loud roaring of the great "Steamboat Geyser."*   The steam of this Geyser issues with great force from a hole about two feet in diameter, and it is so heated as to be invisible until it has risen to some height from the

* This Geyser is shown in the view of "Geyser Cañon."   It is the upper large column of steam on the left side of the cañon ; the one below it, and nearer the spectator, is the "Witches' Cauldron."   The foreground of the view is occupied by the "Mountain of Fire," from which the steam issues by a hundred different apertures.

ground. It is highly dangerous to approach very close to it unless there is sufficient wind to blow the steam aside.

But the most startling of all the various sounds was a continuous subterranean roar, similar to that which precedes an earthquake.

We must confess, that when in the midst of all these horrible sights and sounds, we felt very much like suggesting to G—— the propriety of returning, but a fresh handful of Epsom salts and alum, mixed, stopped our mouths, and by the time we had ceased sputtering over the puckerish compound, the "Witches' Cauldron" was reached. (See vignette.) This is a horrible place. "Mind how you step here," said G——, as we approached it; and, with the utmost caution, we placed our *tens* in his tracks, that is, as much of them as we could get in.

The cauldron is a hole, sunk like a well in the precipitous side of the mountain, and is of unknown depth. It is filled to the brim with something that looks very much like burnt cork and water (we believe the principal ingredient is black sulphur). This liquid blackness is in constant motion, bubbling and surging from side to side, and throwing up its boiling spray to the height of three or four feet. Its vapor deposits a black sediment on all the rocks in its vicinity.

There are a great many other springs—some two hundred in number—of every gradation of temperature, from boiling hot to icy cold, and impregnated with all sorts of mineral and chemical compounds; frequently the two extremes of heat and cold are found within a few inches of each other. But as all the other springs present nearly the same characteristics as most of those already referred to, it would be but a tedious repetition to attempt to describe more. They are all wonderful. The ordinary observer can only look at them, and wonder that such things exist; but to the scientific man, one capable of divining the mysterious cause of their action, the study of them must be an exquisite delight.

It is worth the traveller's while to climb the mountains on the north side of the Pluton, for the fine view which their summits afford on every hand; toward the north, a part of Clear Lake can be seen, some fifteen miles distant. But, perhaps, the scene which

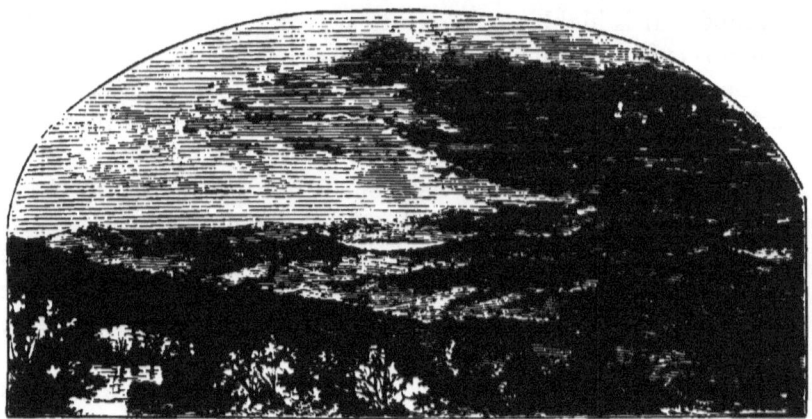

CLEAR LAKE, FROM THE RIDGE NEAR THE GEYSERS.

would delight a lover of nature most, can be obtained by rising early and walking back half a mile upon the trail which descends to the hotel. It is to see the gorgeous tints of the eastern sky, as the sun comes climbing up behind the distant mountains, and afterward to watch his long slanting rays in the illuminated mist, as they come streaming down the cañon of the Pluton, flashing on the water in dots and splashes of dazzling light, and tipping the rich shadows of the closely-woven foliage with a fringe of gold.

Some people have said that California scenery is monotonous, that her mountains are all alike, and that her skies repeat each other from day to day. Believe them not, ye distant readers, to whom, as yet, our glorious California is an unknown land. The monotony is in their own narrow, unappreciative souls, not in our grand mountains, towering, ridge upon ridge, until the long line of the furthest peaks becomes blended with the dreamy haze that loves to linger round their summits. And the gorgeous glow of our sunrises, or the still more gorgeous green and orange, and gold and crimson, of our sunsets, reflect their heavenly hues upon dull eyes, indeed when they can see no beauty in them.

The route most generally travelled, from San Francisco to the Geysers, is as follows: At 8 o'clock A. M., or at 3:30 P. M., take steamer at the Vallejo Street wharf for Vallejo—distance twenty-five miles—time about two hours—fare, $1. Thence by the Napa Valley Railroad to Calistoga—distance forty-four miles—time two hours—fare, $2.50. Thence by Foss's stage, *via* the new road, to the Geysers—distance twenty-eight miles—time about five and a half hours—fare, $6.

The better time to leave San Francisco would be at 3:30 P. M., arriving at Calistoga at about 7:30 P. M. Leave there about 7:30 A. M. the following morning, after breakfast, and arrive at the Geysers about 1 o'clock P. M. As the sun "eats up" the steam from the springs during the heat of the day, the best time to see them is after a good rest, and when the shadows of evening have filled Geyser Cañon; or, early in the morning, before sunrise. When leaving the Geysers on the return trip, it is a good plan to have a cup of coffee before starting, and, taking the old road, make Foss'—and a good breakfast—at 9 A. M., Calistoga about 12 M., and San Francisco about 4 P. M.

The beautiful and singular scenery; the different methods of travel—by steamboat, by railroad, and by stage-coach; and the world-renowned driving of Foss';—are all recorded in the note-book of memory kept by every visitor to "The Geysers."

THE RIFFLE-BOX WATERFALL, DEER CREEK.

CHAPTER XI.

THE RIFFLE-BOX WATERFALL.

"Who lives to nature rarely can be poor."
YOUNG.

THIS beautifully picturesque and romantic waterfall is situated on Deer Creek, about nine miles below the large and populous mining town of Nevada. To those who are unacquainted with the technicalities of mining, the meaning of the above name, when applied to a waterfall, may be somewhat of a mystery. To make it plain to every reader, perhaps it will not be uninteresting to describe one of the implements of mining called the *Long Tom*. This ancient, and now almost obsolete mining tool, if such it may be called, consists of a long flatish box or sluice, from ten to fifty feet in length, and from one foot to three feet in width, and open at the top; into this the dirt is thrown, and through it a stream of water is turned. The back end being elevated, gives sufficient fall for the water to pass down with considerable force. At the lower end there is a plate of perforated iron, called, a *Tom Iron*, through which the water, dirt, and gold pass into a "riffle-box" underneath; where the gold is saved. This box has narrow strips of wood across the bottom; and when one end is elevated the water makes a fall, or riffle. Hence, from the great resemblance in the shape of the above falls to a riffle-box, comes the name of Riffle-Box Falls. During the winter season, when the water rushes over with an impetuous sweep, it is remarkably wild and tumultuous.

In 1852, a company was formed to test the richness of this great riffle-box of nature; and to accomplish which a tunnel was cut through a hill of solid rock, about three hundred feet in length, at a cost of twenty thousand dollars. Through this tunnel the waters of the creek were turned, and by which the falls were drained.

The water had worn deep holes in the bed of the creek, and to pump these dry, seven thousand dollars more were expended in machinery, &c. When this was accomplished and the "box" was made dry, *the whole of the gold that was taken out was only about two hundred dollars.*

This is one of the many enterprises into which the Californian enters, and where his money and time—frequently all that he possesses—are embarked, in a single venture, and he thrown penniless upon his own energies to begin life again—as he terms it. This will give friends in the East at least, one idea *why* the miner frequently remains from dear friends and home so long, when his hopes of returning were built upon the success of his undertaking —and which too often proves a complete failure.

CHAPTER XII.

LAKE TAHOE.

LAKE TAHOE.
Sketched from nature, by George H. Goddard.

UNTIL the discovery of the rich silver mines of Washoe, this remarkably beautiful lake was known only to the few. It is true
that the footsteps of the old mountaineer, the early explorer, and
the pioneer emigrant, trod its silent shores at a very early day;
and in later years the hardy prospector, in search of Gold Lake,
and other fabulous localities of supposed wealth, looked upon the
burnished waters, and cloud-draped crags that encompass this
beautiful sheet, with charmed eyes. But it remained for the liv-

ing tide of population that poured into that region over the sierras, in search of the precious ores, during the excitement of 1860,
and subsequently, to make this scene become extensively familiar;
inasmuch as a magnificent view of Lake Tahoe can be obtained,
on reaching the summits of the surrounding mountains, from nearly every northern trail into Washoe, especially that from Placer-
ville, without even turning aside from the road.

It may not be generally known, that, at the heads of nearly
every stream originating among the snows of the Sierra Nevada,
there are extensive lakes, or fertile valleys, from the Siskiyou
mountains to Fort Yuma. To these retreats the stock raisers of
the midland counties take their droves, when the feed in the Sacramento and San Joaquin valleys becomes scant, or dried up during the dry months of summer.

Since the excitement before alluded to, numerous companies
of prospectors have gone out in the hope of finding rich veins of
silver-bearing quartz; and, in addition to discovering the valuable
mines of Mono, Esmeralda, and others equally rich, they have returned with ever-to-be-remembered mind-pictures of those scenes
of beauty and of grandeur, that lie slumbering in lofty solitude
among the rocks and peaks and stunted pines of this great mountain chain.

During the year 1855, Mr. George H. Goddard, civil engineer,
in charge of the state wagon-road survey, visited this spot, and
favored us with the following sketch:

"This beautiful lake is situated in a valley of the Sierra Nevada,
at the eastern base of the central ridge, a few miles north of the
main road of travel to Carson Valley. It lies at an elevation of
some 5,800 feet above the level of the sea, and about 1,500 feet
above Carson Valley, from which it is divided by a mountain ridge
three to four miles across.

"The southern shores of this lake were explored during the state
wagon-road survey of 1855, and its extreme southern latitude determined at 38° 57'. The 120th meridian of west longitude divides
the lake pretty equally, giving its western shore to California and
its eastern to Utah. Its northern extremity is only known by re-

port, which is still so contradictory that the length of the lake cannot be set down with any thing like accuracy. It can hardly exceed, however, twenty miles in length by about six in breadth;
notwithstanding, it has been called forty, and even sixty miles
long.

"The surrounding mountains rise from one to three, and, perhaps, in some cases, four thousand feet above the surface of the
lake. They are principally composed of friable white granite,
so water-worn that, although they are rough, and often covered
with rocks and boulders, yet they show no cliffs or precipices.
Their bases, of granite sand, rise in majestic curves from the plain
of the valley to their steeper flanks. Many of the smaller hills
are but high heaps of boulders, the stony skeletons decaying *in
situ*, half buried in their granite *debris*. The shores of the lake,
at least of its southern coast, are entirely formed of granite sand;
not a pebble is there to mar its perfect smoothness.

"A dense pine-forest extends from the water's edge to the summits of the surrounding mountains, except in some points where a
peak of more than ordinary elevation rears its bald head above
the waving forest. An extensive swampy flat lies on its southern
shore, through which the Upper Truckee slowly meanders, gathering up, in its tortuous course, all the streams which flow from the
south or south-east. The deep blue of the waters indicates a considerable depth to the lake. The water is perfectly fresh. The
lake well stocked with salmon and trout. It is resorted to at certain seasons by the neighboring Indians, for fishing.

"Although lying so near the main road of travel, little has been
known of this lake until quite a recent period. There is no doubt
this is the lake of which the Indians informed Colonel Fremont,
when encamped at Pyramid Lake, at the mouth of the Salmon-
Trout or Truckee river, and which he thus relates, under date of
January 15, 1844: 'They made on the ground a drawing of the
river, which they represented as issuing from another lake in the
mountains, three or four days distant, in a direction a little west
of south; beyond which they drew a mountain, and farther still
two rivers, on one of which they told us that people like ourselves

travelled.' How clear does this description read to us, now that we know the localities!

"Afterward, when crossing the mountains near Carson Pass, Colonel Fremont caught sight of this lake, but, deceived by the great altitude of the mountains to its east, and the apparent gap in the western ridge at Johnson Pass, he laid it down as being on the California side of the mountains, at the head of the south fork of the American River. In the map attached to Colonel Fremont's report, it is there called *Mountain Lake,* but in the general map of the explorations by Charles Preuss it is named *Lake Bompland.* In Wilkes's map, and others published about the period of the gold discovery, it bears the former name. When Colonel Johnson laid out his road across the mountains, the lake was passed unnoticed, except under the general term of Lake Valley. General Wynn's Indian expedition, or the emigrant relief train, first named it Lake Bigler, after our late governor. Under this name it was first depicted in its transmountain position in Eddy's state map, and thus the name has become established.*

"There is no lake in California which, for beauty and variety of scenery, is to be compared to Tahoe Lake; but it is not its beauty of situation alone that will attract us there. A geological interest is fastening upon it, for there we see what so many other of the great valleys of the sierra once were. The little stream of the Upper Truckee, though but of yesterday, has yet carried down its sandy deposits through ages, sufficient to form the five miles of valley flats, from the foot of the Johnson Pass to the present margin of the lake, and still the work progresses. The shallows at the mouth of the river are stretching across toward the first point on the eastern slope of the lake, and at the same time the water level of the lake is evidently subsiding."

---

* In 1862 the name of this lake was very properly changed to its present Indian one, of "Lake Tah'oe"—pronounced, however, by the Indians, Tah'oo—which means, "big water," and as such, it has since been known to every tourist.

ALABASTER CAVE, EL DORADO CO., CALIFORNIA.

THE PULPIT, IN THE ALABASTER CAVE.

CHAPTER XIII.

Whenever nature steps out of her usual course to make any thing very beautiful or very wonderful, it is not unreasonable to expect that men and women, generally, will be gratefully willing to go out of their way to see it. It is true that many men love money more than they love nature, others love nature more than money, and yet often feel too poor, almost, to gratify that love; others have become so much habituated to the same stool in the counting-house, the same old chair in the office, and the same familiar standing-place in the store, and the same spot in the workshop, mine, or field, that nothing short of an earthquake, or revolution, could induce them to turn aside from the well-worn highways of business habit, to see any thing beyond themselves and their business routine. In their eyes it is the Alpha and Omega of life, the beginning and end of all things, yea, life itself. Unfortunately, habit unfits them for any thing beyond the man-machine. The blue sky, the bright sunshine, the flower-carpeted earth, the foliage-clothed trees, the moss-grown caverns, the mighty hills, or the forest-formed harps, touched by the fingers of the wind, and playing their grand old anthems of praise, have an inviting and suggestive voice, that "man was made for enjoyment as well as duty —for happiness as well as business;" and the probability is apparent, that the godlike faculties bestowed upon him, enabling him to hold communion with the beautiful and the ennobling, the sublime or wonderful, would not have been, if man were not expected to be something loftier than a mere humdrum business machine.

Nature sometimes turns over some new and wonderful pages in her glorious old volume, and discovers to men such morsels as the groves of mammoth trees, the Yo-Semite Valley, the Geysers, the natural bridges, and caves; and, more recently, the Alabaster cave, of El Dorado county. On such occasions there are many persons who will find time to open their sight-seeing eyes, and take a glimpse, if only to say that they have seen them, lest they should be deemed behind the age, or out of the fashion; but there are others again, and their name is legion, who adore, yea almost worship, the beautiful, the grand, the astonishing; from the handful of soil, that gives out so many varieties of rare and fragrant flowers and lucious fruits, to the vast cathedral-formed arches and intricate draperies of stone, produced by chemical agencies and mystical combinations, in one or more of nature's great laboratories beneath the surface of the earth. With the latter class it is always a pleasure to be in company; as a pleasure shared is always doubled; besides, kindred spirits have a happy faculty of reproduction, denied to others.

THE DISCOVERY OF THE EL DORADO COUNTY CAVE.

A ledge of limestone rock, resembling marble in appearance, cropped out by the side of the El Dorado Valley turnpike road, which, after testing, was found to be capable of producing excellent lime. Early in the present year, Mr. William Gwynn employed a number of men to quarry this rock and build a kiln. To these works he gave the name of " Alabaster Lime Quarry and Kiln." On the 18th of April, 1860, two workmen, George S. Halterman and John Harris, were quarrying limestone from this ledge, when, upon the removal of a piece of rock, a dark aperture was visible, that was sufficiently enlarged to enable them to enter. A flood of light pouring in through the opening made, they proceeded inward some fifty feet. Before venturing further, they threw a stone forward, which falling into water, determined them to procure lights before advancing further.

At this juncture Mr. Gwynn, the owner, came up; and upon being informed of the discovery, sent for candles, to enable them to further prosecute their explorations. The result of these, after several hours spent, cannot be better described than in Mr. Gwynn's own language, in a letter dated April 19th, 1860, addressed to Mr. Holmes, a gentleman friend of his, residing in Sacramento City; and first published in the Sacramento *Bee*:

"Wonders will never cease. On yesterday, we, in·quarrying rock, made an opening to the most beautiful cave you ever beheld. On our first entrance, we descended about fifteen feet, gradually, to the centre of the room, which is one hundred by thirty feet. At the north end there is a most magnificent pulpit, in the Episcopal church style, that man ever has seen. It seems that it is, and should be called, the 'Holy of Holies.' It is completed with the most beautiful drapery of alabaster sterites, of all colors, varying from white to pink-red, overhanging the beholder. Immediately under the pulpit there is a beautiful lake of water, extending to an unknown distance. We thought this all, but, to our great admiration, on arriving at the centre of the first room, we saw an entrance to an inner chamber, still more splendid, two hundred by one hundred feet, with the most beautiful alabaster overhanging, in every possible shape of drapery. Here stands magnitude,·giving the instant impression of a power above man; grandeur that defies decay; antiquity that tells of ages unnumbered; beauty that the touch of time makes more beautiful; use exhaustless for the service of men; strength imperishable as the globe, the monument of eternity—the truest earthly emblem of that everlasting and unchangeable, irresistible Majesty, by whom, and för whom, all things were made."

As soon as this interesting announcement was noised abroad, hundreds of people flocked to see the newly discovered wonder, from all the surrounding mining settlements, so that within the first six days, it was visited by upwards of four hundred persons; many of whom, we regret to say, possessed a larger organ of acquisitiveness than of veneration, and laid Vandal hands on some of the most beautiful portions within reach, near the entrance. This determined the proprietor to close it, until arrangements could be made for its protection and systematic illumination; the better to see, and not to touch the specimens.

At this time, Mr. Gwynn leased the cave to Messrs. Smith & Halterman, who immediately began to prepare it for the reception of the public, by erecting baricades, platforms, &c.; and placing a large number of lamps at favorable points, for the better illumination and inspection of the different chambers.

The discovery being made in the spring, considerable water was standing in some of the deepest of the cavities; but signs were already visible of its recession, at the rate of nearly six inches per day; and in a few weeks it entirely disappeared, leaving the cave perfectly dry. This afforded opportunities for further explorations; when it was found that a more convenient entrance could be made, with but little labor, from an unimportant room within a few feet of the road. This was accordingly done, and this, in addition to its convenience, allows of the free circulation of pure air. Having thus given an historical sketch of the discovery, with other matters connected with its preservation and management, we shall now endeavor to take the reader with us, at least in imagination, while describing it and

SOME SCENES BY THE WAY.

As a majority of visitors will, most probably, be from San Francisco, it may not be amiss, with the reader's permission, to present a brief outline of some of the most interesting sights to be witnessed, from the deck of the steamboat, on our way up the Sacramento. A large portion of the route, from that great mercantile metropolis of the Pacific to the mouth of the San Joaquin, has been already illustrated and described in the first chapter of this work, to which we would again refer his attention.

On page twenty-nine, we have described the course of the Stockton boat as to the right; while that bound for Sacramento City sails straight forward, toward the west end of a large, low tule flat, lying between the San Joaquin and Sacramento, named Sherman's Island, and here we enter the Sacramento river. The Montezuma hills, seen on our right, and a few stunted trees on the left, are the only objects in the landscape to relieve the eye, by contrast with the low tule swamp, until we approach the new and flourishing little settlement of Rio Vista. "This town," writes Dr. C. A. Kirkpatrick, the obliging postmaster, "is situated about forty-five

SCENE AT THE LOWER JUNCTION OF THE MAIN SACRAMENTO RIVER, AND STEAMBOAT
SLOUGH.

miles below the city of Sacramento, and below the outlets of all
the large sloughs, or at least two of the largest, Steamboat and
Cache Creek sloughs—uniting with the main, or old Sacramento
river, just above this place; making the stream here about one-
third of a mile wide. The reader will see that, being upon the
main river, so near its outlet into Suisun Bay, not over twenty

18

NIGHT SCENE ON THE MAIN BRANCH OF THE SACRAMENTO RIVER.

miles, and so far from the mining region, there is a clearer and larger body of water than can be found anywhere else on the river. It is to this place that the salmon-fish now resort. Before taking the final plunge, they seem here to have turned at bay, and are eagerly caught in the following manner:

THE SALMON FISHERY ON THE SACRAMENTO.

"Nets are constructed of stout shoe-thread, first made into skeins, then twisted into a cord about the size of common twine, after the fashion of making ropes. It is then, with a wooden needle, man-ufactured into a web of open network, from 780 to 1200 feet, or 130 to 200 fathoms long, and 15 feet wide. On both sides of the net are small ropes, to which it is fastened. On the rope designa-ted for the upper side, are placed, at intervals of five or six feet, pieces of cork or light wood, for the purpose of buoys; while on the other line bits of lead are fastened, to sink the net in the water. Now attach to one end of the upper line a small buoy, painted any dark color which can be easily distinguished, and at the other end make fast a line fifteen or twenty feet long, for the fisherman to hold, while his net floats, and the net is complete.

SALMON FISHING, PAYING OUT THE SEINE.

"Whitehall boats are those most generally used in this branch of state industry; they are from nineteen to twenty-two feet in length of keel, and from four to five feet breadth of beam; this size and style being considered the best. Now, the next thing wanted, are two fearless men; one to manage the boat, and the other to cast the net. The net is then stowed in the after part of the boat, and every thing made ready for a *haul.*

"Being at what is called the head of the *drift,* one of the men takes his place in the stern of the boat, and, while the rower pulls across the stream, the net is thrown over the stern. Thus is formed a barrier, or network, almost the entire width of the stream, and to the depth of fifteen or twenty feet. The *drift* is the distance on the river which is passed after casting the net, which floats with the tide until it is drawn into the boat. This passage, and the drawing in of the net, completes the process of catching the salmon.

"In coming in contact with the net, the head of the fish passes far enough through the meshes, or openings, to allow the strong threads of the net to fall back of and under the gill, and thus they are unable to escape, and are effectually *caught in the net* and drawn into the boat.

HAULING IN THE SEINE.

"During the year 1852, there were probably as many fish found in that part of the Sacramento river before alluded to, as at any time

previous, and more than at any time since—two men with one
net and boat having caught as many as three hundred fish in the
course of one night; the night being the best time to take them,
on account of their being unable to see and avoid the net.

GROUP OF SALMON ON THE BANKS OF THE SACRAMENTO RIVER.

"The fish which are caught in the spring are much larger and
nicer than those caught during the summer months; the former
being really a bright *salmon-color*, and the texture of the flesh
firm and solid; while the latter, in appearance, might properly be
called salmon-color faded, and the flesh soft and unpalatable. This
difference is no doubt owing to the temperature and composition
of the water in which the fish may be sojourning; the cold, salt
sea water hardening and coloring the flesh, while the warm, fresh
river water tends to soften and bleach.

"They seem to be gregarious in their nature, travelling in herds, or, as the fishermen call it, "*schools*." They do not like a very cold climate, as is indicated by their not ascending the rivers on the northern coast, except in very limited numbers, until the month of July. In those streams where the current is very rapid, their rate of speed is supposed to be five or six miles an hour; but where the current is eddying and slow, not more than two miles an hour. It has also been ascertained that they will stop for two or three days in deep, still water; no doubt to rest and feed, as they choose places where food can be easily procured.

"There seems to be quite a difference in the size, flavor, and habits of the salmon found in the Sacramento, Columbia and Frazer rivers; those of the Sacramento being larger, more juicy, more oily, and brighter colored. They are, however, more abundant in the north, and about half the average weight—that of the the former being about fifteen pounds; although early in the spring some are caught in the north quite as large as any caught in the Sacramento, and weigh from fifty to sixty pounds.

"In the Gulf of Georgia and Bellingham Bay, and on the Columbia, Frazer and Lumna rivers, the salmon are taken by thousands; while we of the Sacramento only get them by hundreds. One boat, last season, on the Frazer river, in one month, caught 13,860. There is also one peculiarity with the fish of the north —every second or third year there are but few salmon in those waters, their places being taken by a fish called the *hone*, which come in great numbers, equal if not greater than the salmon. The two fish never come in any considerable numbers together.

"From facts obtained from the freight clerks of the C. S. N. Co.'s boats, we learn, that from the principal shipping port of the Sacramento river, Rio Vista, there is an average of 150 fish, or 2,250 pounds, sent each day to market, for five months of the year, making a total of 22,500 fish, or 337,500 pounds; the greater part of these are shipped, and used fresh in San Francisco. But this number forms but a small proportion of what are caught, the principal part being retained and salted, or smoked, or otherwise prepared for shipment to various parts of the world—many finding their way to Australia, and the islands of the Pacific, as well as to New York, and other domestic ports on the Atlantic seaboard."

THE HOG'S BACK.

About six miles above Rio Vista is the far-famed "Hog's Back." This is formed by the settling of the sediment which comes down from the rivers above, and is caused by a widening of the stream and a decrease in the fall of the river. It extends for about three hundred yards in length; and at the lowest stage of water is about five feet from the surface, and at the highest point eleven feet six inches. Being affected by the tides, and as they are exactly at the same point every two weeks, during the fall season of the year, for two or three days at each low tide, a detention of heavily freighted vessels, of from one to four hours, will then take place.

Persons when descending the river, as the steamboat generally leaves Sacramento City at two o'clock P. M., have an opportunity of knowing when they arrive at the "Hog's Back" by seeing the mast of a vessel with the lower cross-trees upon it, and sometimes a portion of her bulwarks. This vessel was named the Charleston, and was freighted principally with quartz machinery, a portion of which being for the Gold Hill Quartz Co., at Grass Valley, she had discharged, but, the owners of another and larger portion of it not being found, she was returning with it to San Francisco in October, 1857, but having struck upon this sand-bank, at a very low stage of the water, careened over, and was swamped. Several attempts have since been made to take out the machinery, but as yet it has defied them all, and being filled with sand, it will be a very difficult task for any one ever to set her afloat again, and the reward be but poor, inasmuch as it cannot be in any other than a spoiled condition, from rust and other causes.

STEAMBOAT SLOUGH.

A short distance above the Hog's Back we arrived at the junction of Sutter Slough with Steamboat Slough, and there enter the narrowest part of the stream. As this slough is deep and navigable, and moreover is about nine miles nearer for sailing through than by the main, or "old river," nearly all vessels upward bound take this route; while those on the downward trip (excepting steamboats) generally take the main river, inasmuch as the wind is more favorable for their return to San Francisco.

SCENE AT THE UPPER MAIN JUNCTION OF SACRAMENTO AND STEAMBOAT SLOUGHS.

As we pass through Steamboat Slough, we are impressed with the narrowness of the channel for such large vessels, the luxuriant foliage of the trees that adorn its banks, and the snug little cabins, nearly shut out from sight by wild vines and trees, that are seen at intervals on its margin. Indeed the scenery, as you steam up or down the river, is picturesque in no slight degree. Here and there, as you turn with the sudden windings of the stream, you come upon the little boats of fishermen, and sloops, with their sails furled like the folded wings of a sea-bird, waiting for the wind. The improvements of the husbandman are everywhere seen along the shore—cottages half hidden among the drooping branches of the sycamores, outhouses, haystacks, orchards, and gardens—with their product of squashes and cabbages piled in huge heaps; and here and there a school-house or church gives a cheerful domestic character to the scene. The landscape is diversified by the gnarled oaks, with vines clinging about them for support, and their branches covered with dark masses of mistletoe.

Sailing along, probably we may see a small stern-wheel steam-scow, puffing away like some odd-shaped and outlandish leviathan, named the "Gipsy." She plies between the various ranches and gardens on the river and Sacramento City, taking vegetables, grain, flour, &c., up to the city, and returning with groceries, dry goods, papers, &c. By this means she has created quite a snug little business for herself, and become an indispensable visitor to the residents. In fact they could not conveniently get along without her.

Far away to the eastward, the snow-capped Sierras, with a black belt of pines at their base, and nearer, the mist-draped and purple Coast Range, rise on the view. Along the plains are here and there seen clumps of trees—a sure indication of water; and occasionally, the charred trunk of some burnt and blasted tree lifts its bare branches toward heaven in solitary grandeur. During the season when the immense tracts of tules which cover the low lands are on fire, the conflagration lends a wild and peculiar beauty to the view.

The levee at Sacramento City—with its scenes of bustling activity; its numerous steamboats, dilapidated and otherwise; its locomotive, puffing and snorting; and all the living tide of industry, riding, driving and walking in all directions—is at length in view,

THE LEVEE AT SACRAMENTO CITY, FROM WASHINGTON, YOLO COUNTY.

but we have gossiped so much by the way, that we have not the
space left to devote to a city like this, holding the second rank on
the Pacific coast, and possessing a population of 14,000 souls, and
about as many objects of interest as does the City of the Bay; so
that we content ourselves by making the best of our way to the
station, and prepare for

A RIDE ON THE SACRAMENTO VALLEY RAILROAD.

This great private enterprise and public convenience was commenced in March, 1855, and is the first passenger railroad built in
California. On the 11th of August of the same year, the first car
was placed upon it; and on the 3d of February, 1856, it was completed to Folsom, a distance of 22¾ miles.

Leaving the depôt, at the corner of K street and Levee, we continue along the eastern bank of the Sacramento river to R street,
where a turning is made to the eastward; then, passing the beautiful gardens and cottages on the suburbs of the city, we emerge upon
a broad oak-studded plain, where the handiwork of the agricultu-
rist and richness of the soil are everywhere visible, in the luxuriant
crops seen on every side. Herds of cattle and bands of horses start
at our approach, as if to make us believe they are frightened at
the shape and speed of the puffing fiery monster that is advancing. Here we see a cross-road; yonder a "station;" now we rum-
ble over a viaduct; then, rattle through an excavation; amid farm-
houses and mining settlements, gardens and orchards, until, after
a ride of an hour and a quarter, we arrive at

FOLSOM.

This is a perfect stage-coach Babel; for, awaiting the train, we
find conveyances to almost every section of the central mines. As
our destination, now, is for the "Alabaster Cave," let us be upon
the look-out for a quiet-looking, open-faced (and hearted), middle-
aged man, who is patiently sitting on the box of his stage, his
good-natured countenance invitingly saying: "If there are any
ladies and gentlemen who wish a pleasant ride to-day, to 'Alabaster Cave,' let them come this way, and then it shall not be my

fault if it is not one of the most agreeable they ever took." That gentleman is Captain Nye. We ask, somewhat hastily, if his is the conveyance for the Cave, when a bluff and kindly response is, "Yes, sir; but don't hurry yourself, I shall not start for a few minutes, and the day is before us."

It may not be amiss here to remark, that the Alabaster Cave is located on Kidd's ravine, about three-quarters of a mile from its debouchment in the north fork of the American River; twelve and a half miles from Folsom, by the " Whiskey Bar" road; and ten miles by the El Dorado Valley turnpike; but, let us give a table of distances from all the surrounding country.

Rattlesnake Bar,	1¼ miles.	Georgetown,	18 miles.
Pilot Hill,	4 "	Diamond Sp's. & El Dorado City,	20 "
Gold Hill, Placer Co.	6 "	Iowa Hill, Placer Co.	20 "
Mormon Island,	6¼ "	Forest Hill,	20 "
Auburn,	8 "	Placerville,	23 "
Negro Hill,	6 "	Grass Valley,	30 "
Greenwood Valley,	9 "	Sacramento,	32¾ "
Lincoln,	9 "	Nevada,	34 "
Folsom,	10 and 12¼ "	Marysville,	36 "
Uniontown and Coloma,	16 "		

FROM FOLSOM TO " ALABASTER CAVE."

As our coachman is ready, and has given the well-known signal "All aboard;" moreover, as he has way-passengers on the El Dorado turnpike route, and none on the former, we, of course, give it the preference.

From Folsom, then, our course lies over gently-rolling hills, with here and there an occasional bush or tree, to Mormon Island. Here, peach-orchards and well cultivated gardens present a grateful relief to the dry and somewhat dusty road.

Crossing the south fork of the American by a long, high, and well-built suspension-bridge, we ascend, on an easy grade, to a mining camp, named Negro Hill. Threading our way among mining claims, miners, and ditches, we pass through the town into the open country; where buckeye bushes—now perhaps scantily clad in dry brown leaves, that bespeak the approach of autumn—the nut pine, and the dark, rich foliage of white oaks, dot the land-scape.

Presently we reach the foot of a long hill covered with a dense growth of chapparel, composed mostly of chemisal bushes. As we ascend, we feel the advantage of having an intelligent and agree-able coachman, who not only knows but kindly explains the lo-calities visible from the road.

From the summit of Chapparel Hill, we have a glorious pros-pect of the country for many miles. There, is "Monte Diablo," sleeping in the purple distance; yonder, "Sutter's Buttes," which bespeak at once their prominence and altitude; while the rich valley, and the bright silvery sheen of the Sacramento and its tributaries, are spread out in beauty before us. The descent to the cave on the other side of the hill is very picturesque and beautiful, from the shadowy grandeur of the groups of mountains seen in the distance.

Arriving about noon, a good appetite will most likely be sug-gestive of a substantial lunch, or dinner. This being quietly over, let us indulge in a good rest before presuming to look upon the marvels we have come to witness; and not be like too many, who do injustice to themselves and the sights to be seen, by attempt-ing them hurriedly, or when the body is fatigued, and consequent-ly the mind unfitted for the pleasing task.

ALABASTER LIME-KILN.

On leaving the hotel, it is but a short and pleasant walk to the cave. At our right hand, a few steps before reaching it, there is a lime-kiln—a perpetual lime-kiln—which, being interpreted, means one in which the article in question can be continually made, without the necessity of cooling off, as under the old method. Here a large portion of the lime consumed in San Francisco, is manufactured. It is hauled down to Folsom or Sacramento in wagons, as return freight, and from thence transported below. To see this kiln at night, in full blast, as we did, is a sight which alone would almost repay the trouble of a visit. The redhot doors at the base, with the light flashing on the faces of the men as they

THE ALABASTER LIME-KILN BY MOONLIGHT.

stir the fire, or, "wood-up," with the flames escaping out from the
top; and when to this is added the deep ravine, darkened by tall,
overhanging, and large-topped trees and shrubs; while high aloft
sails the moon, throwing her silvery scintillations on every object
around, from the foliage-draped hill, to the bright little rivulet
that murmurs by—description is impossible.

At these works, there are forty barrels of lime manufactured
every twenty-four hours. To produce these, three and a half cords
of wood are consumed, costing, for cutting only, $1 75 per cord.
To haul this to the works, requires a man and team constantly.

Two men are employed to excavate the rock, and two more to attend to the burning—relieving each other at the furnace every twelve hours; from morn to midnight.

The rock, as will be seen in the engraving, is supplied from the top, and is drawn from the bottom every six hours, both day and night.

THE ENTRANCE.

When entering the cave from the road—as indicated in the engraving, by the group of figures opposite the two trees behind the lime-kiln—we descend some three or four steps to a board floor. Here is a door that is always carefully locked, when no visitors are within. Passing on, we reach a chamber about twenty-five feet·in length by seventeen feet in width, and from five feet to twelve feet six inches in height. This is somewhat curious, although very plain and uneven at both roof and sides. Here also is a desk, on which is a book, inscribed, "Coral Cave Register." This book was presented by some gentlemen of San Francisco who believed that "Coral Cave" would be the most appropriate name. The impression produced on our mind at the first walk through it, was that "Alabaster Cave" would be equally as good a name; but, upon examining it more thoroughly afterward we thought that—a greater proportion of the ornaments at the root of the stalactites being like beautifully frozen mosses or very fine coral, and the long icicle-looking pendants being more like alabaster— the former name was to be preferred. But, as the name of "Alabaster" had been given to the works by Mr. Gwynn, on account of the purity and whiteness of the limestone found, even before the cave was discovered, we cheerfully acquiesce in the nomenclature given. The register was opened April 24th, 1860, and on our visit, September 30th ensuing, 2,721 names had been entered. Some three or four hundred persons visited it before a register was thought of, and many more declined entering their names; so that the number of persons who entered this cave the year of its discovery, must have exceeded three thousand.

Advancing along another passage, or room, several notices attract our eye, such as, "Please not touch the specimens," "No

smoking allowed," " Hands and feet off," (with *feet* scratched out)
—amputation of those members not intended! The low shelving
roof, at the left and near the end of the passage, is covered with
coral-like excrescences, resembling bunches of coarse rock-moss.
This brings us to the entrance of

THE DUNGEON OF ENCHANTMENT.

Before us is a broad, oddly-shaped, and low-roofed chamber,
about one hundred and twenty feet in length by seventy feet in
breadth, and ranging from four to twenty feet in height.

Bright coral-like stalactites hang down in irregular rows, and
in almost every variety of shape and shade, from milk-white to
cream-color; standing in inviting relief to the dark arches above,
and the frowning buttresses on either hand; while low-browed
ridges, some almost black, others of a reddish-brown, stretch from
either side, between which the space is ornamented with a peculiar
coloring that resembles a grotesque kind of graining.

Descending toward the left, we approach one of the most beautiful stalactitic groups in this apartment. Some of these are fine
pendants, no larger than pipe-stems, tubular, and from two to five
feet in length. Three or four there were, over eight feet long;
but the early admitted Vandals destroyed or carried them off.
Others resemble the ears of white elephants (if such an animal
could be known to natural history), while others, again, present
the appearance of long and slender cones, inverted.

By examining this and other groups more closely, we ascertain
that at their base are numerous coral-like excrescences of great
beauty; here, like petrified moss, brilliant, and almost transparent; there, a pretty fungus, tipped with diamonds; yonder, like
minature pine-trees, which, to accommodate themselves to circumstances, have grown with their tops downward. In other places,
are apparent fleeces of the finest Merino wool, or floss silk.

Leaving these, by turning to the right we can ascend a ladder,
and see other combinations of such mysterious beauty as highly
to gratify and repay us. Here is the loftiest part of this chamber.

Leaving this, you arrive at a large stalagmite that resembles a tying-post for horses, and which has been dignified, or mystified, by such names as " Lot's wife" (if so, she was a very dwarf of a woman, as its altitude is but four feet three inches, and its circumference, at the base, three feet one inch), " Hercules' club," " Brobdignag's fore-finger," &c.

Passing on, over a small rise of an apparently snow-congealed or petrified floor, we look down into an immense cavernous depth, whose roof is covered with icicles and coral, and whose sides are draped with jet. In one of these awe-giving solitudes is suspended a heart, that, from its size, might be imagined to belong to one of a race of human giants.

On one side of this, is an elevated and nearly level natural floor, upon which a table and seats have been temporarily erected, for the convenience of choristers, or for public worship. It would have gratified us beyond measure to have heard these " vaulted hills" resound the symphonies of some grand anthem from Mozart, or Haydn, or Mendelssohn. Many of the pendant harps would have echoed them in delicious harmonics from chamber to chamber, and carried them around, from roof to wall, throughout the whole of these rock-formed vistas.

We must not linger here too long, but enter other little chambers, in whose roofs are formations that resemble streams of water that have been arrested in their flow, and turned to ice. In another, a perfectly formed beet, from one point of view; and from another, the front of a small elephant's head. A beautiful bell-shaped hollow, near here, is called " Julia's bower !"

Advancing along a narrow, low-roofed passage, we emerge into the most beautiful chamber of the whole suite, entitled

THE CRYSTAL CHAPEL.

It is impossible to find suitable language or comparisons with which to describe this magnificent spot. From the beginning, we have felt that we were almost presumptuous in attempting to portray these wonderful scenes ; but, in the hope of inducing others to see, with their natural eyes, the sights that we have seen, and enjoy the pleasure that we have enjoyed, we entered upon the task,

19

even though inadequately, of giving an outline—nothing more.
Here, however, we confess ourselves entirely at a loss.   Miss
Maude Neeham, a young lady visitor from Yreka, has succeeded
in giving an admirable idea of this sublime sight, in some excellent drawings, made upon the spot; two of which we have engraved, and herewith present to the reader.

The sublime grandeur of this imposing sight fills the soul with
astonishment, that swells up from within as though its purpose
was to make the beholder speechless—the language of silence being the most fitting and impressive, when puny man treads the
great halls of nature, the more surely to lead him, humbly, from
these, to the untold glory of the Infinite One, who devised the
laws, and superintended the processes, that brought such wonders
into being.

After the mind seems prepared to examine this gorgeous spectacle somewhat in detail, we look upon the ceiling, if we may
so speak, which is entirely covered with myriads of the most
beautiful of stone icicles, long, large, and brilliant; between these,
are squares, or panels—the mullions or bars of which seem to be
formed of diamonds; while the panels themselves resemble the
frosting upon windows in the very depth of winter; and even these
are of many colors—that most prevailing being of a light pinkish-
cream. Moss, coral, floss, wool, trees, and many other forms, adorn
the interstices between the larger of the stalactites. At the farther end is one vast mass of rock, resembling congealed water,
apparently formed into many folds and little hillocks; in many
instances connected by pillars with the roof above. Deep down,
and underneath this, is the entrance by which we reached this
chamber.

At our right stands a large stalagmite, dome-shaped at the top,
and covered with beautifully undulating and wavy folds. Every
imaginary gracefulness possible to the most curiously arranged
drapery, is here visible, "carved in alabaster" by the Great Architect of the universe. This is named "The Pulpit."

In order to examine this object with more minuteness, a tempo-
rary platform has been erected, which, although detractive of the

THE CRYSTAL CHAPEL, IN ALABASTER CAVE.

general effect, in our opinion, affords a nearer and better view of all these remarkable objects in detail.

This spectacle, as well as the others, being brilliantly illuminated, the scene is very imposing, and reminds one of those highly-wrought pictures of the imagination, painted in such charming language, and with such good effect, in such works as the "Arabian Nights."

Other apartments, known as the "Picture Gallery," &c., might detain us longer; but, as they bear a striking resemblance, in many respects, to other scenes already described, we must take our leave, in the hope that we have said enough to enlist an increased attention in favor of this new California wonder.

The ride being agreeable, the fare cheap, the coachman obliging, the guides attentive, and the spectacle one of the most singular and imposing in the state, we say to every one, "*Go and see it.*"

Those who prefer going by railroad from San Francisco to Sacramento instead of by water, can make choice of two routes: *First, via* the California Pacific Railroad as follows:—Taking steamboat at Vallejo Street wharf at 8 o'clock A. M. and at 3:30 P. M., arriving at Vallejo in about two hours. Thence by C. P. R.R. to Sacramento, arriving at 12:15 o'clock P. M. and at 7:45. P. M. Distance 85 miles, 25 by steamboat and 60 by railway. Fare $3. *Second, via* the Western Pacific Railroad, through Stockton to Sacramento, as follows:—Start from Alameda Ferry at 8 o'clock A. M. and at 4 P. M., reach Oakland in thirty minutes. Thence by W. P. R.R. to Sacramento, arriving at 2 o'clock P. M. and 10 P. M. Distance 138 miles, 8 by steamboat and 130 by railway. Fare $3. Both routes are picturesque and full of interesting changes of scenery.

ERRATA.

On page 92, 10th line from top of page, leave out, " Here we change horses."

"   115, for " 2550," read " 2634."

"   130, 15th line from top of page, "*Œnothera* " should come after "primroses."

4

www.ingramcontent.com/pod-product-compliance
Lightning Source LLC
Chambersburg PA
CBHW021040030726
47496CB00006B/1623